NORTH WOODS UNIVERSITY BOOK TWO
THE DARE

USA TODAY BESTSELLING AUTHOR
J.L. BECK &
C. HALLMAN

© Copyright 2019 J.L. Beck & Cassandra Hallman

Cover Art by: Black Widow Designs

Editing: Ellie Mclove at My Brothers Editor

Proofread: Stacie McGlaughlin

All rights reserved. This book or parts thereof may not be reproduced in any form, stored in any retrieval system, or transmitted in any form by any means—electronic, mechanical, photocopy, recording, or otherwise—without prior written permission of the publisher, except as provided by United States of America copyright law.

PROLOGUE

Ava
Five Years Ago

Racing across the back yard, I chase after Vance. He's always faster, and of course makes it to the treehouse before me. The long grass tickles my legs and I almost trip in a hole, missing it just by a hair. I'm too busy paying attention to Vance running ahead of me. Looking at me over his shoulder, his eyes twinkle in the moonlight, his brown hair looks as if it could use a good cutting, or at least that is what Mom says.

"You're so slow, Ava. The Ice Age could beat you to the treehouse," he teases, just as he always does. Mom says it's because he likes me, but I don't think Vance likes me, at least not more than a friend. Not that I would ever kiss him. Kissing is gross. Reaching the treehouse, I put my hands on my hips and narrow my gaze. It's hard to see this far away from the house and a shiver ripples through me as a cold gust of wind blows through my damp hair.

"Not all of us were born with daddy long leg, legs." Being the jerk that he is, he doesn't even respond. Instead, he places one foot in front of the other and races up the wooden planks and into the treehouse, his body disappearing from view a second later.

Shaking my head, I climb up the wooden planks as well. The very first time I climbed into the treehouse, my legs were shaking, and my stomach was aching like someone had punched me in it. Now, I race up the steps like it's second nature. Popping my head through the square cut-out in the floor, I find Vance sitting Indian style in his usual spot. He's staring out the giant window that overlooks the yard.

This high up, I like to think we can see everything, the town we live in, even my best friend Mallory's house. But we can't... see everything that is. Climbing up and into the small space, I take a seat in a similar fashion.

As soon as I'm seated, Vance turns his attention to me. His green eyes are soft and remind me of a vast forest full of trees standing tall and proud even in the worst of circumstances. When he smiles, a weird tingle fills my belly, and I don't understand why it does that. It happens often though, almost every single time he smiles at me.

My eyes roam over him. He's wearing a ragged pair of jeans and a plain cotton t-shirt. My dad says his parents don't have a lot of money because Vance's father lost his job and that he can't afford new clothes right now so I shouldn't tease him or be mean, but I think his clothes look just fine. This is also why his family is living with us for a few weeks, just until his dad finds a new job. Either way, I'm fine with them staying with us. I don't have any siblings, and I like having Vance here to hang out with when he isn't being a jerk, or beating me to the treehouse.

With the moonlight shining into the treehouse, it's easy to see Vance's face. He rubs at his jaw and scrunches his eyebrows together, the look is one I've seen grace his face before. Anytime he looks like this, I know he is thinking hard, digging deep inside his *head to try and come up with something worthy of a dare. This is a game we play a lot, and by a lot, I mean nearly every day. Truth or Dare. Or as Vance always says, truth, since that's usually all I ever choose.*

Tonight, however, I chose dare. I don't know why I did it. I guess I'm just feeling adventurous. Or it could be because I'm tired of Vance always teasing me about picking truth.

When a huge grin spreads across his face, I know he's thought of something that he deems good enough for the game. I'm a little worried what he's come up with, and almost change my mind, telling him truth instead. Before I get the chance, his mouth is opening.

"I dare you to...sneak into your parents' bedroom."

"My parents' bedroom? I'll get into so much trouble if my mom catches me!" I whisper-yell. My dad is at work, so it's only my mom sleeping in their room. But it's the middle of the night and I'm supposed to be in bed and asleep, but instead I'm in my treehouse with Vance playing Truth or Dare. We'll both be in big trouble if our parents find out we're out here instead of in bed.

"Aw, are you chickening out on me?" he teases, a mischievous twinkle in his eyes. My lips set into a firm line, heat creeping into my cheeks at his statement.

"No, of course not." I lift my head high, my chin jutted out. "Not only will I go into the bedroom but to prove that I did I will also get something out of my mom's jewelry box."

"Ooooh, the stakes are high." He rubs his hands together. "I'll be waiting here for you."

"Don't worry, you won't have to wait long. I'll be back in no time wearing my mom's pearl necklace." I smirk, confident as can be. Vance rolls his eyes at me, obviously not believing me, which only makes me want to prove him wrong more.

There's a knot in my belly as I climb back down the wooden ladder, making my way through the yard and into the house I snuck out of a few minutes ago. My pulse rises and my breathing speeds up as I tiptoe up the stairs missing all the creaking spots. I don't know why I'm so nervous about this. So what if my mom wakes up?

I could always tell her that I had a bad dream or something and even if she doesn't believe me, what's the worst thing that could happen? Focusing on my thoughts, I miss the last creaking spot at the top of the stairs, my foot pressing against the squeaky floorboard, the sound bouncing off the walls and down the hall. Freezing, I hold my breath, my ears perking up while my heart thuds so hard inside my chest, I worry it might explode.

The sound of whispering meets my ears a second later...

There are two voices, but the only one I can make out is my mother's.

Why is she whispering? Who is she talking to? Vance's mom is at the hospital for her nightshift as a nurse and his father's room is downstairs, he shouldn't be here.

For a moment, I consider turning back around and crawling into my bed, leaving Vance and his stupid dare alone for the night, but I can't. I want to prove him wrong, that I'm not a chicken.

Tiptoeing down the hall, I get closer to my parents' bedroom. The whispers get louder, and my eyes widen when I hear who my mother is talking to. The words I hear are ones I'll never be able to forget. Ones that I'll never be able to let go of.

This was the night that changed my life forever.

1

AVA

*P*icking at the pink polish on my nails, I wonder how I got to this point. How I managed to find my way back to North Woods after five long years of being gone. Five years, that's how long I spent away from my childhood home town. A place I had grown up, a place that I missed more and more every single day that I was gone. It wasn't the friends I had made or known my whole life, or even the house that I missed, it was the physicality, of knowing a place, of having grown up in it. I had nothing to fear in this town. It was my world.

After that night of Truth or Dare with Vance, my father kicked out Vance's family, leaving them homeless. Then he took my mother and me and moved us across state lines. We just left, we didn't even get to take all of our stuff. My parents sold the house not even a month later and I knew we would never come back. I'd cried, begged and pleaded with my father but it did me no good. We still moved, my whole life flipping completely upside down and all because of one secret. Gritting my teeth, I shove the memory away and into the darkest crevices of my mind.

My parents stayed married for two years after that, even though I think they knew they would have been better off getting a divorce. Those two years were ones that I didn't really care to remember. Full of fighting, of anger and blame. Every day I saw their hate for one another grow. Then it finally happened, they got divorced and I stayed with my dad.

My mom moved away shortly after things ended, claiming she couldn't find a job as a secretary where we were living and my dad of course was not willing to move, nor was I. High school was hard enough without having to move to a brand new school and I wasn't about to pack up my life again and start over wherever the hell it was that my mother wanted to move. That, and a part of me was still angry with her. Angry for ruining my life, her life, my dad's life. It was because of her selfishness that we left in the first place.

When she moved back to North Woods, I didn't really think anything of it. That was until she called me last Christmas.

"Hey sweetheart, did you get the Christmas presents in the mail?"

"Yes, Mom, thank you. The only thing that would've made it better was spending the day with you." There was nothing like spending Christmas with your family... though I wouldn't truly know since I hadn't spent a holiday with my mother since she left. It was just Dad and I and even then, sometimes it was just me.

"I know, me too." Her words didn't match her tone of voice.

"If it's okay with you, I was thinking about coming down for a few days next week since I'm still on break. We can watch *Elf* and make Christmas cookies." The mere thought of spending time with her left me feeling whole again. Even if I was pissed off at my *mother for not visiting me, or making an effort, it didn't mean I didn't want to spend time with her, if given the chance.*

"Yeah...maybe." *She paused and I couldn't miss the nervous tone that overtook her voice. It sounded like she was going to say something she thought I might not like.*

"You know, honey, I've been meaning to tell you something..." *There was another pause, and I gripped the phone tighter in my hand. When I didn't say anything, she continued a long sigh filling the speaker.*

"I've been seeing someone...it's... it's um... Henry."

My hold on the phone slackened and I nearly dropped it.

Holy shit. She didn't actually mean Henry...

Shaking my head, I somehow manage to find my voice.

"Henry Preston? Vance's dad?"

"Yes, we met again a few months ago. He and Tonya got divorced as well. I swear to you we were only looking for friendship but, sometimes the heart has other plans. Anyway, we started going out and I figured you should know. I don't want to keep anything from you."

She figured I should know? Ha, that's funny. She could miss Christmas with me and barely pick up the phone to call me but felt like I should know about her love life.

Someone should get her an award.

Mom of the year here.

There's a permanent sour taste that coats my mouth every time I think back to that phone call. No, I take that back, it's actually all of *it*. All of this leaves a bitter taste in my mouth.

Everything about my life is fucked up. Her moving away. My dad making me stay with him, even after he started drinking. My mom never coming back for me, even when she knew I needed her. Her absence only drove the knife of betrayal deeper into my chest.

Which leads me to this moment. An eighteen-year-old

high school graduate without a single dime to her name because her dad drank and gambled her college fund away. I was the poster child for fucked up, going nowhere real fast.

My mom insisted on me coming to live with her but not until *after* she found out about my father's wrongdoings. Anger bled at the edge of my tongue. I wanted to ask her where she was a couple years back, but what was the point.

Nothing she did now could change the past. The only good thing that came from moving in with her was her promise that she and Henry would pay for my college and give me a place to live while attending the local university. After the shit show my mother had left me in, I was seriously considering saying no.

I prided myself on being a smart girl and I wasn't about to fall into that trap again. She had let me down more than once in my life... I had no reason to trust her...but what else was I going to do with my time?

With my dad in some high-end rehab facility across the country and the house being foreclosed on. It was only a matter of time before I could add being homeless and jobless, to my long resume of fuck ups. I knew what the outcome would be if I didn't take my mother's offer. And as stubborn as I wanted to be, I couldn't give up my dream of going to college.

So I took the offer. It was a cute little deal tied up with a red ribbon, like those stupid presents she had sent me last year. I couldn't pass it up, not even if I was still angry at her for being absent for nearly all of my teenage years.

Looking up at the elaborate mansion Henry bought my mother, I try not to cringe. Stone masonry, a huge three car garage, in a secluded area. The icing on the cake the *Welcome to our home* sign blowing back and forth in the wind.

It's like a red flag calling out to my rage, and I'm the bull, ready to dig my horns into it.

There was a point in time when the Preston's had no money, not even two quarters to rub together. Then, according to my mom, Henry struck it big, partnering up with some big wig.

Oh how the times had changed. Something told me Henry had more money than God if he could just pull houses out of his ass and throw bribe money at me like it was pieces of confetti.

Which is what this was... a bribe. Maybe I should be a little more grateful, but who the hell was I kidding. I didn't want to be here anymore than I'm sure he wanted me to be, than his son will want me to be.

Vance Preston.

The name in itself makes me shiver, and not with fear. I'm not bitter, totally not bitter or angry, or any of those things. It's not Vance's fault that my life fell apart like a bad game of Jenga. We were just two kids caught in the crosshairs of an adult situation.

Smoothing my hand over my hair one last time, I look down at my clothing. Skinny jeans and an *ACDC* shirt. I hope she didn't expect me to show up wearing a dress? They might regret inviting me after all.

The suitcase is heavy in my clammy hand as I walk up the front steps, stopping at the front door of the place I'll call my new home. Home isn't really what I would call this place. It's more like one of those houses you see in a magazine.

Glamour, over the top.

The only thing it's missing is a fountain out front but give them a little time, they'll have one built. The taxi driver didn't even bother helping me inside, instead he sped off giving me just enough time to get my bag out of the back. Staring at the door, I give myself a couple seconds to gain my composure. *One. Two. Three.* Exhaling all the air from my lungs out my mouth I let air filter in through my nostrils as I reach out and press the little doorbell button. While I wait, I force a smile to my lips.

Truthfully, my feelings for my mother are confusing. It's a slippery slope of loathe and love. I want to see her more and spend time with her, far more than I care to admit even to myself, but of all the times to come back into her life it had to be on her wedding day? And to be married to Henry? Yeah, I was pretty sure the universe hated me.

The door swings open a millisecond later and my half-dressed mom appears in the doorway. "Oh Ava, my sweet baby girl. I'm so happy that you made it." She throws her arms around me, pulling me into her chest, wrapping me up in a hug that's far tighter than a woman as tiny as her should be able to give. In the process of hugging me, she pulls me into the house as well. It's almost like she's afraid I'll turn around and run away if she doesn't.

Sucking in a greedy breath of her floral scent I'm taken back to a time when my mom was really my mom, when she didn't make selfish choices, when she ran my baths, and told me I was the prettiest girl in the entire world. It seems like a lifetime ago and somehow, I wish I could go back.

"Don't mess up your makeup, Linda," some lady scolds from inside the house. When the hug ends, I'm left feeling cold. My mom takes my hand into hers and pulls me deeper into the foyer. I barely manage to get the suitcase over the door jamb before she's closing the door behind us. *Jesus.* My gaze sweeps across the room and through the house as my mother tugs me along. It looks unlike anything I've seen before, marble, crown molding, high ceilings. It reminds me of nothing from the home we shared when we were actually a family and not broken pieces in a picture frame.

The walls are painted a light beige that makes the room

seem light and airy. Signs with different quotes adorn the walls, along with photos that I don't care to look at.

We enter the living room, which is basically just one giant room. There's a huge leather sectional, fireplace, and flat screen TV set up. Built-in bookcases are on the side of the room and my fingers itch to run along the spines of the books.

The living room opens up into the kitchen, which is all white marble and stainless steel appliances. It looks like something out of a Sears catalog.

In fact, this entire house looks like a catalog.

Like a designer came in and put everything in its perfect place.

"Please, come and sit with me while they finish up my hair and makeup. We have so much to catch up on, sweetie." I open my mouth to say something, but she continues to tug me down a hallway that leads off the kitchen.

"I'm sorry I couldn't pick you up at the airport. I would've but as you can see." She waves a hand in front of her, like I can't see it myself.

"It's okay," I lie. The hallway is long and there are a few doors, all of which are closed hiding their contents inside.

"This place is huge." The words slip past my lips before I can stop them. I mean to say them inside my head rather than speak them out loud, but obviously my mouth had other thoughts.

"Believe me, I know. I feel bad for the cleaning ladies sometimes, I cannot even imagine the amount of time it takes to clean this place. I told Henry a simple apartment would suffice, but he demanded the best." She grins at me over her shoulder, and then turns, pulling me into a room that looks like a professional makeup studio.

Mirrors and hair products and makeup litter every surface. There are three ladies standing in the room, with smiles on their faces, but impatience in their eyes. My mother shoves herself down into a seat and forces me to take the one beside her.

I do not fit in here. No way, no how.

Once seated, she releases my hand, and I take the moment to wipe the sweaty palm she was holding against the front of my jeans. My eyes roam over my mother's disheveled form that I somehow missed when she answered the door. I wasn't really looking at her then, but looking right through her.

A pink robe is wrapped around her slim frame, and slippers that say *The Bride* on the front of them cover her feet. Huge curlers have her chestnut brown hair, the same shade as my own, wrapped up tightly. She looks like she's getting ready for a beauty pageant, not a wedding.

"You have no idea how happy I am to have you here, sweetie. What's it been, three years?" She bats her long eyelashes and smiles at me. I can't miss the fakeness of her tone, or the fact that she's talking to me like I'm one of her Stepford house friends rather than her daughter. It sickens me, but what am I supposed to do?

"Yeah, three years, *Mom*," I say, my words clipped.

My intentions when coming here had nothing to do with making my mom feel like shit for not being there for me. Sooner or later, she would realize what she had done. Instead, I set out to better my life. I wanted to go to college, wanted to enjoy life, instead of worrying about what bill we were going to pay next.

If I thought my life was hard after we moved, it became a shit storm after my mother left. This was my one and only chance at doing something for myself, and even if I had to use Henry's money and deal with my fake mother to get it, I would. There were worse things I could be doing with my life.

One of my mother's makeup artists chose then to appear in

front of her, like a magical fairy dabbing at her face, painting on her mask. For some reason, I was uncomfortable. I felt like an outsider, like I didn't belong.

"Look, I'm sorry, honey. We might as well get this out of the way. Me leaving had nothing to do with you. I just needed space and time. Things weren't good between your father and me and there was no work to be found in that godforsaken town." She pauses for a moment as if she's thinking over what she just said before continuing, "The past is the past though. Now we have years upon years to look forward to."

Go figure she would be happy go lucky about this, telling me to move on from something that she didn't have to endure. The world was full of people telling you to get over your problems, the last thing I needed was my mother joining in on the fun.

"I didn't come here to discuss the past. It can't be changed. I'm going forward. I just want to have a decent end of the summer, register for classes, and enjoy your wedding." The last part was a lie. I would rather eat glass then suffer through her wedding, but it's part of the agreement, and if there is anything you should know about me, it's that I always follow through.

She beams at my words. "Of course. I have your dress laid out in one of the guest bedrooms that I had put together for you. Once you get settled in, you can decorate it however you would like. Vance and Henry are beyond excited to see you."

I fidget with my hands nervously. Vance. Five years have passed since I saw him last. Back then, we were friends, middle-schoolers with nothing but time on our hands, now we would be strangers that somehow knew each other at one point and time.

I won't lie and say I'm not curious when it comes to him. I've wondered about him often over the years. What he was doing? If he still ate his bologna sandwiches with ketchup and cheese?

Puke.

We might not ever agree on condiment choices, but other than that, we were friends. Upon my life falling apart, I lost someone that I considered to be my best friend.

God, life was cruel.

"The joy." I roll my eyes. "If you're okay with it, I'm going to go and try on that dress and put some of my stuff away."

My mother smiles as one of the ladies checks the curlers in her hair. "That's fine. You'll need to get your hair and makeup done next so don't run off. Go up the stairs and take a right, your room is the last one on the left. I'm so excited to have you here. Life's going to be much better sweetie, you'll see."

Ha. I want to tell her life would be better had she not fucked up, but don't. It wouldn't be worth it. Instead, I get up and walk out of the room, tugging my impossibly large suitcase behind me. Home sweet home.

I get the feeling that living here is going to be anything but sweet...

2

VANCE

"I want your cock." Sarah purrs, her big brown eyes peering up at me from her position on the floor. She's kneeling before me like I'm her king and strangely, I guess I am. The king of orgasms. Tossing the stupid tie my father had me wear to his even stupider fucking wedding I reach for her, pinching her chin between two fingers.

She's pretty enough, with red lips, and fuck me eyes. She'll never be *it* for me though.

"And you'll have my cock in your mouth soon enough." I wasn't always this big of an asshole. Tonight was different. Tonight I was on edge, hanging off the cliff by my fingernails, and all because of *her*.

My dream.

My nightmare.

One would've thought five years would be enough time to let go of the pain, of the anger, of the betrayal but seeing her again, it only ignited the barely cooled embers of hate in my heart. It didn't help her bitch of a mom marrying my father either. That was another knife to the back, and another gallon of gasoline poured on my rage.

Flicking the button on my dress slacks, I watch Sarah's eyes fill with excitement. I'm going to use her throat before discarding her like I do all the other girls that come and go. Fucking them is fun. Listening to them whine and cry afterward, not so much.

Shoving my boxers down, I pull my diamond hard cock out. I palm the fucker a couple times, warming him up. Precum beads at the tip and a groan of pleasure resonates through my chest when Sarah's warm mouth makes contact with the head. She sucks it into her mouth, flicking her pink tongue over the slit at the top before taking more of my length into her mouth.

Fuck, she's like a porn star.

When she starts to suck, I'm reminded why I always call on her when I want a good fucking blow job. Because she sucks like she's a Hoover fucking vacuum cleaner, that's why. She makes a gagging sound when my cock hits the back of her throat, the sound sending zings of pleasure through my ball sack. For a moment I forget about my father, the man I've looked up to my whole life, of Laura, my new stepmother.

My thoughts catch on *Ava*. My ex-best friend, and new stepsister. She looks gorgeous tonight, curvy, with her hair curled, looking like a fucking angel, though she's anything but that. She's the devil, a fucking liar wrapped up in a tight little bow.

And even though I wouldn't put my dick in her, I wonder if she would let me use her throat like Sarah is? Images of her on her knees before me, looking up at me with her big eyes, me punishing her with my cock, coaxing the truth right out of her pretty little mouth. My eyes fall closed and all I see is her.

Threading my fingers into Sarah's mass of blonde hair, I

imagine its Ava's mousy brown. I hold her face right where I want it and fuck her throat, listening to her gags and soft mewls. I bet she's drenched for me, just waiting for my cock to make her come, would Ava be like that? Would she be soaked with need for me? I bet she fucking would. She's a fucking liar, but even she can't hide the evidence of arousal.

Momentarily, I consider pulling my cock out of Sarah's throat and fucking her pussy, but I don't. It's bad enough I'm thinking about my lying bitch of a stepsister while fucking her mouth.

Fuck that, not tonight. Tonight she'll have to use one of my friend's dicks to get off.

Thrusting my hips savagely, my head tips back and I let the euphoric pleasure overtake me. Piercing green doe eyes, and creamy white skin. All I see is Ava inside my head. With Sarah's warm mouth wrapped around my dick and forbidden thoughts plaguing me, I fall apart, shattering into a million pieces, roaring as I explode into the back of her throat. She makes another gagging sound but then swallows around my softening length.

Fucking, fuck, fuck.

Waves of pleasure wash over me, and I take a step back, my cock falling from her red painted lips. My heart hammers deep inside my chest, confirming that it still lives there. Once the pleasure fades into the darkness, I shove myself back inside my boxers and pull my dress slacks back up. Ava's already got a hold on me and she hasn't even said a fucking word yet. I guess the good news is I hate her too much to listen to a word she has to say. The bad news is that my cock likes the image of her on her knees.

I can feel Sarah's eyes on me, burning through my clothes and into my flesh.

"What about me?" She pouts.

"What about you?" I question, tucking my shirt back in. "Go ride Clark's dick. I'm sure he'll show you a nice time." My response is not one she wants to hear, and she shoves from the floor wiping at her mouth with the back of her hand, anger boiling over in her features.

"Why do you always have to be a dick?" she growls, smoothing a hand down the front of her pink chiffon dress. Sarah is what you would call a princess. She likes things that glitter, and people she knows her parents would hate to see her with, and though I'm not *that* bad of a guy, I'm not what you would call honorable either. Her country club father would never be okay with her being with me, no matter how much she wants me.

My lips tip up into a smile. "I can't help it, sweetheart. I'm just a big ass dick. Now get the fuck out of here, and don't let anyone see you walking out."

She rolls her eyes at my demand but does as I say, scurrying from the room like someone lit a fire under her ass. The door opens and closes with a soft click and I'm finally left to my thoughts. Exhaling a ragged breath, I run a hand through my brown trusses. Sarah's pretty, in fact, all of the women I've screwed are pretty, I'll give them that, but they aren't *her*.

Ava Wilder.

I can't get her out of my mind. She's fucking with my head, my thoughts, and my feelings. Her name alone feels like acid raining down on me. She's haunted me for years, her memory digging its claws deep into my mind. Time was supposed to heal wounds, but it only made mine fester. And seeing her tonight, it ripped open every single one of those wounds. They were sleeping with hate, while blood dripped down my chest. The pain of seeing her angered me so much that I had to walk away after the ceremony.

It made me want to hurt her, destroy her. And yet there

had been a time I would've done anything for her. She didn't look at me like the other kids did back then, like I was some charity case. She wanted to be my friend, or at least that's what I thought. Back then, I never would've touched her, or even thought of hurting her, but now... the inky thoughts consumed me. A memory from when we were kids pops into my head and I'm drawn back in time.

"Johnny said that he kissed Sierra," I announced as we walked down the street and toward our bus stop.

Ava shrugged like she didn't care. "So, who cares, kissing is weird."

It was weird, but I wanted to do it, more with Ava than any of the other girls in school. She wouldn't laugh at me if I messed up or did something stupid. We were friends, and she was there for me.

"What would you say if I wanted to kiss you?"

Her green eyes widened, and she stopped mid-step right before she shoved me in the shoulder. Those little fists of hers were curled. She was cute when she was mad.

"I would tell you to go away because kissing is gross and I would rather chew on a piece of bubble gum that was chewed on by three other people before I kissed you."

Grinning, I tugged on her ponytail. "Good, I wouldn't kiss you either."

I smile faintly at the memory. That was before she was a liar, before she took everything away from me. I wasn't sure which hurt most, her betrayal, the lies, or losing her as a friend. I forgot all about my selfish pain when she came walking into the church with a smile on her face, acting like she hadn't done a damn thing.

Like she hadn't ruined my fucking life. She had done nothing short of destroy my family and force us into a homeless shelter. Her lie ripped us apart. It ended my parents' marriage. She didn't deserve to be here, to enjoy the fucking hors d'oeuvres or drink the wine.

No, she deserves heartache, and I hope like hell, that she doesn't plan on staying, because if she does, I'm going to break her, destroy her. I'll send her back to wherever the fuck she came from crying, and she'll think twice before crossing paths with me again.

Tonight I'll give her a warning, the one and only time I will show her an ounce of mercy. Her mother may have weaseled her way into my father's life but there is no way in fucking hell Ava's going to find her way back into mine.

Stepsister or not, she's dead to me.

She was dead to me the night she lied about me to her father.

A few minutes later, I leave the backroom of the clubhouse and sneak back into the reception without even a second glance from any of the patrons. I'm sure no one even noticed I was gone. They're all much too busy gushing over Laura and her designer dress to care about me and my explorations.

Not that it would matter if they were, my father isn't paying me any attention today anyway, matter of fact, ever since he started dating Laura a few months ago, he hasn't paid me a lick of attention. I try not to dwell on it. It's not like I'm a child anymore who needs his father's affection left and right. I just don't want Laura getting any ideas.

My gaze sweeps around the room, it looks like a bridal magazine had a baby with pink glitter in the reception area. There's a sculpture of a swan carved from ice near the bar that's puking wine and I can't comprehend why my father would spend money on all this bullshit.

My eyes clash with Clark's. Best friend and confidant, he's been there through it all with me. Besides Ava, he's the only one who *knows* me. A year after Ava left, he showed up with his father after losing his mother to cancer. We didn't like each other right away but shared a mutual disdain for life. It was cruel and we were bearing the brunt of all of its wrongdoing. Crossing the room, I come to a stop right in front of him.

"You look like you just got laid."

"I'll never kiss and tell." I give him a cheeky smile.

"No, you just fuck and tell, which means you got your dick sucked."

"You know me so well."

Clark shook his head. "A beer, my friend?"

"Thought you'd never ask." I grin, taking the beer from his extended hand. We're just shy of drinking age, but no one gives a shit and we've done worse things than underage drinking before. Bringing the bottle to my lips, I take a long pull of the beer and turn around surveying the room. The cold beer cools my heated inside. I can't stop myself from seeking her out. It's almost like we're magnets being pulled toward each other, the pull too intense to break.

"She's pretty," Clark says nonchalantly.

Pretty? She's gorgeous, out of his league but she's like poison, killing you slowly.

"Don't let her pretty face fool you. She's also a master manipulator and the enemy, the fact that she has a pussy makes her even more dangerous. She'll fuck you if she has to get what she wants, guarantee it. So, please, don't go there, Clark." My fingers grip onto the beer bottle, tightening.

"Whoa, that sounds a lot like jealousy, Van. Are you jealous?" His voice is teasing, light, and I glare at him in response.

He's trying to stir the pot and as much as I usually like his antics, tonight isn't a good night for that shit. I'm not jealous of Clark hooking up with Ava, in fact, I don't give a fuck who he sticks his cock in. The lying bitch can get her heart broken for all I care. But that's all I'll let it be is a quick fuck.

"Jealousy isn't what I would call what I'm feeling. It's more like burning fiery rage. I want to hurt her," I murmur, turning my attention back toward our guests.

I drink Ava in like she's a glass of water and I'm near death from dehydration. She's stunning, her silky brown hair falls in soft curls down her back, framing her delicate heart-shaped face. Her skin is creamy white without a single blemish. She looks like an actual princess, delicate, fragile. Her full lips are painted blood red, but her eyes look innocent, which is funny since she's anything but that.

"Maybe fucking her would help then?" Clark suggests, and my face deadpans.

"Fucking her? Really?" I lift a brow. "I don't think fucking her would help at all. I don't want her lying pussy wrapped around my dick. I want her crying, not writhing in pleasure, asshole."

Clark shrugs, taking a drink of his beer. "Then I don't know what to tell you. What can you do that doesn't involve physically hurting her? And plus, who knows, maybe she just showed up for her mother's wedding? Maybe her intentions aren't as bad as you're making them out to be?"

Always the benefit of the doubt kind of guy. Clark has no idea what he's talking about.

"She better hope for her own sake that, that's all she's here for," I ground out.

Though it's doubtful. I'm pretty sure I heard my father talking to Laura about inviting Ava out to stay with us. If she's smart, she won't take the offer. She'll run for the fucking hills.

Like a creep, I stare at her, watching her smile, and talk amongst the guests. There's a darkness inside of me, an anger that's laid dormant for a very long time, and it's returning, rising up inside me like lava pushing out of a fucking volcano and when I erupt, she's the first person I'm coming for.

"Ladies and gentlemen, it is time for the first dance. Please, Henry and Laura, come and let us see those sweet dance moves," Steve, my father's best man's, voice which also happens to be Clark's father, rattles through the speakers.

The crowd parts making way for my father and his new *wife*. Everyone grows quiet as the music starts to play, all eyes on them, including my own. They dance, my father holding her close, while leaning in to most likely whisper sweet nothings in her ear.

Their smiles are dazzling and filled with love, so much love it's truly disgusting. I take another swig of my beer to stomach the image before me.

No way can I bring myself to feel even an ounce of happiness for them. It will never happen, no matter how much Laura tries to warm up to me. In my eyes, she'll always be the enemy's mother. Resentment pools in my belly as they continue to dance. This stupid marriage was both a blessing and a nightmare.

A nightmare because it made Ava my stepsister, and a blessing because it brought her back to me, making it possible for me to get revenge, something I had told myself a million times over I would never get.

That night when we left with nothing but a few belongings after my father told me what she had done. I vowed to get even with her, and maybe it wouldn't have been so bad, maybe I could've let it go, but then my parents divorced, and that drove the knife of betrayal deeper into my chest. Channeling all my feelings over it, I placed that blame on Ava as well, knowing that if I ever got the chance to see her again, if she ever showed her face in this town again, I would ruin her. And lucky me, her stuck up mother fell for my filthy rich father.

I try not to think about Laura being married to my father, basking in his riches while my mother got nothing after the divorce, not a single dime. I give her a few hundred dollars each month from my allowance so she can get by. I don't give a shit about the money, I would give her thousands if I could.

When the song ends and their dance is over, and thank god, I was close to puking, Steve's voice booms through the room again causing me to roll my eyes. Enough with the sappy speeches and corny jokes already. Let's just get drunk and forget this nightmare ever happened.

"Now as requested by the bride and groom, I would like to invite Vance and Ava to the dance floor to join their parents."

The fuck? No way.

No. Fucking. Way.

The beer bottle in my hand almost slips to the floor. A wave of ahhs and ohhs whisper through the crowd, and all I can do is stand there, mouth parted in shock, unable to believe the words I just heard. No way, no motherfucking way.

"Here's your chance…" Clark nudges me in the side.

"Now don't be shy, you two. Get out here, and show your folks how it's done," Steve chuckles into the mic.

My gaze swings to my father who is giving me a *don't make a scene* look. He told me to play nice and welcome Ava into the family, probably to please his new wife. But I'm never going to welcome her back into my life, not ever.

Grinding my teeth together so harshly I think I might chip one, I shove my beer into Clark's chest and make my way out onto the dance floor.

Ava scurries across the dance floor meeting me in the center, she's fidgeting with her hands, nervousness flickers in her green eyes. Does she expect me to reassure her, to tell her everything's going to be okay? I almost expect her to run away, surely she knows I won't let her stay here after what she did?

I've successfully avoided her all night while knowing this moment would come sooner or later. I just didn't think we would have the entire fucking guest list staring at us when it did. That kind of makes saying what I want to her without everyone hearing or seeing obsolete, and if I fuck up, ruining my father's wedding by being an asshole, then he'll hand me my ass ten-fold. The next song starts, and I take a predatory step toward her.

Run. Run as fast as you can....

Forcing my curled fists to uncurl, I reach for her, grabbing her by the hip, pulling her into my chest before offering my other hand like a complete gentleman. She gasps softly through her parted lips at the contact and I take pleasure in knowing that I can get even the simplest of a reaction out of her.

Hesitantly, as if she already knows what will happen to her, she places her much smaller hand into mine and this weird electric current zings through me. It feels like I've stuck my finger in a light socket, and I want it to go away, but in order to do that I would have to let her go, and I'm not ready to do that, not yet.

No matter how much I try, I can't help but notice how soft and warm her hand is inside of mine, the warmth of her touch seeping deep into my veins. *Warm? Soft?* What the hell, when did I grow a pussy? Why the hell am I thinking about her hand, about how tiny it is? She's nothing, nothing but a fucking con-fucking-artist. I hate how she makes me feel, that she can evoke feelings from deep inside me that I shouldn't feel for someone like her...for anyone, for that matter.

So fragile, soft, warm.

"Hi," she whispers, her voice like a wisp of air blowing through the trees, as we start dancing. *Hi?* That's what she says after all this time. After what she did to me...what she did to my family? *Hi? What the fuck?*

She should be crying, begging me to forgive her, not

rambling some fucking *hi* like we're long lost best friends or something. The blood in my veins boil, but I rein in my anger. When I don't answer her, she keeps talking, carrying on like the last five years didn't happen.

"So, I guess we're going to the same college?" she asks, peering up at me through thick lashes. Up close, she looks breathtaking, which only drives my stake of hate for her deeper.

"Don't!" I scold, through clenched teeth. "Don't fucking pretend we are friends."

Her whole body stiffens at my words, and my grip on her hip tightens. Shock flashes over her features and again, I'm baffled by how ignorant to this situation she is acting.

It's an act. Plain and simple.

She might be able to fool everyone else, but she can't fool me. I won't be ensnared by her beauty. I mean, what did she think was going to happen? That she could just come back here and I would forgive and forget that she fucked me over?

Wrecked my family and my life, just to save her ass. It was a simple dare, but it ripped my entire world to pieces. We were only kids, but there were consequences for your actions and while she carried on with her fucking perfect life I suffered.

Unable to stop myself, I pull her closer, so close that her perky breasts are almost touching my chest. I can't stop myself from looking at them. The last time I saw her, she was hardly a woman, and now she's grown into herself, her body finally taking shape, her hips flaring, her breasts heaving.

Her sweet scent permeates the air, filling my nostrils. Maybe if I didn't hate her so much, I'd find it appealing, but instead, I tell myself it's revolting. Ignoring the way she feels against me, and the urge to inhale her, I lean down, my mouth pressing to the shell of her ear.

"This innocent act you've got going on, it's cute and all, but

I see right through it. I can smell bullshit a mile away and you smell like you've bathed in it."

"Wh...what?" Her body trembles in my hold and her breath hitches in her throat like she might be scared. Be scared, cry, run... get as far away from me as you can.

"This is your only warning. Leave, go back to wherever the fuck it is you came from...and I'll take mercy on you, just this once." I lick my lips, pulling back, letting my eyes drop to her slender neck. I can see her pulse thrumming beneath the skin, giving away her fear and I can't stop the sinister smile that appears on my lips. I shouldn't crave her pain, her fear like I do. I know it's fucked up, but I didn't do this. She did.

My body tingles, my heart jack-hammering in my chest. Her fear is like my own personal brand of heroin and I'll do anything I can to get another hit.

"Stay, and I'll make you wish you never met me. One way or another, I'll send you back to your daddy. I'll make you pay..."

The song ends right then, and I release her like she's a venomous snake that'll strike at any second, refusing to give in to the need burning through me, the need to make her hurt, to feel my pain. Turning around, I stalk off the dance floor and back over to Clark, who is smiling like a fucking asshole. I hate her, but I also want her.

I grab my beer from him and down the entire thing at once. I don't want to see her face again. I can't handle seeing her play the innocent little girl when I know all too well that she's a liar. A beautiful one at that.

3

AVA

What the hell was that?

My whole body is shaking as I watch Vance walk away. I'm not sure what I expected our first interaction to be like, but it certainly wasn't like that. My hand is still warm from where he was holding onto it and I think he burned a hole in my dress where he was touching my hip.

Why is he so angry with me?

I've been watching him from afar all day. Too scared to talk to him after so long. It didn't take but one look for me to know that the boy I had known since I was a young child was no longer a *boy*, but now a man.

A dark, broody, man that apparently had it out for me. His warning rung inside my head. Disdain dripped from his words, there was venom in his eyes and he wanted to inject me with it, but why?

I couldn't take my eyes off of him, or forget the way he looked down at me during our dance. The image will forever be ingrained in my mind, and I don't understand why. He's handsome as sin, his hair the same russet brown, but cut shorter on the sides and longer on top. His jaw is sharp, and his cheekbones are high. And those green eyes of his, seem darker now, holding secrets that I plan to expose. Obviously time has been good to him, he looks like he walked off the cover of a GQ magazine.

Shaking my head, I will the images away. Trying to forget how it felt when he touched me. Those butterflies I got in my stomach all those years ago, it felt like there was an entire zoo of them taking up residence inside me. His sudden hate for me is nothing but confusing. It should be me who is mad, not him. I've lost everything, and he...he got it all. Just like Henry and my mother, he got everything he wanted.

The poor boy he used to be, the one with nothing had everything now, and the roles were reversed. The girl who once upon a time, had it all, had nothing.

People start to flood back onto the dance floor, and I realize that I'm still standing in the middle of the room. Everyone joins in to celebrate the happy couple and I force my lips to pull into a smile as I smooth a nervous hand down the front of my dress.

I feel dizzy, drunk, and all from one simple dance.

It takes me a moment to compose myself and get my legs to start moving again, but once they do, I find my way out of the crowd, walking toward the bridal party table. I look around, trying to find my mother in the sea of bodies, but all I see is hundreds of faces that I don't know.

All my fears start to trickle into my mind. A knot forms in my throat. I've never felt so out of place in my life. Like a flower in a sea of weeds, I stick out, drawing unwanted attention.

I heard some of the guests whispering about me, about how my mother only married for money, and how my father was a drunk. Their words stung even if they weren't directly said to me. It almost hurt more that they said them behind my back.

Trying to soothe the ache in my chest, I remind myself that I'm not here for anyone else, but still Vance's warning isn't something I can just shake off. Surely he didn't mean what he had said? Maybe he was joking? *Yeah, I don't think so...*

I glance around the room again, silently searching for him, but he's nowhere in sight. And suddenly I'm reminded of why I never should've agreed to come here.

Everyone around me seems to be having the time of their lives, drinking, dancing, and singing while I'm standing in a corner of the room alone. I don't need anyone to tell me that this isn't where I belong, that this isn't where I should be. Vance and my mother have already proven that tonight. And yet I have nowhere else to go, nowhere else to be. And somehow, I wish my past was my present. Where Vance and I were friends again. Where my parents were still together, and I had never discovered the one secret that shattered my world.

AFTER THE WEDDING last night I went to bed, tears filling my eyes while I prayed the next day would be better. All thoughts of Vance were pushed to the back of my brain, along with his anger toward me. College was what I needed to be focusing on, making something of my shit life. All I could do was keep pushing forward, remembering that things could be worse.

Waking up the next morning, I had hoped I could spend some time with my mom before she and Henry left for their honeymoon, but it was obvious that wasn't going to happen as soon as I woke up. I had barely seen her yesterday and today she was absent, nowhere to be found in this enormous house. In fact, I hadn't seen anyone except the housekeeping crew.

Disappointment settled heavy in my gut. When will I ever come to terms with the fact that my mom is and always will be, absent from my life. Five years ago, I didn't just lose everything, I lost my mom. Finding her that night, seeing her...

Squeezing my eyes shut, I will the memory away. I press my curled fists into the Tempur-Pedic mattress and exhale through my mouth. After a few moments, I feel calmer and open my eyes.

At least I haven't run into Vance yet, and after his cryptic threat last night I'm more than thankful for that. I'm not quite sure what to make of him. I was too shocked by his words to form a single sentence last night. I wanted to respond but I couldn't, my vocal box refusing to work.

Most of the morning is spent hiding in my room, sneaking out to grab some breakfast from the kitchen before retreating back inside it. It feels weird staying here, eating food without asking. This doesn't feel like a home to me... it feels like I'm more of a guest...an unwanted guest at that. When I hear voices carrying through the house, I pop my head out my bedroom door and into the hallway.

I don't see anyone, but I can hear my mom's high pitched giggles and Henry's deep laugh. I bound down the stairs like a kid on Christmas morning, beyond excited to see my mother, and maybe get a chance to spend some time with her. When I reach the bottom step, I'm met with disappointment once again because I know my mother isn't staying here. Not with them pulling luggage out of the hallway closet.

"Hey, sweetheart. We're about to head to the airport," my mom greets me.

"Oh, okay," I say, trying to hide the hurt from my voice.

Shouldn't I be used to the let down by now? I feel like one of those kids that wait outside all day for their parents to pick them up, but they never come. That's my mother, never showing up, never caring.

"Sorry we weren't here when you woke up, we had some last minute errands to make," she explains while looking through her carry-on bag. She doesn't even look up at me as she's talking, which only grates on my nerves further. I'm her daughter, not some piece of crap, the least she could do is give me a sliver of her attention.

Henry starts to wheel out the first suitcase and that's when I spot someone moving behind him, walking through the door.

Vance. The air around me becomes electrically charged. The fine hairs on my arms sticking up at his entrance. When we were kids, I thought he was disgusting. I mean, I thought all boys were. But now... now I've come to realize that Vance is anything but disgusting. He's sin dipped in chocolate.

"There you are. I need to talk to you before we leave," Henry says, propping the suitcase up against the door.

"What is it? I'm busy," Vance snaps, his gaze on his phone rather than his father. His muscles tense and as if he feels my eyes on him, he lifts his eyes to mine, giving me his full attention. I should look away, it would be the smart thing to do, the safe thing. But, I've never taken the easy route and it's not like he doesn't already know he's disgustingly gorgeous, drawing all the attention and air out of the room.

I'm simply window shopping, looking is just fine. Plus, he hates me anyway, and I'm totally not checking him out. Taking in his appearance, I see he's wearing a pair of jeans, Wrangler, I think, that hang low on his hips, rather than a designer pair. He's matched his simple jeans with a plain cotton t-shirt, and a pair of black boots. He looks more like the boy from my past than he did yesterday in his suit and tie.

Swallowing, I imagine the body he's hiding beneath that

cotton shirt. Does he have a six-pack? Are his muscles stone, and chiseled from rock? God, I need to stop thinking about him. Somehow I snap myself out of the trance his presence has put me in and lick my dry lips. Hopefully, I'm not drooling. The last thing I want is for him to know that I'm attracted to him.

Henry ignores his son's attitude. Obviously he's used to it. "There's been some changes… I know I've told you both that you could live on campus after classes start, but Laura and I decided it would make more sense if you guys just lived here instead—"

"You've got to be fucking kidding me," Vance interrupts his father, his gaze turning murderous.

"It's only a twenty-minute drive to campus, plus you can ride together. It will be good for you two to spend some time together. Catch up," Henry adds.

Vance makes a snorting noise, his eyes rolling so far to the back of his head I'm afraid they might get stuck back there.

My mom smiles nervously, her gaze moving over each of us, as if she's trying to avoid confrontation. How typical of her. Always avoiding the important stuff.

"We can talk about this more later, but I want to make it clear to you right now…" Henry's staring at Vance and using what I would call his authoritative dad voice. "I want you to watch out for Ava. Show her around, treat her as a friend. Remember when you guys used to be friends? Maybe you can find your way back to that?" He pokes fun, but nothing about this scenario is fun. I'm stuck in a house with a man that hates me for no apparent reason and has a serious anger problem that apparently only I see.

Speaking of an angry man, his hard eyes cut to me. "She's a big girl. She can take care of herself. Can't you, *Ava?*" I don't miss the dig he makes at me, but I don't give him the satisfaction of responding either. The dude clearly has got some mental issues, and there's no way in hell I'm tangling myself in that web of bullshit. I've got my own problems, no need to add his to my heaping pile.

Henry sighs impatiently. "Watch out for her, Vance. I mean it. If you don't, there will be consequences."

The warning is clear like a neon sign hanging in a bar window, fail to comply and his father will bury him. In what way, I don't know, but I'm curious. Vance doesn't take me as the kid that will just take his punishment and let it be, plus he's an adult. What can his father do to hurt him? Take away his trust fund? I almost chuckle at my own joke. Silence settles over the four of us. It's uncomfortable and makes me want to retreat back to my bedroom.

"Oh, I'll watch out for her..." Vance finally says, his lip curling, a sinister smile forming on his sensuous lips. I can't help but gulp at the intensity of hate in his eyes. My skin burns and my cheeks heat without permission. It sounds more like a threat than an obligation to actually protect me and I vow not to put myself in a situation that will require me to need him. I can't rely on him, just like I can't rely on my mother.

Before anyone can say anything else, he turns and walks out of the room. Tension clings to the air, like peanut butter stuck on the roof of my mouth and my lungs burn as I release the breath I wasn't even aware I had been holding in, my chest sagging as I do.

I want to ask where he's going, but it's not really any of my business and I tell myself I don't care, even though I kinda, sorta do. He can do whatever he wants. I mean, it's better like this anyway. Maybe if I stay out of his way, he'll stay out of mine. No conflict means no problems. Hopefully we can get along, at least until our parents get back.

"When I get back, we can have a spa day, and maybe do

some shopping for your bedroom." My mother's singsong voice meets my ears and I skew my facial expression, giving her a megawatt smile instead of a disappointed frown.

"Of course, that sounds great." And it does, but it would've sounded better three years ago. God, I need to let go of my disappointment in her, of the past. There isn't shit that can be done to change what happened. Life is cruel sometimes, suck it up and move on, right?

"Good, good. Well, I love you, sweetie. I have a flight to catch. I'm sure everything will be fine with Vance. He's a little moody sometimes, but don't let him get you down. He'll come around." My mother gives me a hug and a kiss on the cheek before walking away.

Henry gives me a soft smile a moment later before following behind my mom, a checklist of things rattling from her mouth. I stand there in the entryway, my feet cemented to the floor for a long moment.

Alone. All over again, I am alone. Tears sting my eyes, and I try to swallow the emotions down but just like vomit, refusing to be subdued, the tears keep coming.

"It's sad, isn't it?" *His* deep voice sounds against my ear a moment before his scent meets my nose. Citrus and soap. Clean, spicy. I whip around, wiping the tears from my eyes.

Where did he come from?

"What's sad?" I croak.

Those green eyes of his narrow in on me and his head cocks to the side in amusement, or maybe curiosity. It's almost like he's trying to read my soul, trying to suck the secrets right out of me. *No.* No, I won't show him how weak I am. How broken I feel on the inside, that I'm one pull string away from unraveling completely.

He steps closer, his firm chest pressing against mine. Caging me. He's all perfectly sculpted muscle and stupid gorgeousness and I want to rip my gaze away, but I can't. I'm pretty sure he means to intimidate me, and he does, easily since he's a whole foot taller and has at least one hundred pounds on me but there is another feeling, rising up, poking through the tremble of fear and it's a strange one, one that spreads warmth through my belly.

I'm forced to crane my neck back to keep eye contact with him. Breathing deeply, I suck more of his intoxicating scent into my nostrils, my nose wrinkling at the scent. Not only is he stupid gorgeous, but he also smells like a fucking supermodel.

Who the fuck is this guy?

"The fact that she doesn't care about you. The fact that you're here and she still doesn't want you. Why don't you face the facts, Ava, no one wants you. No one. You're an unloved liar."

He could have slapped me, and it would've hurt less than hearing him speak my truths. Curling my hand into a tight fist, I try and tell myself it's not worth it to punch him in his fucking face, because I really, really want to punch him in the face.

He doesn't know what my life has been like since that night five years ago, and I guess a part of me should blame him...if he hadn't dared me...

He leans into my face, his eyes flicker to my lips and for a moment, I think he might kiss me and I kind of want him to. I want to bite his lip, draw his blood, and make him feel the pain that resonates deep within my chest every time I take a breath. But as fast as the thought appears in my mind, it disappears at the sound of his gravelly voice.

"If you were smart, you would leave now. With both our parents gone, there won't be anyone to protect you...no one to save you from me."

He can't possibly be threatening me again, and yet that's what it sounds like, no, it's not a threat. It's a promise.

"I'm not scared of you, Vance. What reason would I have to fear you? And why are you so mad at me anyway? It's not my fault our parents got married and you got stuck with me for a stepsister," I sneer, the closeness of his body to mine making me dizzy.

His head tips back and a bitter laugh fills the space. "You think this has to do with our parents getting married?"

My brows knit together in confusion. What the hell else could it be about? I've done nothing to him, hell I haven't even seen him in five years. He must be mentally unstable, conjuring up things inside his head.

When I don't say anything, he starts to shake his head in disbelief, his body vibrating with rage that reaches inside me and sticks to my bones.

"Liar. That's what you are. A fucking liar. And guess what, you can't lie your way out of this one, nothing will save you from me. I've seen the truth, heard it first hand and I'll get my revenge on you, Ava. I'll hurt you until you beg me to stop."

"I..." Words lodge in my throat. "I don't understand." I blink rapidly, his frame still towering over mine, making me feel as if I'm an inch tall.

"You will soon enough, and if I were you. I would watch my back. You never know when someone's going to lodge a knife in it." With one last cold sweep of his eyes, he pushes past me and out the front door. His words leave me feeling cold, and a sliver of fear cuts through me.

Whatever happened to the boy with soft eyes that never stopped smiling?

4

VANCE

*B*eads of sweat slip down my face blurring my vision. I hit the punching bag at the gym until my knuckles scream at me to stop and the muscles in my arms shake with exhaustion. The rage inside my veins dull to a low simmer, instead of torrid fire. That lying minx thinks she can come back into my life and play me for a fucking fool. Batting her eyes at me like she is an innocent little girl.

Fuck her.

"Jesus, dude," Clark exclaims next to me. "Calm down, you're showing off your hulk skills. Everyone's going to be jealous."

Glancing over at him, I see genuine concern flash in his eyes, even though his words are playful. I stop throwing punches and place a hand against the punching bag, leaning against it.

"Just getting in a good workout," I half lie. Clark knows all too well about my boiling rage and need for vengeance. Usually my temper is in much better check, but with Ava around, I'm one match strike away from exploding.

"Okaaaay." Clark rolls his eyes, a critical expression on his face. There's no point in lying, I know that he knows that this is more than exercise for me. When something bothers me, I come to the gym and let it out. Better than getting into fights with other guys like I used to. There are only so many times a lawyer can get you off assault charges without jail time. Although, maybe jail wouldn't be so bad right now, at least it would get me away from *her*.

"Look, I know your dad getting remarried sucks, you just have to hang in there, buddy. A few more years, and you'll be done with college, and you won't need him anymore...or her," Clark tells me, handing me a bottle of water. "Speaking of your new *stepsister*...she is kinda hot," he continues.

I untwist the bottle cap and start chugging the water, letting the cold liquid cool my throat.

"Yeah, any fucker with a dick would notice that, but my hatred for her runs too deep to fuck her. That, and she doesn't deserve the pleasure my cock would bring. My cock knows she's sexy, but my brain knows she's a lying bitch."

"What about me fucking her? Would you be cool with that?" Clark questions, and a nasty wave of jealousy washes over me. I hate it, I hate the way she makes me feel, the power she holds over me. Somehow, and thank god, I manage to hide the jealousy.

"You can fuck her all you want, as long as that's all you are doing with her. I don't want her to hang out with us and shit. Not unless you want me to kill her." I kid. I might talk a big talk, but I wouldn't ever lay a hand on her, at least not one that didn't inflict pleasure.

"Of course that's all I want to do with her. You know me." He grins. Yes, I do know him. He's even worse than me. Being a dick to girls is his thing...well, mine too. The difference between him and I is that I tell the girl up front that sex is all I want. I'm the *what you see is what you get* kind. Clark, on the other hand, doesn't give a shit. He'll tell the girls whatever they want to hear, making promises that he'll never keep. Once he gets what he wants, he drops the girl faster than he drops the condom in the trash after fucking her.

"Then go for it, she's all yours." At my words, a sinister grin spreads across his face.

"I'm gonna head back home and grab a shower. Want to go out later? Ren invited us to a party, and I could use some pussy and a little weed," I ask as we leave the gym together.

"Sure, just come to my place whenever you get done."

I nod and we part ways in the parking lot. I get into my car and start the engine. Normally I'm relaxed after a session at the gym, far too worn out from my work out to be concerned about anything.

That's not the case today, today I feel as on edge as I did when I walked into the gym. All thanks to the witch living down the hall from me. The drive home is quick and by the time I park my car in front of our house, I'm calm enough to not punch the first person I see in the face. I walk inside and up the stairs, planning to go straight to my room and hop in the shower, but within a few feet of her room, I halt.

There's something about her, something that nags at me. I want to see her again, watch her tremble as I threaten her. I'm fucked up, so fucked up, but I don't care. I'm beyond rational thinking right now.

Stepping closer to the door, I listen intently for any kind of noise. When I don't hear anything, I grab the doorknob and twist it, not bothering to knock. Frowning when I realize it's locked, I knock on the door. You can only lock the door from the inside, so I know she's in there. Probably hiding, coming up with her next lie.

Impatience encases me, and when she doesn't answer, I

knock again. She must be in the bathroom, probably taking a bath, or maybe she's sleeping? My cock twitches in my gym shorts at the thought of her naked body behind that wall. I almost turn and leave, but then I remember that we have one of those wire keys, you can use to open a door from the other side.

I walk down the hall to the guest bathroom and raise my arm, using my hand to feel along the doorframe. *Bingo.* With the key in my hand, I make my way back to her door and unlock it. With a smile on my face, I place the key on top of her door frame to use in the future.

Stepping over the threshold and into her empty room, I find that it is truly *empty*. There's not a single item inside it to showcase that it's hers, no personal touches, pictures or even trinkets. The only thing giving away her occupancy in the room is her unique scent, some kind of flowery smell. I can't pinpoint the scent, it's just feminine and it makes my mouth water. I'm used to women who wear overpowering perfume and cake their faces with makeup. Of course Ava doesn't do either of those things, making her ten times more appealing to everyone with a dick and eyes.

Now that I'm in the room, my ears perk up at the sound of the shower running through the closed bathroom door. What a shame it's closed. I wouldn't mind sneaking a peek. I guess I can wait. Flopping down onto her bed without taking my shoes off and I fold my arms behind my head, waiting so very impatiently for her. I monitor the bathroom door, anticipating the moment she's going to step through it...hopefully naked.

When the shower finally turns off, I almost lose it from the possible image I'm about to see. The door opens a moment later and she steps into her room a towel wrapped around her slim body. *Ahhh... shit.*

"I'm disappointed in you. I was really hoping you would be naked." My lips turn into a pout.

Ava's eyes flick to mine in an instant and her plump pink lips let out a loud shriek. She clasps the towel to the front of her chest like it has the power to save her from me.

Funny, nothing can save her now. My gaze travels down her creamy bare legs, appreciating at least that small glimpse. It's not her tits or her ass but I'll take what I can get. Then again, I didn't come here to check her out...I came here to keep her on her toes, to remind her who is in control.

"What the hell are you doing in here?" she yells at me, her chest rising and falling quickly, while drawing attention to the swell of her breasts.

"Just making sure you're uncomfortable, *stepsister*."

Her lips pucker like she's eaten something sour. "Well, consider it done. Now get the hell out of my room!"

I rub at my jaw. "No, I think I would rather watch you change."

Her green eyes widen, fear flickering in the depths. *Yes*. Give me your fear, your tears, your heartache.

"What is wrong with you? Get out. There is no way in hell I am changing in front of you."

Again, somehow she manages to look seriously surprised by my actions. When is she going to stop playing the victim? Stop acting like she doesn't know what she did or that she doesn't deserve anything less than my hate. Her ignorance of the heaping pile of shit she put on my life sends me into a barely restrained fit of rage.

"Drop the towel," I order, ignoring her question.

"No! There is seriously something wrong with you. Do you have a mental disorder or something? You might not be used to women saying no to you, so let me spell it out for you. Get. Out." Her voice is shaky now.

She's trying to appear strong, like a lighthouse standing tall against the coastline but what she doesn't know is I'm so much more than I appear to be and right now I'm a fucking category five hurricane coming right for her.

Her knuckles turn white as her grip on the towel tightens. One single piece of fabric separates us, and I'll be damned if I'm going to let her keep hold of it.

Swinging my legs off the bed, I shove into a standing position. At my sudden movement, she takes a step back, colliding with the wall behind her.

Run princess, run as fast as you can....

Prowling across the room, I close the distance between us until nothing but a few inches separates us. I'm inches away from her now and she's pressing herself flat against the wall as if she's hoping it will swallow her.

I won't let her get away that easily.

"Drop. The. Towel." I enunciate each word. She's so much shorter than me that I have to tilt my head down to look at her face. Her eyes refuse to meet mine, either out of defiance or fear, but I'm banking on the second one from the way her tight little body is trembling.

Her eyes flicker to the door and I think she's about to make a run for it. Before she can make up her mind, I grab the towel and yank it out of her hand, tossing it behind me. I grin, amused with her behavior. Her eyes go impossibly wide at the loss of the towel and her arms flail as she makes a feeble attempt to cover herself up.

"Don't hide," I growl into her face, my fingers circling her wrists before I pin them above her head and against the wall. Her chest heaves up and down like she just ran a triathlon.

"Don't," she whispers, her voice nothing more than a caress against my cheek. My nostrils flare and I inhale her scent again, needing it to clear my head before I do something stupid, like kiss her.

I take both of her slim wrists into one hand and use the other to touch her. She flinches at first contact as if I would use my hands for anything but pleasure on her, though she doesn't need to know that.

My fingers trail over her collarbone, her skin so smooth it feels like cashmere and for a moment I imagine things are different, that we're just two normal college kids sharing an intimate moment, but we aren't, not really. There isn't anything intimate about us.

This is about fear, about power, about control and I'm going to show her that. She wiggles in my grasp, and my attention drops to her perky breasts, her light pink nipples are hard and begging to be in my mouth. I bite my bottom lip stifling a groan as my gaze sweeps farther down her body, my fingers ghosting against her sternum along the way.

There's a slight tremble to her body, the muscles of her smooth tummy ripple beneath my fingers.

So soft, so fucking perfect. My cock is aching, the fucker wishing to be deep inside of her. *Enemy. Enemy. She's the fucking enemy.* I remind myself over and over again as my gaze travels lower, falling onto the smooth flesh between her thighs.

Fuck. Her pussy is silky smooth, and completely bare of hair.

"Please...don't." Her voice meets my ears and I swallow down the arousal that's building inside me. I could have her if I wanted her. I could take from her until there was nothing left to take, but I won't. I can't. I want to hurt her, but I don't want to *hurt* her like that. Looking up at her I notice the shaking of her lips. Her fear is real, and it only makes my cock harder.

"I'd like nothing more than to run my hands all over your cunt, to dip my fingers inside and see if it's as wet as I think it is..." I pause, leaning into her face, my thumb drawing tiny circles directly above her mound.

"But I don't fuck liars, so..."

Her cheeks flush pink and her lips part. "I don't care what you like, and I wouldn't fuck you if you were the last person on the planet, so I guess we agree on one thing." She curls her lip before pulling her wrists from my grasp, using her hands to shove at my chest. Her weak attempt at moving me makes me grin, and she glares up at me with a fury that could almost rival my own...*almost*.

It takes her another second before she finally moves. Scurrying to the side as not to touch me, she heads to her dresser. I twist around and watch her bare ass jiggle lightly with each step. My dick is so hard, the fucker has created a sizeable tent in my shorts, giving away my want, my need. She rips open the first drawer, her hands shaking as she plucks a shirt from inside and quickly pulls it on, and over her head. Then she does the same with a pair of leggings, my eyes following the fabric up her legs.

"No underwear, huh?" I lift a thick brow. "Not that I'm complaining. It'll be easier for me when I come for you in the middle of the night."

Fuck, what's wrong with me? Threatening her. Scaring her.

She's driving me insane.

"Fuck you! Touch me again and I'll cut your balls off," she yells before dashing out the door.

What the hell is wrong with us? It's like an intense game of tug of war. I should just leave her alone, but I can't. I stand there for a long moment, my chest rising and falling rapidly.

I hate her, but I'm not dumb enough to deny the fact that I'm attracted to her. For a second, I let myself wonder where she's going, but then I shut that shit down. I don't give a fuck what she does or where she goes.

With an iron rod between my legs, I make my way to my bedroom and then into the bathroom where I strip off my clothing before stepping into the walk-in shower.

Twisting the knob, water sprays from the shower head and the first few seconds are ice cold the beads of water pelleting against my skin like hail.

Even that doesn't help my painfully hard cock.

Without thought, I wrap a hand around the beast and stroke him a couple times. I'm so horned up and ready to go that I know it won't take much to get me off. Images of Ava's naked body shaking with need beneath mine filter through my head, my soft strokes turning to strangling jerks.

Another image of her eyes pleading and her bottom lip trembling. Fuck, I want to suck on that lip, bite it, and lick it. Thinking about that mouth of hers has me conjuring up all kinds of things. Ava on her knees, her lips parted as I thrust my cock all the way into her mouth and deep in her throat until she gags around my length. I wonder if she's ever been fucked, ever had a man use her throat as a pussy.

I keep stroking myself furiously while thinking about her. The wrongness of it all only heightening my lust. It doesn't take me long before my balls drag together and an orgasm ripples through me. Tossing my head back, I squeeze my eyes shut as ropes of cum shoot out of my cock and onto the shower floor. Even if I don't want to admit it, she has some type of control over me. I want to own her fear, her hate, and her anger.

Fuck.

5

AVA

My heated cheeks cool under the soft breeze as I run out the back door and into the yard. I have no idea where I'm going, all I know is that I need to get away from him.

The grass is soft under my bare feet and the breeze feels nice against my skin as I aimlessly run away from the house, trying to make sense of what just happened. My eyes fill with tears as the anger and shock are replaced with confusion and shame.

Confusion because I don't understand why he is doing this to me and why he keeps calling me a liar. Shame because part of me likes what he was doing, liked how he touched me and talked to me crudely. What the hell is wrong with me? There must be something wrong with me too if I liked him threatening me like that?

When I finally stop running, my lungs are burning, and I can barely suck in enough oxygen to breathe normally. I lean against a tree while catching my breath and let my gaze sweep over the property. It's beautiful, spacious, and helps me clear my head.

Not ready to go back yet, I sit down behind the tree, leaning my back against the trunk. It might be childish to hide out back here, but right now, I don't really care what anyone thinks of me, least of all Vance. My brain feels like it has just been through a blender. My emotions are all over the place. I have no idea what to do.

Can I even live here safely? I remember his threat to come in my room tonight and a shiver runs down my spine, but only partly from actual fear. I can't help but imagine him coming to me in the middle of the night, sneaking into my room through the darkness.

Climbing into my bed... I squeeze my thighs together, feeling the moisture, and warmth build there thinking about him, and what he would do to me.

Yes, there is definitely something wrong with me.

For a long while I sit there, breathing in the fresh air and wondering what my life would be like if I hadn't played Truth or Dare that night five years ago. Maybe my father would have never found out, he would have never turned into an alcoholic, barely holding onto his sanity. Maybe my parents would still be together, we would still live in our old house, and we would still be a family...and Vance would still be my friend, maybe even more.

He probably wouldn't hate me.

What if...

Feeling that it must be safe to go back inside, I walk back across the yard, and enter through the backdoor, closing it quietly behind me. The entire house is quiet, too quiet as I tiptoe through the kitchen and into the hallway, going completely unnoticed. That is until I turn the corner to head to the staircase and my body crashes into another. Startled, I stagger backward, almost tripping over my own feet. I'm seconds away from beefing it on the polished floor when someone grabs my arm, steadying me.

My mouth opens to yell at *him* to take his hands off of me. I would rather fall on my ass than have Vance catch me, but I realize a second later that it's not Vance holding onto me, it's another guy. He looks oddly familiar. High cheekbones, chocolate colored brown hair that's cut stylishly, and a pair of hazel eyes filled to the brim with mischief.

"You okay?" he asks, his voice friendly and his eyebrows drawn together with concern.

"Yeah, sorry, I uhh..." I apologize and he lets go of my arm. My tongue feels heavy inside my mouth.

"You're Ava, right? I'm Clark," he introduces himself with a grin showing off his perfectly straight white teeth.

"Yes, I'm Ava. It's nice to meet you, Clark."

"I was actually looking for you. Looks like you found me first," he says playfully, his eyes twinkling.

"You were?" I squeak, unsure why he would be looking for me.

He nods. "Yeah. I was wondering if you wanted to hang out. I know how hard it is to be the new kid, plus Vance can be a pain in the ass, so I thought maybe you could use a friend to hang out with."

I get the feeling he doesn't just *hang out* with girls often, not without having his dick inside them and if he's friends with Vance well that's enough said.

"Oh, that's...well, that's sweet of you. I would like that." Clark's smile turns wolfish and only then do I remember my lack of underwear and bra. Of course I would run into a gorgeous Greek god without either item on. All the blood inside my body rushes to my cheeks, giving my embarrassment away.

"If you're free tonight, you could come out with us..." Clark's voice trails off.

"No fucking way. She's not coming out with us." Vance's voice booms down the staircase a moment before he appears at the top of the stairs. He's changed and is now dressed in a dark pair of jeans and gray button-up shirt, looking annoyingly handsome as always.

Beads of water cling to the strands of his russet brown hair. My eyes are drawn to his pink lips, and even after what he did to me earlier, I still want him. It's stupid, and wrong beyond measure since he's not only my stepbrother but obviously the enemy.

"What are you even doing here? I told you I'd come to your house," Vance says bitterly.

I wonder how he keeps friends when he talks to them like that.

"I was tired of waiting, asshole. You took forever and I have zero patience, so here I am. Also, she can come if she wants to, it's a party that the entire campus was invited to. Let the woman choose for herself," Clark responds to Vance who snorts before turning to me.

"Ava, do you wanna come with us? I promise to keep Vance's asshole tendencies to a minimum."

My lips tip up into a small smile.

"No, thank you. I would rather stay home tonight..." *or nail my hand to the wall.* Clark gives me a small pout.

"Maybe, next time?"

"Sure," I mumble, trying to avoid another confrontation with Vance who is walking down the stairs, heading straight for me.

"Maybe you'll put on a bra then, unless the super slutty look is what you were going for," Vance sneers in passing and I curl my hand into a tight fist.

All I need to do is land one punch, one...

"Just ignore him," Clark whispers before surprising me by leaning in and giving me a light kiss on the cheek. When he pulls away, he gives me one more smile revealing two dimples that make him look even cuter. With a wink, he turns and follows Vance, who is already at the door. I wait until the door closes behind them before I turn around and walk up the stairs. Back in my room, I flop down onto the bed, the smell of citrus, and soap filtering into my nose. My blankets smell just like that bastard.

Can't I get away from this guy?

∽

IT'S the middle of the night when I hear the door open and someone walking in. I go from being half asleep to being wide awake in less than a second. Silently I curse myself for not pushing the dresser in front of the door like I had considered doing.

"Have you been waiting for me?" Vance slurs, walking toward me, his movements sluggish. Oh God no, he's drunk. My heart sinks even farther. Too many nights I watched my dad come home drunk. It's a memory of my last I would much rather not relive.

"Get out!" I try to keep my voice strong, while getting out of bed. I can smell the liquor on him, the distinct scent making me recoil.

"Don't be like that...lie back down," he mumbles as he staggers toward me. When he's close enough for me to touch him, I lift my hands and press them to his chest to give him a gentle push toward the door, but his body's firmer than a brick wall and my tiny push doesn't even make him budge.

I don't know why but for some reason, I thought in his

drunken state I would somehow be able to overpower him. Unfortunately, I underestimated him. I was wrong...so very wrong. I shove against his chest as hard as I can, but he doesn't budge. Instead, he grabs me by the arms and pushes me backward and toward the bed.

Alarm bells go off in my mind. This is bad, very bad. I'm completely alone with him. He's much stronger than me and on top of that, he's drunk. I'm so fucking stupid for believing that staying here would be a good idea.

He warned me, told me that he was going to come for me tonight and I ignored his warning. I fell right into his trap.

"Vance..." I say his name, but it comes out more like a whimper.

"Shhh, just lie down," he orders and gently nudges me down until I'm lying on the bed. I push up onto my elbows and try to get away, but he's faster and springs on me like a jaguar, his large frame pressing me into the mattress. Panic claws at me, and inky dread coats my inside, my whole body shaking with fear. He's going to hurt me, he's going to make me pay for something that I'm not even sure I'm guilty of.

"Please," I beg, hoping that he's not too far gone, that he doesn't *really* want to hurt me.

"Please what?" he whispers into my skin with his face buried in the crook of my neck. He smells like vodka and bad decisions. I can't let him do this to me, whatever *this* is. "Please fuck me? I told you...I don't fuck liars. But I did have some girl at the party suck me off...I thought about *you* while I fucked her throat. I was thinking how you would like my cock in your mouth...wouldn't you, Ava?"

"No..." *not like this anyway.*

"Liar...all you do is fucking lie," he growls before slapping a hand over my mouth to shut me up. "I'm done listening to that pretty little mouth spew lies."

I don't understand anything that he's saying, and I squeeze my eyes shut, waiting for whatever he is going to do to me to happen, but I'll be waiting for a while because he doesn't move an inch. It's almost like he's a statue, the weight of his body pressing me further into the mattress. His body blankets mine, his breath moving my hair across my neck with each breath he takes. Strangely, some of the fear starts to ease out of me, and for the first time ever, I don't feel alone.

"Why? Why did you have to fuck everything up?"

He's just venting, talking more to himself than to me. It doesn't stop me from wanting to ask him what he's talking about.

"You could have just kept your mouth shut. You didn't have to tell your dad anything. You didn't have to ruin it all."

I blink rapidly, realization dawning on me.

Is that what this is about? Is he mad at me for telling my dad what happened that night? I want to say something so badly, talk to him, make him understand that I didn't know what else to do, that I was only a kid, but his hand remains securely over my mouth.

Anything I would say would come out as a mumble.

"If you would've just kept your mouth shut, everything would still be the way it was supposed to be. Maybe I wouldn't hate you...maybe we'd still be friends," he whispers, and my chest constricts, a sob lodging deep in my throat. He just rubbed my own worst fears right in my face. Slapped me with them. He answered a question I've been asking myself for years.

What would have happened if I didn't say anything?

All my doubts, worries and fears... they're projected right before my eyes.

Maybe he's right, maybe it's my fault.

The tears start to fall without warning and slip down the

sides of my face. It feels like my heart is ripping in two, the pieces being discarded like trash. For a few minutes, I sob, uncontrollably beneath him. The weight of his body comforts me more than I want to admit and I wish he would touch me, wipe away the tears, tell me it isn't my fault, but he won't because deep down I know he thinks it's all my fault. He blames me for all of it and he plans to slice the knife of a betrayal deep into my chest.

"Shhh, it's too late for your tears now. They won't save you. Nothing can save you from me." He lifts his head, his warm lips ghosting against my cheek. Green eyes reflect back at me. They're glassy and I wonder if he's crying too?

For the loss and the pain that we both obviously endured. I don't get the chance to ask him, not even as he removes his hand from my mouth and pushes up off the bed. My throat is too tight to speak, the words I want to say lodged deep inside the knot forming there. I didn't realize how much comfort I was taking in his body until he was gone.

Stumbling backward, he gives me one last once over before jerkily walking out of the room, closing my bedroom door softly behind him. The room is so quiet now that I'm reminded of how alone I am, how alone I've always been. A quiet sob of pain pushes past my lips, my chest aches at the pressure inside of it.

"Nothing can save you from me..." His words haunt me all night long while I'm lying in my bed cold and alone.

Always alone.

Always cold.

"Nothing can save you from me...." I repeat his words back to myself.

Maybe I don't want to be saved, maybe I need Vance's hate as much as he needs to give it to me.

6

VANCE

Waking up the next morning, all I can think about are all the shitty choices from the night before. *Too much vodka. Sarah. My need to be close to Ava.* My head throbs like someone took a sledgehammer to it. Showering takes an enormous amount of time and effort and by the time I'm done, all I want to do is climb back into bed.

I'm never drinking again, though I suppose I wouldn't have gone balls to the wall if it wasn't for the fucking girl across the hall. She's stupidly beautiful and nothing like my typical flavor of women, which only makes me want her more.

Why did drunk me feel the need to talk to her? I know *why,* but that doesn't mean I want to admit it to myself. Truthfully she needed a hug just about as much as I did, and I guess my drunken self, thought right then would be a good time to give her one.

All night I had thoughts about her, about her lips, her face, the way her fear smelled earlier when she thought I was going to hurt her. I thought about how all I wanted to do was be back at the house tormenting her, breaking her down.

Which in turn led me to drink a lot more than I meant to just so I could stop myself from coming back here. Which was all for nothing, 'cause I still ended up home and in her bed.

Shaking the thoughts away, I somehow manage to get dressed and slip into the hallway. I need to eat something before I barf. Fuck me, I'm never letting Clark pour me shots again.

Even though I tell myself no, my mind reflects back to the way she felt beneath me last night. I wanted to stay in bed with her, hold her in my arms, piece us both back together, but I also wanted to hurt her. Slice her with my words, feel her pain as it poured out of her.

Her tears had surprised me. I didn't expect her to start crying, and when she did, I couldn't stop myself. I had to stay, just for a while longer.

When my feet hit the bottom stair, the smell of freshly brewed coffee tickles my nose. I enter the kitchen to find Ava dancing around in a pair of cute little sleep shorts and cami, headphones in her ears as she pours what looks like pancake batter into a pan. I didn't even know we had pancake batter.

She shakes her cute ass and rolls her hips to the beat of the music that's blasting in her ears. Fuck, I can imagine my hands gripping onto those hips as I rail into her, over and over... Turning around, she gasps, her eyes raking up and down my body at a snail's pace.

She might not like me very much, but she definitely likes what she sees. Pulling out the earbuds, she tosses them onto the counter along with her phone that she has shoved into her bra.

"I...I didn't know you were there."

I roll my eyes. "Obviously." There's a coolness to my voice that doesn't quite match the heat radiating throughout me.

Every time I'm in her presence, I feel like I'm one volcanic eruption away from wiping out the human race forever.

She nibbles on that plump bottom lip nervously and my cock hardens. He needs to stay the fuck out of this. My feelings for her are nothing but hate and revenge. I don't need to add *fucking* her to the list.

"I made you breakfast, I mean… if you want some…"

A long stretch of silence settles over us. Her doe eyes stare up at me. Why the fuck is she looking at me like that? Like she can see right through me? Suddenly I feel vulnerable and I don't like it, not one fucking bit.

Smoke billows from the pan behind her and I grin. "You mean the breakfast that you're currently burning?"

Whirling around with a shocked look on her delicate face, she grabs the pan, a slew of curses fill the air. She tosses the burnt pancake into the trash before setting the pan back on the stove. She pours more batter into the pan, her body fidgety as hell.

"My mother called me this morning," she says with her back to me. For some stupid reason, I enter the kitchen and take a seat at the island. I haven't eaten breakfast in here since the house was built.

"Yeah, and why the fuck should I care?"

"Because it has to do with you." I don't miss her exhale, or the sadness that seems to coat her words. Minutes ago she seemed at ease, but now she seems, heartbroken, like someone kicked her fucking dog or something.

"Well speak… I don't have all day, and I don't particularly care for what you have to say. Liars are and always will be liars." Even with my nasty remark, she turns and places a plate of pancakes and bacon in front of me. Her green eyes harden, and I watch her visibly swallow.

"Our *parents* are extending their trip. Apparently they want to go to the Bahamas next, or something..." Her tone is bitter, a clear indication that her relationship with her mother is just as strained as my own with my father. I slather the pancake in syrup and cut a piece off, shoving it into my mouth before I can say something that would make it sound like I give a fuck, because I don't. I really don't give a fuck.

Pushing all the words away, I take a bite, and then another, Ava's eyes remaining on mine the entire time. I don't like the way her eyes feel on me, like she's able to see through the walls I built up around myself. Like she fucking knows me. She doesn't, no one does.

"You sound bothered by that, any particular reason why?" I ask, grinning. I'm sure I have something to do with her obvious bitterness. Probably because she doesn't want to be alone with me and I relish in the thought of how uncomfortable I make her.

Get used to it, princess...

She shrugs. "I don't know. I was hoping to spend some time with her before classes start. I haven't seen her in three years. It would be nice if she could slow down for five seconds and talk to me like I'm her daughter, or pay me even an ounce of attention."

I stop mid-bite, the fork hovering in the air.

What did she just say?

Three years? Damn. I almost feel bad for being a dick, *almost.*

But then that little nagging feeling in the back of my mind reminds me that she brought this on herself. She did this to both of us.

And if there's anything I can't stand, it's a liar, and that's what she is, a liar.

A liar with a pretty fucking face, and a broken heart.

It's clear her mother has let her down in more ways than

one, and stupidly for a fraction of a second, I wonder what happened to her after that night. What happened between her parents that led her to me, that led her down this road?

Her lie destroyed my life, but what did it do to hers? I never really thought about it, to be honest, and I still don't care enough to ask her. It's her own fault. If she would've only been truthful... I mean, we were just kids, she didn't have to do it if she didn't want to. Maybe in her eyes it was just a white lie, something to save her ass, but to me, it was the end. It's where my life started to spiral out of control.

Everything changed because of her stupid lie.

I lost everything... my father's love, my mother, my life fell into shambles because of her. I watch her make her own plate out of the corner of my eye. She takes a seat at the kitchen island, but not next to me. She leaves two chairs between us as if she knows better than to try and sit beside me. *Thank, fuck.*

An uncomfortable silence settles over us and I try to shove the last remaining forkfuls of food into my mouth. I have to get out of here, I have to get away from her. Away from her floral scent, her heart-shaped face, her sad fucking eyes. The blood in my veins is reaching its boiling point. All these unsaid words and questions hang between us.

I want to hurt her with my lips, break her with my touch... I want to tell her she's not truly that unlovable, but that would go against everything inside of me. That would be like betraying myself, and I have to remember why we're enemies, why her being here is a fucking problem. I can feel her green orbs on my skin... Why isn't she eating, why is she staring at me like I can provide her with all the answers in the world.

"About last night..." She starts and I tighten my hold on the fork, the metal digging into my palm. Does she really want to see me lose my shit? Obviously so, because she continues the words pouring out of her mouth like acid.

"What did you mean last night? You keep saying I lied, but I don't know what you mean. If I knew, maybe I could understand, maybe I could make this..." She moves a hand between us. "Make this hate go away."

I think maybe she has a death wish... bluntly attempting to act innocent right to my face.

"Are you fucking serious right now?" I can feel my skin heating, the zing of anger pulsing through me. For so long, I've held that pain inside, I've let it eat away at my soul, my spirit and now she's here, the cause of it, right in front of me and all I want to do is make her own it. Make her take it from me.

Dropping the fork to the marble, I curl my hand into a fist and slam it down on the counter, making her jump in her seat and my head throb at the clatter. Pain radiates through my hand and up my arm, but I love it. I fucking love it. It reminds me that I'm still alive and that the pain is real. There's a tiny tremble to her body, her chest rises and falls and a pink flush creeps onto her cheeks. She looks scared, but she also looks...I don't let myself finish that sentence. Instead, I bask in the glory of hate.

How dare she sit here and pretend she doesn't know what I'm talking about? Liar, all the fucking lies. Every word off her tongue is a lie.

I can't stand to be in this room with her a moment longer. Shoving my seat backward, I let it topple over, slamming into the hard floor. The sound makes me wince, the throbbing behind my eyes becoming more and more annoying. That coupled with her presence and I'm a second away from losing my shit.

Grabbing my plate, I stomp to the trashcan and dump the rest of my food into the garbage before throwing my plate in the sink. It lands with a loud clack, most likely breaking. Hell, it wouldn't be the first time I broke something in this house in a fit of rage.

"Your pancakes taste like shit, just like the fucking lies that you spew," I yell, turning around to face her, to drive the knife a little deeper. Her shocked face peers up at me, and my fingers curl into the countertop. It's either I grab this, or her, and I don't want to touch her, not right now. Not with this much anger, this much madness spiraling out of control inside of me.

I lean into her, ignoring her scent and the fear that circulates through her eyes. She needs to know that I fucking mean what I say, she needs to know that I'll only ever hate her. Always.

"Just tell me, Vance." Her bottom lip juts out and it looks like she's about to cry. She's begging me to tell her what happened, but she already knows. She's the one that did this, not me. The sound of my name falling from her lips sends me over the edge and I release my hold on the countertop and instead grip her by the chin, pulling her forcefully into my face.

"Oh, how the mighty fall. One day you had it all and now you have nothing... it's strange how the tables turn, how one lie can make an entire world crumble overnight." My lip curls with hate, her tiny hand clasping onto my wrist in an effort to get me to release my hold. But I'm not done yet, not by a long fucking shot.

"You might be able to shed some tears and get other people to feel sorry for you with that look, but believe me when I say this, you'll never get an ounce of pity from me. You deserve everything you've got and everything that's coming to you!" I release her like she truly has the power to destroy me and stomp out of the room before I do something I can't take back.

My intentions have always been to hurt her, to break her

down, to show her that she's nothing, but having her here, smelling her sweet scent all around me, feeling her skin, it's almost like she's hurting me instead of me hurting her. And I can't let that happen. She's already owned too much of me, of my thoughts, of my past. I'm Vance Preston. I lost my heart years ago, because of a lie that destroyed my family, because of a threat that wasn't true.

Had she told the truth...had she never made me out to be the criminal then maybe I wouldn't be the man I am today. Maybe there wouldn't be a gaping wound inside my chest, maybe I wouldn't need to taste her fear, to feel her pain.

Maybe we would be more than enemies.

Or maybe we wouldn't.

7
AVA

It's the dreaded first day of school and I try not to dwell on the fact that my mom still hasn't returned from her honeymoon. Or that my dad still hasn't called me, or that Vance still seems to hate my entire existence.

At least he's ignored me for the last few days, sticking mainly to his bedroom. It's much nicer than him actively trying to hurt me and make me uncomfortable. Living with him is like living with a ticking time bomb. There's a constant ball of anxious anxiety inside of me and I hate it. I never know what to expect with him... is he going to hurl an insult at me, or is he going to hug me like he did the night he got drunk?

I wear the least eye-catching attire I have. A pair of skinny jeans and free-flowing blouse that hangs off one shoulder. It's cute, but it's not going to draw every single eye to me. *I hope.* I leave an hour before my first class is scheduled to start, and chew on a granola bar on the way there. I didn't dare to ask Vance if we could ride together so I'm taking the Honda that was parked in the garage to class.

I'm avoiding my tormentor at all cost. The last thing I want is for us to have another duel. I'm hoping if I stay out of his way, he'll stay out of mine and that when our parents get back, we can forget about the verbal sparring we did while they were gone.

When I get to campus, I park in one of the student parking areas and get out my class schedule and the map I printed out. Then I'm off with my Converse-covered feet beating across the pavement. It doesn't take me long to find the building I need to be in, and once I do, I find a small bench just outside the building and get out my biology book, flipping through the first few pages.

My eyes skim over the material, and I suck in as much knowledge as I can so I'm prepared for what's to come. To most kids, college is a drunken sex fest, where you grow, and make friends, but not to me. To me, college is my way out... my key to getting the fuck away from all the people that don't care about me.

After a few minutes of studying, other college students start to appear, walking past me, they're lost in conversation, laughing and smiling. Someone opens the door to the building a moment later and I get up from the bench, walk down the sidewalk and inside. I take a seat in the back, spreading my stuff out on the table. A second later, a girl comes walking in and takes a seat to my left, situating her books in a similar fashion.

The air in my chest halts. I notice right away that her book looks different from mine.

My gaze narrows in on the book.

The cover reads *Abnormal Psychology*. Quickly, while trying not to draw any attention to myself, I look around the classroom and realize that all the students, at least the ones in this classroom, have that same psychology book.

I swallow down the panic that's creeping in on me and turn to the girl beside me.

"Hey, can you tell me what class this is?"

"Psych 301," she says and graces me with a soft smile.

"Thanks," I mumble before grabbing all my things and speed walking out of the room. I look at the building number on my way out to make sure it is building nine and it is. I double check my class schedule and the map again.

According to it, I'm at the right building, and in the right class, but the book I have doesn't match the class I was just in.

What the actual hell? Panic turns into confusion as I look up and when I spot two guys walking toward me, I know I need to ask for help.

"Hey, can I ask a question?" I fiddle with the strap of my backpack nervously. I'm not this open with people, but I'm beyond confused and don't want to risk missing all my classes for the day because I can't figure out where the hell I'm going.

"Most definitely," one of the guys answers in a flirty tone. He's cute, in an all-American boy way.

"Do either of you happen to know where the nine AM biology class is?"

One of the guys rubs at his scruffy chin as if he's thinking, while his friend elbows him in the side and answers me.

"Biology is usually in building two." He hooks a thumb pointing in the direction behind him. *Motherfucking shit.*

"Okay, thanks," I mumble, returning my attention back down to the map. My gaze roams over the map key and all the buildings. When my eyes lock on the number two, I curse.

"Shit!" I tilt my head back and look up at the blue sky. Why, why does the world have to shit on me? Building two is all the way across campus. It's going to take me forever to get there, but since I had to park pretty far away, I think I'm still better off on foot than driving and trying to find a spot to park again.

Exhaling a frustrated sigh, I swing my bag over my shoulder and start running down the sidewalk to the other buildings, my feet slapping against the concrete. I probably look like a crazy lunatic, as I hurry past everyone in my way. By the time I get to the building, I'm ten minutes late, sweating like a whore in church and completely out of breath.

Just how I wanted to start my morning, stinky and late.

The room is packed, but somehow, I manage to find a seat. Whispers meet my ears, some quiet, some loud, but I don't pay anyone an ounce of attention.

The rest of the class I spend frazzled and feel as if I'm trying to play catch up. I hate being late. Hate it. It ruins my day and gets me off schedule. Maybe it's a form of OCD, but when it comes to being somewhere, I'm always on time. *Always.* I end up dropping my pencil twice, and misspelling words left and right. My notes end up in the wrong notebook, and now I'll have to copy them into the right one.

Something is wrong with me.

After what seems like an eternity, the professor releases us. I gather up my things and walk out looking for my next class, which luckily doesn't start for another half an hour. Hopefully this time I can be on time, and in the right room.

My class schedule says it's in building five, but when I walk over to the sign, it says *Administration Building.* I clench my jaw, a low simmering anger rippling through me. Why would my English literature class be in the admin building?

Vance. It hits me then. He must've done this, done something with my classes. There's no other explanation for it. When I got my class schedule, all my classes matched up with the books that I bought, but the classes on my schedule now, don't.

Stupid, Vance. He thinks he can mess with me. I kick at the pavement out of anger and stub my toe. *Jesus*. I'll find a way to get him back, but for now, I need to fix the problem that he's caused. Walking inside the building, I peer around, trying to find someone who can help me. It's the first day of school you would think this building would be the busiest of all, but it seems it's the most vacant.

There's no one sitting at the front office, instead there's a sign that says *OUT* in big bold letters. Who works in an admin building at a college and just doesn't show up for their job? It's not lunch time, so what does the *out* mean? Shaking my head in frustration because today has already been a clusterfuck, I walk down the long hallway looking for someone, anyone.

Out of nowhere, a door opens right in front of me, and I almost run into it face first.

"Oh, sh— I'm sorry..." the guy who almost hit me with his door says, his eyes finding mine. They're a vivid blue, so blue that for a moment I forget what the hell it is that I'm doing.

"Are you okay? Are you hurt?" His deep baritone voice breaks the trance and I find my voice through the fog.

"Yes, I'm fine...well, besides this... it seems the building numbers on my class schedule are messed up. I ended up in the wrong building and then late for my first class because I had to run across campus." I blow out a frustrated sigh. It's not his fault, I know that, but I can't help but vent.

"Why don't you come into my office and I'll see if I can help you with that," he says, holding the door open for me. I walk in and take the seat at the front of his desk. It holds a little metal plague that says **S. Miller, Dean's Assistant.** Looking at him, he doesn't seem to be much older than me, and though I know it's none of my business, I wonder how he got into a position like this.

I hand him the piece of paper as he sits down in the chair

on the other side of the desk. I take him in, he's handsome, young, and could pass for a student that goes here. His eyes glance over the paper his eyebrows pointing down, his features turning serious.

"I think someone was trying to play a prank on you." He frowns a moment later.

His assumption isn't just correct it's spot-the-fuck-on. "Yeah, I figured as much...my stepbrother thinks stuff like this is funny. This is my first day here and I missed move-in day and orientation so I have no idea where anything is. Figures he would turn my first day of classes into a real-life nightmare."

"Ah, brothers of all kinds can be a pain in the ass. I have two. I know all about it, and I'm the middle child so I have to deal with both at the same time."

I'm only slightly surprised by his use of words, after all, he isn't much older than me.

"Let's turn your crap day into a better one. I'll print you the right schedule right now and you can get back to your classes, hopefully on time."

He types some stuff into the computer, his long fingers stroking over the keys. A second later, a soft knock sounds on the door, making us both look up. The door, which wasn't closed all the way, swings open a few inches, revealing a woman my age.

"Oh, gosh. I'm sorry I didn't know there was anyone in here," she apologizes, her cheeks tinting pink as if she's embarrassed or something.

"It's fine, you can come in, Jules." He waves his hand, motioning for her to walk in, a smile on his lips.

"This is..." He looks down at the paper in his hand. "Ava. She's new, today is her first day. Maybe you could show her around campus? From the sound of things she's not having a very good time." A soft chuckle passes his lips and I wouldn't be surprised if he has women throwing themselves at him. I swing my gaze back to the girl, *Jules* as he called her, feeling sorry that he put her on the spot like that. She doesn't seem to be bothered by it though and graces me with a bright smile.

"Sure, I would love to," she answers, the genuineness of her tone telling me she isn't lying. "When is your next class?"

I blink. "In twenty minutes...but if you're busy. I mean, I'd understand if you can't do it. If you have something else that you needed to do—" I try to give her a way out, but she shakes her head the mass of blonde ringlet curls bounces with the movement.

"No way Jose. I have plenty of time, most of my classes are in the evening and only a few times a week. Plus anyone that's a friend of Seb's, is a friend of mine."

Friend? I don't know if we're friends. It's kinda his job to help me, though he certainly doesn't have to be nice to me while he does it.

"Oh okay..." I smile, feeling a little better knowing that I won't be burdening her. The last thing I want is to make her feel like she has to help me. I'm used to doing things on my own. I've done it this way for three years, and if she couldn't help me, then I would have figured it out myself. I'm a big girl, as Vance would say.

"How about I take you to your next class and maybe later we can get some coffee and I can show you around the rest of the campus?"

"That would be great," I sigh. *It really, really would.* I need this, so much, so much more than I want to admit.

"Perfect!" she exclaims, her eyes moving back to Mr. Miller. "I'll call you later, Sebastian."

"Tell Rem I said hi, and that he should show his face more than once a week," Mr. Miller teases, and I get the feeling that these two know each other on a personal level.

"Will do. He's been buried in homework lately," Jules responds.

"Homework, you say?" He lifts a thick brow and grins before averting his eyes back to the computer. Jules' cheeks heat, and she nibbles on her bottom lip. Oh, yes, these two definitely know each other, and whoever Rem is, he's with Jules. It doesn't take Sebastian long to get my schedule printed and send me out the door.

Jules walks me to class and for once, I feel like I might have made a good choice with coming to school here. She tells me about her boyfriend Remington, and how Mr. Miller is actually *Sebastian*, and Remington's brother. She asks me a few questions about myself that I answer with a vague response. I don't want anyone to know how fucked up my situation is. Everyone has problems, that doesn't mean we need to broadcast them.

"Here, let me text you. Then later, when you finish up classes for the day, we can meet up. Oh, and if you have any questions, give me a call. I'll help you however I can. I know all too well what it's like to be the new girl." She smiles and makes me feel like there is more to her story. I rattle off my number and she sends me a quick text, my phone signaling the incoming message from my pocket.

"Thank you, and I truly do mean it. It was very nice of you to... to do this." My thanks is awkward, but Jules doesn't say anything about it. She just gives me a soft smile and then a hug, as if she knows how badly I need to be hugged right now.

"It gets easier. I promise," she whispers into my ear before releasing me. I really hope she's right, because if it gets worse, I'm not sure what the hell I'm going to do. Vance successfully ruined the start of my first day of classes. I guess there was a silver lining in all of this. I had made my first friend. I bet Vance Preston wasn't expecting that to happen.

My next three classes fly by and before I realize it, it's the afternoon and I haven't eaten a thing, the rumbling of my stomach providing proof.

Rubbing the organ, I promise to feed it as soon as possible and head toward a coffee shop I saw on the corner while leaving one of my classes earlier. Fishing my phone from my pocket, I check the time, when that one single distraction sends me colliding into another body, or brick wall. Before I can stop it, I'm tumbling backward, my ass cushioning my fall as I land hard against the sidewalk. Pain radiates up my spine at the impact.

"Watch where you're going," somebody sneers, but as soon as I hear the icy tone of his voice, I know who it is that just sent me falling to my ass.

And the universe just keeps shitting on me.

"Sorry," I mumble, shoving up from the ground, ass aching as I do. I drag my eyes up his stupidly gorgeous body, stopping on his arrogant face. Tight jaw, firm lips, piercing eyes that look like daggers are growing inside of them.

Yup, that's Vance Preston. Brooding, angry, and with a chip the size of Texas on his shoulder. I hate that I find him attractive, while also wanting to sucker punch him in the throat. While most chicks throw themselves at him, I just want to throw *shit* at him.

"Heard you were in the dean's office earlier." His eyes narrow. "Did you use that *thing* between your legs to get your schedule changed or something?"

First, how the hell did he know I was in the dean's office, does he have eyes everywhere?

And two, why is he referring to my vagina as a *thing*, while accusing me of whoring myself out to get a schedule change.

Taking a step back, I crane my neck up at him. "Excuse me?"

I'm not even shocked to hear him talk so shitty about me, but I am shocked that he would do so in such a public place. Then again, he probably doesn't care what people think about him, not that it matters since no one would dare say something so vile to him.

His lips twist into a grin. "Your pussy, did you use it to manipulate the dean? It wouldn't surprise me. Master manipulators have a tendency to do that kind of thing. I wouldn't expect anything less from you."

My teeth grind together... *don't say anything, don't say anything...* I tell myself, but my mouth pops open anyway, because who the hell does he think he is? My resolve snaps and I take a giant step forward pressing a finger into his very firm, very well defined chest.

"What is your problem? I didn't lie about anything and I wouldn't have been in the dean's office if it wasn't for you and your cruel little joke," I yell, drawing attention from a passersby.

His icy gaze drops down to where my finger is touching him, and he grabs said finger, tossing my hand back as if I'm a piece of garbage. He leans into my face, piss and vinegar marring his features. He's like a bull that's been poked with a hot branding iron and I'm the one holding it.

"*You.*" The growl that rumbles out of his chest vibrates through me. "You are my problem and until you leave, running back to wherever the fuck you came from, you will continue to be. Want it to stop, just say the word. Leave, and it will all end. Stay, and I'll break you so badly you won't even recognize yourself."

My lips curl without thought, and even though I don't have a mean bone in my body, I can't help but say the first words that come to mind. "Fuck you, Vance. You don't own me, or this school, so do your worst, you can't break something that's already broken."

I'm not dumb, truly I'm not. I know I shouldn't taunt him, push him, but it's so hard to allow him to say the shit he is about me. His face turns emotionless and I shiver at the image before me. It's worse than the icy gaze he was giving me moments ago.

"Checkmate, Ava, checkmate," he whispers against the shell of my ear before shoving past me. I'm not a dog, and I won't roll over and play dead. If he wants to hurt me, he's going to have to try harder than that.

∼

Not wanting to go home and face Vance yet, or worse yet nothing at all, I decide to do a little shopping. By the time I get home, the sun is setting, and my stomach is grumbling, demanding me to feed it. The shower is calling my name and I have a paper to write. Oh the joys of the first day of classes. I pull onto the long driveway that leads to the house and immediately see cars lined up along the road and in front of the house.

What the hell is going on?

I can already feel my blood boiling in my veins. People scurry across the driveway as I press the garage opener in my mom's car, only to find there's nowhere for me to park since there appears to be a game of beer bong taking place in my parking space.

He's got balls… massive ones, if he thinks this is going to fly. And who has a house party on a Monday, anyway? Doesn't anyone care about classes? Sleep? Throwing the car into park, I get out, my teeth grinding so hard I wouldn't be surprised if one of them cracks.

The music inside the house is so loud I can hear it outshide, the ground shaking from the bass. This asshole is going to get the police called on us. My appearance draws the attention of a bunch of people that are standing in the yard, red cups in hand. A few of the girls sneer at me, while the guys stare at me like I'm a fawn entering the lion's den.

Grabbing my shopping bags out of the car in a haste, I march up the walkway and onto the front porch. If this asshole thinks he can ruin me by doing some adolescent bullshit, then he's got another thing coming. I'm shutting this shit show down, right now.

8

VANCE

I feel her before I see her. That's the strange thing about being drawn to someone you have no business being drawn to. You feel them deep inside you, like your soul is speaking what your mind refuses to acknowledge.

"Heads up, little stepsister alert. And she's looking hot as fuck, and a little bit psycho," Clark chuckles, a billow of smoke escaping his lips. Sarah is slung across my lap, acting as if she belongs there, and though she doesn't, I don't have the patience to tell her otherwise. She twirls a piece of blonde hair around her finger, looking bored.

She's not who I want...who my blood sings for... As if my body knows she's close, the hairs on the back of my neck stand on end. A second later Ava appears in the foyer, her hands filled with bags, a scowl the size of Texas on her face. Like the perfect mix of drugs, her presence sends endorphins racing through my veins. It cripples me, making me weak, but it also gives me the edge I want. The edge I need to hurt her.

Her cheeks are dark pink, and frustration creases her forehead and I know I've hit my mark. The schedule switch was supposed to be a little fun, just something to humor myself, but then I heard she had befriended Jules Peterson, and I couldn't have her thinking her first day turned out okay.

So like always, Clark came to the rescue with the back-to-school-bash. A few texts and the mention of free beer and word spread like herpes on spring break.

"Hey *stepsister*," I greet with a smug smile. Her hands curl into tiny fists and she looks like she has the urge to throw her shopping bags at me. She's kinda adorable when she's mad, her mousy brown hair pulled into a tight ponytail, her outfit sexy, but not overly eye-catching. I bet she had a guy or two lusting after her today.

Sarah wiggles in my lap, her well-manicured hand running over my chest possessively. Normally I would tell her to cut it out, she means nothing to me, has no hold over me, but right now I don't mind it so much, not when I see jealousy flash in Ava's emerald eyes.

"How was your first day? Did you find all your classes alright?" A couple of the guys chuckle beside me.

"Great, thanks for asking," Ava sneered sarcastically, her eyes rolling to the back of her head. "If you wouldn't mind, I would really appreciate it if you could quiet it down. Most of us have classes tomorrow and I have homework already, so..."

The fuck? Who does she think she is? Obviously, I need to bring her down a couple notches, show her who is really in control here.

"What are you, eighty? Just go to your room and close the door. It's not like you were invited, and if I don't want to see you, then I can guarantee no one else in this room does." I hate myself a little bit more as I say the words, because while they're mean, they stoke the fire of resentment toward her.

"Baby," Sarah coos, her feral gaze turning toward Ava. "Give her a break. This is a big change for her. I mean, I can't imagine how hard it must be for trailer trash like her to suddenly be living in a nice place like this. Especially with her dad being in rehab and all. She's probably over the moon."

Sarah's words almost wipe the smile off my face. *Trailer trash? Rehab?* If it wasn't for the sudden change in Ava's demeanor, I wouldn't even believe Sarah's words. But seeing Ava's eyes fall to the floor and the slump of her shoulders tells me that it's true and I swear to God if she starts to cry again, I might lose it.

"Go on... run up to your room... no one wants you here..." Sarah cackles, shooing her with her hands, and I feel the sudden urge to shove her off my lap and go to Ava. This is wrong, treating her this way, breaking her down. But it's right too.

She deserves this, deserves to feel pain, sadness. No matter if her father is in rehab, she probably didn't spend the last three of the five years we've been apart struggling. She probably had a good fucking life, probably still does even living here and that alone solidifies my choices. I can't let doubt lead me astray. I *won't* let it.

Clark exhales a long sigh beside me before shoving up from his seat. My mouth pops open, words piercing the edge of my tongue, but I don't say shit. She's fresh meat, and I hold no stake over her. If he wants to befriend her and fuck her into next week, then he can. It's none of my business. I don't care. *Or at least I shouldn't.*

He leans down and whispers something into her ear. He's close enough that if she turned at the right angle, their lips would touch, and for some reason, that pisses me off. Stupid, this is fucking stupid. Her being here, it's toying with my emotions.

I try and force myself to look away, but I can't. I'm transfixed on them, needing to know for sure that Clark doesn't do something. Whatever he says to her causes her to shake her head, the movement slow and causing small wisps of hair to fall onto her face. She's beautiful, so beautiful that it's sickening. I want to brush those strands from her eyes, kiss her pink lips, and feel her tiny body beneath mine.

Then as if she can feel my gaze on her, her eyes lift to mine. For a fraction of a second, our eyes meet... the world is suspended in time around us. It's just her and I. I'm not the bully anymore, and she isn't a victim to my rage. Clark's mouth starts to move again, and the moment between us ends.

I see her lips form the word *sorry*, and then she's walking out of the room, just as Sarah had instructed, thankfully leaving Clark behind. He twists around, a dazzling grin on his face. His hazel eyes filled with mischief. I'm not sure what I would've done had he followed her upstairs. He's my best friend, yeah, but I don't think I could've handled it, not without lashing out in some way.

"What a loser." Sarah purses her red lips, throwing her arms around me while trying to place a kiss on my lips. Yeah, no. I don't kiss, and if I did, it wouldn't be Sarah. She's had a lot of dicks pass her lips, and I'm not about kissing anyone that puts dick in their mouth like most chew gum. And with Ava out of sight, there's no need to keep Sarah on my lap. My need for her presence is done.

"Get away from me," I growl, unwrapping her arms from me before shoving her off of me and onto the couch cushion. She's so surprised by the movement that she almost slides off the couch altogether. I feel dirty, filthy for the things I've said to Ava, and for letting Sarah sit on me like that. Like a small toddler that's been told no, Sarah stands, stomping her wedged heel against the wooden floor.

"What are you doing, baby?"

"Stop calling me baby, in fact, keep my name out of your

mouth. We're not a couple. You suck my dick a couple nights a week, that's it. Giving good head doesn't make you girlfriend material, and while you have a pretty face, you have a shit fucking attitude. Now leave me the fuck alone." I don't even look at her, I know damn well she is glaring daggers at me, probably thinking about taking her shoe off and beating me with it. Wouldn't be the first time something like that happened.

Needing a drink, and some air, I get up from the couch and make my way into the kitchen. The place is a fucking disaster with open liquor bottles scattered across the countertop, and dirty glasses piled up in the sink. There's trash laying around on the floor, as if that's the place to be putting empty beer bottles when the perfectly empty trashcan is sitting right fucking here. *Assholes.* Though I would love to see my father's face if he came home to this mess. He would shit bricks.

Ignoring all of that, I walk straight to the bottle of whiskey, find myself a cup and pour it into a glass. I'd drink right from the bottle, but that would be dangerous as fuck and I don't want a recap of what happened last time I got drunk.

Ava doesn't need to get any more ideas about the person I am. A heavy hand lands on my shoulder and I swing around, ready to slug whoever it is when my eyes meet Clark's. Worry creases his forehead. The jackoff looks like he walked off the cover of a magazine. Where I'm ripped jeans, t-shirts, and boots, Clark is polos, designer jeans, and Nike.

We shouldn't be friends at all, not even run in the same circles and yet I wouldn't trade the fucker for the world.

"She's fucking pissed," he tells me, as if I don't already know it.

"Yeah." I shrug. "So? What's your point? So was I when I found out she was a fucking lying pig. Don't let her doe eyes fool you, she's a lying bitch."

Clark's gaze widens a bit and I know he's taken back by my words. Usually I'm not such a dick, but with Ava reappearing in my life, it seems a new shade of asshole has risen from inside of me.

"How long are you going to play this game? What's the end result? Should I wait to sneak in to fuck her until after you've broken her?"

My jaw tightens. "First, it isn't a game, second, the end result is always going to be the same. I won't stop until she's admitted that she lied. Until I feel that she's suffered enough humiliation and disappointment."

Clark nods. "And what if it's never enough? Hurting her won't change the past. She seems like a nice girl. I mean Sarah said her dad's in rehab, maybe some shit went down that we don't know about. I can find out - I mean if you want me to, that is."

I can feel my hand curling around the cup. The temperature rising. Forcing myself to inhale, I take a gulp of the dark liquid, letting it burn down my throat, and settle deep inside my stomach. Instead of it cooling my body, it warms it, making me feel ten times hotter than I already am.

"She seems like a nice girl, because that's what she *wants* you to see. Nice girls don't lie. They don't destroy families for fun. Nice girls are *nice*. Ava isn't nice. As for the past, it might not change what happened, but it'll certainly make me feel better." I bring the cup to my lips again and swallow down the rest of its contents.

My insides are blanketing with warmth once more, the dull ache in my chest becoming less noticeable.

"And what about her father? Do you want me to...?" Clark's voice trails off as the lights flick off and the room goes dark. Panic ensues, and people start running for the door, the sounds of screams and feet stomping across the wood floor fill the room. I don't move though. I let everyone filter out first.

What. The. Fuck.

"What the hell? How did you lose power?" Clark asks, a perplexed look on his face. There's an uptick in my blood pressure, a shift in the air. I can taste the rush of adrenaline. Gritting my teeth, I crumple the cup in my hand as if it's a piece of paper.

She wouldn't...would she? Not unless she had a death wish, right?

Who am I kidding, she would, and I suppose I wouldn't expect any less of her after the way Sarah embarrassed her. But nonetheless, this is *my* party and *my* fucking house, and if she's going to shut down my shit for the night, then she's going to have to entertain me in other ways. I hope she's the praying type because she's going to need all the prayers she can get.

"Make sure everyone gets the fuck out. I don't want any stragglers left behind. I'm going to take care of the brat," I tell Clark, and swipe at my bottom lip with my thumb. I toss the cup onto the counter and stomp off in the direction of the garage, little tendrils of excitement slither down my spine.

This cat and mouse game we're playing has my cock permanently hard. I've never been so hard for a girl before, let alone one that I hate. It's like my body isn't getting the fucking memo. She's not worthy of my dick, no matter how soft, how beautiful, how tempting she is.

As I suspected, the door is closed when I reach it. Grabbing onto the knob, I twist it, the lock firmly in place. *That fucking witch.* Anger slithers through me like a fire spreading through a forest after a drought, devouring everything it touches.

Taking a step back, I look at the door one last time. I could kick the fucker in, but I've got a better idea. Retreating down the hallway off the kitchen, I stop and lean against the wall, waiting, watching. The house grows quiet, so quiet I can almost hear myself think.

I lick my lips, the anticipation building.

My cock is rock hard. The words I'm going to say right on the edge of my tongue.

She has to come out eventually.

The minutes tick by... she probably thinks she's safe, that I've run off, but no way in hell am I letting her push me out of my own house. Nope, tonight Ava Wilder is going to pay, she's going to give me a slice of that sweet little body of hers.

Patience isn't really my strong suit, but I'll wait knowing that the reprieve will be worth it. After a short while, a noise perks my ears, the sound of the lock disengaging, and the knob twisting. The hallway is submerged in near darkness, the moonlight coming from a nearby window allowing a sliver of light inside, though none of it reaches the wall I'm leaning against. I can hear her tiny steps. Unsure, weary.

Come closer...

I hold my breath, making sure she doesn't hear me before she sees me. I'd hate to ruin the surprise. She takes two more steps before she comes into view, her eyes skidding over her shoulder as if she's watching for someone, waiting for someone.

Too bad she doesn't realize that she's already being hunted. My eyes roam over her, eyeing up the prey. She takes one more step, it's tiny, uncertain and I pounce as a loud shriek rips from her throat and I grab her by the shoulders and push her against the nearest wall.

"Did you really think you could do shit like this without consequences? Who do you think you are?"

Her tiny nose wrinkles, her eyes narrowing as she stares at me with disgust. "Who do *I* think I am? Shouldn't you be asking yourself that? You're the one acting like you're above everybody else. Like you're some king when you aren't. For once, someone's knocked you down a peg or two..."

Color me fucking shocked. The girl found some courage, though she's not hiding her fear beneath it all that well, the slight tremor in her voice giving her away. Letting me know that my presence still terrifies her.

She's brave talking to me this way, taunting me. If she wants me to bite, then I'll bite, and I'll bite fucking hard. I'll draw blood. I'll leave a scar, because that's all I've ever wanted to do, was leave a scar just like the one she left on me.

"Maybe I'm not above all else, but I'm definitely above you," I sneer, leaning into her face. She twists in my grasp and tries to shove me away with her hands, but being stronger than her, I easily keep her pinned to the wall.

She's like a gnat, and I'm an elephant. If I don't want her out, I'll squish her.

"Where do you think you're going?" I tilt my head, not really caring to hear her response. I'm just not ready for this game between us to end.

"To my room, to sleep, since it's finally quiet in this jail cell called a house. Now let go of me, before I scream."

Before she screams. My head tips back and a bellow of laughter passes my lips.

"Scream? Go ahead. Yell at the top of your lungs. No one cares. No one will stop me. Hell, no one would believe a word you said, since you're a liar. It's practically your job now, lying, and ruining people's lives." Her jaw tightens, her lips pressing into a firm line, and I can't help myself. I lean in closer, wanting, needing to be closer to her. "You fucked up my party and sent everyone home, so now you get to entertain me for the rest of the night. Sarah never got around to sucking my cock which is truly a shame since she's so good at it, but a warm mouth is a warm mouth and yours looks good enough."

"Fuck you, I'll bite off your dick if you come near me with it!" She wiggles her tiny body against mine in a futile effort to get away from me, but it only makes me crave her more. Pushing my chest against hers, I feel her heart racing, see her pulse throbbing in her throat.

My cock is rock hard, and I lean in, pressing my center into her soft skin. She smells so good, and I bet if I kissed her, she'd taste good too.

Fuck, I'm screwed.

I know she can feel it, the hard ridge trapped inside my jeans.

She whimpers, her eyes flicking up to mine. There's an unsaid plea in those green depths, and I'm not sure what she's asking me for... to stop, to keep going...to put us both out of our misery.

I'm not sure if it's the soft whimper, or her tiny body rubbing against mine, or maybe just the alcohol coursing through my veins. Maybe it's a combination of all of them, but whatever it is, it drives me over the edge, shoving me headfirst off the cliff and into lust-filled waters.

My mind shuts down for a second, all my thoughts fleeting as I let my body's reaction to her take over. I don't let myself think of the consequences, or how wrong it is of me to be doing this. Instead, I let my lips find hers, crashing into the smooth skin with such force the back of her head hits the wall. She whimpers again, but I swallow it up with my mouth. The kiss is teeth, and anger that burns hotter than the sun.

There's nothing gentle about it, nothing tender, or loving. It's raw, it's powerful, it's the kind of kiss that as cliché as it sounds, I'll remember for the rest of my life. I feel it in my bones, in the thundering beat of my heart.

My fingers dig into her shoulders. I want to mark her. Leave bruises on her skin, but in a way that brings us both satisfaction, and I will, soon, so very fucking soon. Snaking a hand into her silky brown locks, I tilt her head back, my teeth biting at her bottom lip hard enough to draw blood. *Hurt her. Ravage her.* Pulling away just enough to see her doe eyes, I watch as they fill with equal amounts of fear and excitement.

The air around us grows electrically charged, our bodies molding together like two pieces of clay. I kiss her again with the same ferocity, but this time she returns my kiss. Her lips move hungrily, as if she's been starving for this same interaction. Those tiny hands of hers go from pushing me away to fisting into my shirt and pulling me closer.

Her lips part and a feminine moan leaves them. It's that sound that suddenly has me snapping out of my lust hazed fog.

What the fuck, Vance?

She's the enemy, a liar, a fucking liar. I pull away abruptly, and her body sags against the wall at the loss of contact. *No!* My chest heaves, my fingers crave to touch her skin again, to mark her, but I can't. I won't weaken myself for this little vixen who wants me to think she's innocent. This has gone far enough. I have to get away from her before I lose control, before I cross that invisible line, the one that I'm already toeing.

Staggering backward like I'm drunk, I harden my gaze. "Entertain me, con-artist, show me another use for that pretty mouth of yours, besides spouting off lies."

"I hate you," she spits through gritted teeth, the lustful haze diminishing in her eyes.

I hate myself too.
For wanting you.
For hating you.
For being stuck in this stupid house with you.
"Come on, we ain't got all night..." I tsk impatiently.

I'm so caught up in taunting her, in feeling the lick of hate that her presence brings me, that I don't notice the slap coming toward my cheek until it's too late. Her hand makes contact with my cheek, and my head flies to the side with the impact of the blow.

My jaw turns to steel and my temper ignites. I'm reacting before I even get a chance to stop myself. Reaching for her, my fingers curl around her throat, my hold is surprisingly gentle for the amount of bitterness flowing through my veins. Ava's reaction to me is petrified fear and she starts to tremble when I lean into her face, giving her delicate throat a firm squeeze.

"If you're going to put your hands on someone, then you better be prepared for them to put their hands on you."

"Don't..." she croaks.

"What? Hurt you?" I tilt my head to the side, eyeing her heart-shaped face. "I could never hurt you like you hurt me, you've done enough of that for the two of us. I'm merely trying to show you a sliver, a fraction of the pain you made me feel." Feeling as if I'm seconds away from crashing and burning, I release her and take a step back. Then I turn to walk away. I'm done. Done with this cat and mouse game.

Her tiny voice meets my ears a second later. "What did I do to make you hate me so much? Just tell me, Vance, please. Tell me so I can fix this. You're making us both suffer for an unknown reason."

"You lied, and like liars always do, they continue to lie to cover up their existing lies."

"What did I lie about?"

There's a plea attached to her question and I'm too exhausted to continue fighting about this right now. She makes me weak, breaks down all my perfectly constructed walls, and leaves me bleeding, always bleeding.

"Everything. All of it. I'm worth the truth, after all this time I deserve it." I sigh and start walking toward the stairs.

"I didn't do anything...I didn't lie that night..." she cries, but I continue walking, each step making my heart heavier, and the knot of pain in my stomach tighter. By the time I reach my bedroom door, there's an inkling of doubt forming. And by the time I step into the shower, it's swirling inside my head, conjuring up different thoughts, and no matter how much I shove it away, it keeps returning.

"Wake up, Vance." My mom's voice drags me from sleep. Wake up, we need to leave." She sniffles and it sounds like she's been crying. When I peel my eyes open and I look at her, the red rings around her blue eyes confirm it. A knot of dread forms in my throat.

"What's wrong? Where are we going?"

"Don't worry about that now, just get up and get dressed, okay?" She wipes at her eyes with the backs of her hands.

I do as I'm told, getting up and dressed in a hurry. Mom and Dad have already packed our suitcases and before I can object to it, or even mutter another question, we are in our car and driving down the road.

"What's going on?"

My dad's jaw tightens at my question and my mother's sobs grow harsher from her spot in the front seat.

"As I'm sure you know, Laura caught Ava sneaking into her room last night?"

"Yeah, I know...we were just playing a game, it was stupid. What happened? Did she get in trouble? I'll explain everything to her mom if you want me to?"

Silence settles over the car. My mom came and got me from the treehouse ten minutes after Ava left. She told me I was grounded for a month, which I didn't even consider a punishment since Ava would have been there regardless. I didn't really understand why I was being grounded. I had done worse things than sneak out of the house at nine at night.

I just assumed it was because Ava had been caught. Oh, how horribly wrong I was. I'll always remember the next words that come out of my father's mouth like they are burned into my memory.

"She told her mom that you forced her to do it. That you threatened her to steal some of Laura's jewelry. Why would you do that, son? Why would you threaten her?" The disappointment in my father's tone sliced through me.

Shaking my head, I will the memory away. *She's a liar.* Through and through. I know what happened that night, and I know that it was her.

She did this to us, and she'll pay.

Pay dearly.

9

AVA

The days pass in a flurry. My mother and Henry still haven't returned home and every second I'm left alone inside this house with Vance, another piece of my thinly worn veil crumbles. He's wearing me down, trying to smash me like a fly, and he gets a little closer to doing so every time he opens his mouth. A tongue may have no bones, but it can break a heart just the same and that's what he does every time he speaks to me - breaks me, and my heart.

He insults me, filets me straight down the middle, gutting me like a fish until my insides are hanging out and my heart is gushing blood across the floor.

"Hey, Ava... wait up," a familiar voice calls from behind me. I don't want to stop though. I just want to keep walking, walk until I'm not alone anymore, until I start to feel whole again. It takes nothing more than a second for Clark to appear beside me and I'm forced to slow to a walk.

"Why the long face, A?"

"A? Is that a nickname or something? I wasn't aware I had made it to that status of cool yet."

"Maybe you haven't in Vance's book, but you have in mine."

"Did he put you up to this?" I question, stopping in the middle of the sidewalk. Clark circles me coming to stand in front of me. He's just about as tall as Vance, but height aside, they couldn't be any more different from each other.

He chuckles. "God no, he's my friend, but he can't dictate who I talk to. I'm a big boy... a *very* big boy, and I make my own choices." He's laying the flirting on thick, like icing on top of a cake, and even though I'm not in the mood to deal with that kind of shit, I can't stop the smile from appearing on my lips. Clark brings a very small piece of happiness to my situation.

"Do you try this hard with all the ladies?"

He inhales a breath before exhaling, his hands gripping the straps of his backpack, "Usually, no. Most of the time it's... *Ooo Clark, please fuck me. Oh yes, Clark. Right there... right there...* Their panties are on the floor, no questions asked."

Snorting, I shake my head. "Now I understand why you and Vance are friends."

"And why is that?" he teases.

"Because you're both arrogant as hell, slightly piggish, and have egos the size of your heads." Clark winces as if I've wounded him, and I feel kind of bad, having just said what I did without really knowing him.

"You wound me, A. Wound me. And yet, you intrigue me all at once. Vance hates you, which I'm sure you know by now..." Reaching out, he grasps onto a piece of my hair, twirling it around, examining it in the afternoon sun. "But I don't... I'm curious about you. I want to be your friend. I want to get to know you."

"You mean you want to get to know my panties."

Dropping the lock, he grins, his smile breathtaking,

perfectly straight white teeth showing from behind lightly pink parted lips.

"Well, of course, I'm a guy, and I have a dick so yeah, I want to get acquainted with your panties, more like your vagina, but I also want to get to know you. We can be friends too. Let's have dinner... we can go to *Slice It*."

Clark's harmless in the big scheme of things, this I know. But, him getting to know me? That can't lead to anything good. I chew on the inside of my cheek, indecision rippling through me. This is a bad idea, a terrible idea, but I'm alone, so damn alone, and I'm tired of it. I'm desperate for some human interaction, even if it's with the enemy's best friend.

How sad is that?

Clark bats his eyelashes and gives me his best puppy dog look. I can't imagine what that look gets him on a regular basis.

"Does that look usually get you whatever you want?" I ask, eyebrow raised.

"All the time, sweetheart," Clark drawls.

Tapping on my chin with my finger, I continue to weigh my options. Go home to face an empty house, and Vance, or go to dinner with Clark, possibly making a new friend and enjoying myself? It can't be that bad, can it? What's the worst that happens? Vance finds out? Then what? He can't hurt me anymore than he already has.

"Come on, it'll be fun. Pizza, endless conversation, and you'll get to chill with me, that's the most amazing part of all."

He's... Jesus, is he full of himself.

"Fine. I'll go, but only if you understand that this is dinner only. Dinner as friends. No date, no kissing, no sex. No funny business whatsoever." I narrow my gaze, waiting for him to answer me. He takes a step closer, and I inhale his scent. Bold and spicy with undertones of vanilla.

"Scout's honor, princess," he promises, holding up two fingers. "Dinner, no funny business, though that is my favorite kind of business."

"Not with me, it isn't."

We exchange numbers, even though I'm pretty sure he already has mine. I think everyone does after Vance's most recent prank where he posted my number all over campus and on Craigslist. The asshole had people blowing up my phone all week asking for nude pictures and booty calls.

"Let's meet back up at four near the coffee shop next to the English building," Clark says, his eyes clashing with mine. "You know where that is right?"

Rolling my eyes, I say, "Yeah, I know where it is. I'll be there. Hopefully you don't regret hanging out with me."

"Never, A. Never." Shaking his head, he backpedals a couple steps. "I'll see you later," he exclaims before disappearing into the mass of students walking in my direction. My phone chimes in my pocket and I pull it out, my eyes falling to the time.

Shit! How the hell am I going to graduate when I can't even make it to class on time?

∼

WE WALK into the small pizza place a few hours later. The aroma of fresh basil and oregano fill the entire place, making my mouth water. I'm starving, my stomach grumbles so loudly I'm surprised Clark can't hear it.

"How about over there." Clark points to a secluded booth in the back.

"Sure." I shrug. He grabs my hand and tugs me along behind him. Gazing down at our joined hands, I'm not sure what to think. He's kind, flirtatious, yes, but he's harmless in comparison to Vance. When we reach the booth, he lets go of my hand and we both scoot into the booth and sit down across from each other.

"So, how are things going on the home front?" Clark asks. I guess no meaningless small talk before asking the personal questions with him. I wonder if he does this on dates? If he dates at all? Probably not.

"You make it sound like it's a war zone."

Clark shrugs, his teeth sinking into his bottom lip in that boyish way that seems to make him more attractive. "I would assume living with Vance is like a war zone. The fucker drives me insane on a daily basis and we don't even live together."

"Well it's not easy, he's constantly harassing me, pointing out my weaknesses and verbally assaulting me."

Clark frowns. "Not that it's an excuse, he shouldn't try and hurt you like he is, but Vance was lost, confused for a long time after you left, fuck, he still is."

For some reason that surprises me. I'm a poster kid for lost and confused. One would think I could recognize that a million miles away, but Vance doesn't seem just lost and confused, he seems livid, angry beyond disbelief.

"He didn't use to be this way," I say, taken aback by how sad the words sound.

I miss the old Vance, I miss my friend. Clark must pick up on my sudden somber mood, because he quickly changes the subject. We talk about classes, his latest hook-up, and the pressure he feels from his father to get good grades, play baseball, and keep up the perfect son image.

I'm glad to have the attention off of me, and as we eat and continue to chat, I feel like I'm actually growing closer to him. When we part ways, I'm a little sad, but we agree to meet up again soon. The entire drive home I'm smiling, carefree, without any weight on my shoulders. Hanging out with Clark wasn't nearly as bad as I had anticipated it to be. In fact, it was much more fun than I expected.

Ten minutes later, I'm pulling into the driveway. I kill the engine, grab my backpack off the passenger seat and walk up the concrete steps to the front door. Like a father waiting for his daughter to be dropped off from her first date, Vance opens the door before I can even grab for the door handle.

"Where have you been?" His tone is condescending and the way he's looking at me has my stomach tumbling into a ball. Nimble fingers thread through his glossy black hair, it looks soft, like cashmere and I want to touch it, run my fingers through it.

"Out," I growl, pushing past him and inside. Our shoulders touch briefly, and my skin tingles, the fine hairs on my arms standing on end. It's almost like I've been struck by a tiny bolt of lightning. Too bad it didn't kill me dead.

"*Out?* Out where? Someone said they saw you with Clark. Were you on a date? Was the lying thief using her tight cunt to con my friend?"

My mouth pops open, shock coloring my features. "Excuse me, but it wasn't a date, and I didn't use my—" I can't even say the word, I'm so flabbergasted. "I didn't have sex with him, if that's what you're insinuating. I'm not some floozy who sleeps with every guy she meets." My mind flashes to Sarah, I'm not like her. He doesn't think I'm like her, does he?

Vance's green eyes darken. "Could've fooled me."

"You're an asshole," I say, attempting to verbally slap him with my words like he does me every time he opens his stupid mouth.

"And you're a liar." He takes a step closer, the heat of his body slamming into mine. His presence makes me dizzy. I don't know if I should slap him or kiss him. I crave his touch, but at the same time, I don't. *This,* whatever it is that's taking place between us, is exhausting.

"Whatever, Vance. You'll think whatever you want to, no matter how much I defend myself." Refusing to give him even another moment of my time, I head toward the stairs. I've got a pile of homework to do and I want to get a little reading in before bed. Neither of those things will get done if I stand here trying to defend myself against someone who refuses to tell me what I've done wrong. I make it all of two steps before his warm hand is circling my arm and pulling me backward.

Bumping into his firm chest, I try and whirl around, but Vance is fast, and using his height and body he easily overpowers me. With both hands gripping onto my arms, he holds them behind my back, guiding me to the nearest wall, only releasing me once my face is pressed against the cream-colored wall.

"Did you think about me when he touched you?" His voice is thick, and I feel my pussy clenching around nothing. Why does he have to be so stupidly handsome, and why do I have to be attracted to him. He hates me, while I pretend to hate him because the alternative would be unbearable.

We can't do this.

We shouldn't be doing this.

"He didn't touch me, and no, I never think about you," I lie. Fuck it. I might as well live up to the name he keeps calling me.

I think about you all the time.

"Me either. I never think about you." His fingers trail down my arm, and goosebumps follow in the wake of his touch. I want to lean into him, let him burn me, because I know if I give myself to him, he will, he'll burn me so badly I won't even recognize myself when he's done with me. His hand drops to my hip, and my chest heaves, my lungs tightening. An entire zoo of butterflies take flight in my stomach.

Oh lord. "Did he touch you here?" Those devilish lips of his press against the shell of my ear, and I tip my head back against his firm chest, my eyes drifting closed while I give myself over to the pleasure of his touch. His deft fingers skim across the front of my yoga pants, and my burning hot center.

"Did he?" he mumbles against my skin, and it feels like I'm on fire, literal fire. He's burning me with the tips of his fingers, branding my flesh with his mark.

"Are you wet with need for him, or is that all for me?"

"No," I whisper, my body humming as he runs his finger over my bikini line and back to my hip, kneading the flesh there.

Something's wrong with me, something's very... I don't even get to finish that thought because he's slipping his hand into my pants, his fingers ghosting over the edge of my panties.

"Tell me to stop... God, please tell me to stop, Ava."

Hunger vibrates from his chest. He wants me just as badly as I want him, and for some reason that gratifies me.

Knowing he wants me while hating me at the same time. It makes me feel powerful, like I actually stand a chance against him. Tension hangs thickly between us, and just like a rubber band snapping under pressure, Vance snaps, losing his ability to make the right choice. His fingers slip beneath my panties, and I suck in a greedy breath, feeling like I'll never be able to breathe again.

"This is wrong...so wrong. But it feels so right, doesn't it? Tell me it feels right." His voice drags on, his lips sucking on a patch of skin beneath my ear.

"Yes," I admit breathlessly, leaning into him even more, wishing there wasn't any fabric at all between us. God, I want to feel him. Want him to touch me. Take from me. I want him to show me how much he hates me, but instead of his words, I want him to use his hands.

Without warning, he rips his hand from my red hot center and spins me around so we are face to face. Facing each other feels more intimate, and suddenly I'm self-conscious my eyes skating down to his well-defined chest.

"Don't look away..." he coaxes with a hand under my chin, tipping my head back up, forcing my gaze to meet his. "I want you to look into my eyes when you fall apart. I want you to feel who owns your pleasure and your hate. So next time you're with *him*, or anyone for that matter, you remember that it's me that makes you feel this way, and that it will always be me."

Releasing his hold on my chin, he moves it to my hip, holding me in place, while his other hand slips back beneath the waistband of my pants.

This time there's an urgency to his touch, he doesn't stop at my panties, his fingers move underneath the thin fabric like they belong there. Those thick digits slide through my already drenched folds and a wicked grin pulls at his lips.

"Of course you're already wet," he says triumphantly as if he knew I would be.

Part of me wants to put an end to this now, to push him away, to prove to him that I'm not as weak for his touch as he is for mine, but I can't.

I just can't. I can't do anything but breathe, and feel, Lord, do I feel. I feel everything, all of him, every inch.

With his thumb, he circles my hardened nub while his finger finds its way to my entrance. It's been so long since I let someone touch me here, since I felt like this. No, I never felt like this before. I've had sex before, but I've never felt like this before, not with anyone else. There's no comparison, it's like nothing else I've ever experienced.

My skin tingles everywhere he touches me. He's like a

thunderstorm, booming, big and powerful, but full of beauty, even in the wake of destruction. I'm so confused by what I'm feeling, by the way he makes me feel. I want to turn the emotions off, forget all about him, but I can't. I can't let him go any more than I can untangle our pasts.

My thoughts float away like clouds whisking through the air. I'm dizzy with need and when he inserts a second finger stretching me in a deliciously slow way before adding pressure to my clit, I know I'll never be the same again.

It's too much, too fast.

His fingers inside me.

My heavy pants.

My eyes flutter closed involuntarily, the sensations mounting.

"Open your eyes," he orders, his fingers digging into my hip possessively. "How long have you been waiting for me to finger-fuck you? Days, weeks? How long have you wanted this, wanted me inside you, owning you?"

God, please, make him shut up.

"I hate you," I murmur, wishing I had the strength to push him away. But I don't, not physically or mentally. He has a hold on me, and I'm caught in his trap, an unwilling victim to his hate, and to his rage.

"I hate you more," he growls, his lips so close he's *almost* kissing me. We stare into each other's eyes, his gaze is hard, but it's brimming with need that definitely mirrors the thrusting his fingers are doing, going even deeper inside of me, curling and hitting a spot that no one else has ever hit before.

I have to concentrate *hard* to keep my eyes open. I want to close them so bad, let my head fall back against the wall, and just give in to the pleasure completely, but I won't. I won't give him that kind of power.

With his thumb on my clit, pressing down on the small

bundle of nerves, he continues thrusting his fingers deep inside of me, his pace increasing, growing furious with each passing second. The sound of his fingers slipping through my arousal fills my ears. It's erotic and reminds me further of how much I despise him.

Warmth gathers deep in my core, and I know I'm close. Judging by the grin tugging on his lips, he knows it too.

Bastard.

"Come, Ava...come all over my fingers. I want to feel you squeeze me." His words set me off. My toes curl in my boots and my spine tingles. The impending climax claiming me with a vengeance. Unable to keep my eyes open a second longer, they close and roll to the back of my head, just as a loud moan rips from my throat.

My whole body tightens, my pussy squeezing his fingers like he wanted me to, but I don't care, not that we crossed a line or that I listened to him.

Right now, I don't care about anything. I feel like I'm high, my mind swarmed with endorphins, my muscles feeling as they went through a deep tissue massage or something. If I wasn't exhausted before, I am now.

My knees wobble like a newborn baby fawn's and almost give out underneath me as he releases me. Vance waits like the perfect gentleman until my pussy stops pulsing and the last tremors of my orgasm have rippled through me before he removes his hand and lets go of my hip. I nearly whimper at the loss of his touch but catch myself a second before I do.

I have to lean back against the wall to keep myself from falling over. Bringing a hand to my chest, I try and steady the muscle beating like crazy inside of it.

Somehow I will my eyes open and find that he is still standing in front of me, eyes gleaming with a noticeable boner pressing against his zipper. For some reason, I expected him to be gone by now, that maybe I had just made up this whole thing in my mind.

But there he is, staring at me recovering from an orgasm that *he* gave me.

"You're welcome," he says cockily, a smile ghosting his lips as he does that weird sexy thing guys do where they rub their thumb over their bottom lip. "Next time, I'll expect you to return the favor."

"Fuck you." The words pass my lips on a whisper. I'm far too tired to fight with him right now. "And this won't be happening again. You. Me. Us. Whatever it is. It's done. I won't let you do this again."

He licks his lips and tilts his head to the side, studying me.

"*Won't* or don't want me to do it again? There's a difference and just as I've always said, once a liar, always a liar. You want this, you want me, and I'll be damned if I don't feed off your biggest weakness. We'll be through when I say we're through."

My mouth pops open to spit off another smart comment, but there's no point, because he's right I am a liar, and I want what we just did to happen again. I want his cock… his hand, his lips.

He doesn't stick around to hear if I'll say anything else, instead, he turns and jogs up the staircase leaving me alone with my treacherous body and thoughts.

I'm a liar, a big fat liar, because I'm falling for the bully, my stepbrother.

10

VANCE

I can't believe the fucker is this late. Clark is usually a stickler for being on time and he said he'd meet me here at eight. It's almost nine and he hasn't shown up, or even texted me for that matter. The party is in full swing around me. Fellow college students are partying away, dancing, drinking, and hell, even a few are having sex.

Normally, I would be right in the middle of all of it, but I'm not in the mood today.

I haven't been in the mood for anything lately.

All I can think of is *her*. She's in my head, under my skin, in my every single waking thought. The only reason I came here was to hang out with Clark and get shit faced, but instead I've been sitting on this couch, a piss warm beer in my hand for the last hour listening to Sarah drone on about how her family isn't going to the Hamptons this winter because her grandmother broke her hip. Her voice is like nails on a chalkboard and I'm seconds away from tossing my beer on her, just to see if it'll make her shut up for a second.

Sarah's voice edges my anger toward Clark up. Fucking asshole, standing me up.

He's going to need to do some major ass kissing for me to let this one go, and his excuse, well it better be fucking epic. My gaze slips around the room. I see a couple football players I know, and a bunch of the douches from the baseball team. Most of them are Clark's friends, not that they wouldn't hang with me, but they aren't really my kind of crowd.

Running a hand through my hair in frustration, I sigh. I should've just stayed home and harassed Ava, which would've been more fun than sitting here, alone, with Sarah. I'm about five seconds away from leaving the party and getting drunk on my own at my place when I spot him across the room heading toward me.

He weaves through the crowd, waving to me when he spots me. Relief floods me, thank fuck he's finally here, and then I notice someone trailing close behind him. My blood turns to ice in my veins.

You have gotta be fucking kidding me.

They get closer and I realize that Ava is not only walking behind him, but that she's also holding his hand.

She's holding his fucking hand.

As soon as Ava sees me, she pulls her hand out of Clark's, as if she didn't want me to see them together. *Too fucking late.*

"Sorry, man, I know I'm late. I had to talk this one into coming with me," he says, hooking a thumb at Ava.

"You were supposed to be here an hour ago!" I yell in his face, rage taking over. Out of the corner of my eye, I see Sarah scooting away from me. I'm sure I look like a douchebag right now.

"Woah, dude. Calm down." Clark's gaze widens as he lifts his hands in a non-threatening manner. "Sorry, okay? I'm here now. I don't know why it's such a big deal all of the sudden, it's not like I haven't been late before."

"No, it's not fucking okay. I'm not some slut who is going to sit here waiting for you. And speaking of *sluts*, what the fuck is she doing here?" I look past Clark, my eyes meeting Ava's razor-sharp gaze. That backbone of hers is getting stronger and stronger, and for some stupid fucking reason, I'm proud of her, proud to see her standing so tall, a pretty little flower standing amongst the weeds.

"Van, sit down and shut up. You're acting like an asshole. Even more so than usual." He tries to brush me off with a joke, like I'm one of his fuck buddies or something and that only fuels my anger.

"Don't fucking tell me what to do," I growl, getting up from the couch. Clark rolls his eyes at me as if I'm being dramatic and my barely restrained anger boils over. I shove at his shoulders and watch him stagger backward and into the crowd.

We've fought before, but nothing like this, and definitely not over a girl at that. His eyes go wide, his mouth popping open in shock like he can't believe I just pushed him.

Believe it, buddy.

He looks at me like he's expecting an apology, but he should know better than that.

I don't apologize, not to anyone, and I'm certainly not gonna start with him. When I don't say anything, his eyes narrow and shock gives way to anger. Curling my hands into fists, I prepare myself for a fight.

"What the fuck is wrong with you?"

"*Me?* That's rich, Clark," I scoff. "You ditched me for pussy." My eyes cut to Ava's as I say my next set of words. "And it's not even good pussy at that."

I have to swallow down the bile that's rising in my throat, burning a path of fire up my esophagus. Fuck. I'm an asshole.

Glancing over at Ava, I see the hurt flashing in her eyes a moment before she spins around and walks away from us.

"Better run after her before she spreads her legs for someone else," I taunt him, wanting him to punch me, to throttle me.

"Vance." Clark's tone holds a warning, but I'm too far gone to give a fuck.

Why the fuck is he sticking up for her anyway? To get in her pants? He could have his pick of any of the girls in this room, but no, he wants the one that's embedded herself under my skin. The one that's driving me insane. This isn't just about him being late, this is so much more than that, but I'm not going to tell him that.

Fuck no.

"Get a grip," he scoffs, and that's when my last bit of restraint crumbles. Without thought, mercy or care, I clench my fist and slug my best friend in the jaw.

His head snaps to the side at impact as my knuckles graze his cheekbone. Pain flares through my hand and up my arm. My punch would have knocked out most guys, but not Clark. He doesn't even straighten up all the way before swinging at me, his hit landing against the side of my face. Pain explodes across my cheek, and I relish in it. Using it to fuel my anger even further, I swing again for him, but he's faster and instead gets me in the ribs.

The hit knocks the air from my lungs. *Bastard.* The crowd around us forms a small circle, people chanting both our names like we're professional MMA fighters. The energy in the room reaches a dangerous high. I only manage to get one more hit in on him, a left hook to the nose before two guys grab onto me from behind, pulling me backward.

I pull my arms back, ready to pummel the bastards holding onto me when I see two more guys doing the same to

Clark, making it so all we're doing now is staring daggers at each other. Looking at Clark, I can see he's pissed, like a bull in a china shop, ready to destroy, I've provoked him. But he provoked me too, bringing her here, antagonizing my anger.

He knows what she did to me, and how much it hurt, and still he brings her around, showing her off like she's a trophy.

They separate us, dragging me out the front door before depositing my ass on the lawn.

"Fuck," I mutter under my breath. When they finally let go of me, I twist around, pushing up from the grass, lip curled, hands balled into tight fists, ready to fight. I'll beat these asshole's asses instead of Clark's I tell myself. That is until I see that it's Remington and Thomas, two of North Woods biggest assholes staring back at me.

Maybe one of them I could handle, but two, no fucking way. Thomas is big, but he doesn't have the stamina I know Remington does. I might be angry, but I'm not stupid.

"I don't know what the hell that was between you and Clark in there, but you can't just go around slugging people in the face. And I'll warn you now, you're not getting back inside the house until you chill out. If I have to separate you two again, I'll kick both your asses."

I've never seen Remington this pissed off before, there's a vein bulging on the side of his neck and I get the feeling if Jules, his girlfriend, wasn't standing five feet away, he would kick my ass, but since she is, I guess it's my lucky day.

"What about Clark?" I ask, wondering if he's getting the same treatment as me. Now that I'm away from Ava, her floral scent not sticking to my nostrils like honey I can actually think again.

Shit. I fucked up. I'm a horrible fucking friend.

"He's cooling off in the backyard. You're more than welcome to come back in when you are done with...whatever this is, and if you want to talk, well I'm all ears. I know what it's like to be angry, boiling over with rage."

"Fine." I roll my shoulders, trying to loosen the tension from my muscles. Remington gives me a hard look, as if he's psychoanalyzing me. I heard about what happened between him and Jules, the bet gone bad.

Maybe he thinks I'm like him, or the way he used to be. I don't know, but I don't like the way he's looking at me right now. Like he can somehow fix this, or fix me. As if he can hear my thoughts being projected onto him, he takes Jules' hand and walks back into the house with Thomas.

Alone at last, I take a few deep breaths to clear the blender also known as my mind. I shouldn't have punched him, I know that, but I was angry, hell, I still am. Even so, he didn't deserve it. No one deserves to have to deal with my piss poor attitude tonight.

Swallowing my pride, I walk around the house and find Clark sitting in a lawn chair in the backyard. He frowns when he sees me coming toward him, but doesn't say anything. He probably thinks I'm going to slug him again. Taking the chair closest to him, I ready myself to apologize, I open my mouth to speak when the sliding door to the backyard opens and Ava walks out, holding two ice packs in her hands.

She walks up, and this time I can't help it, my eyes rake over her body, the skinny jeans that hug her ass and legs like a glove, the simple NWU t-shirt. Her mere presence breaks me, and I hate it. I hate that I'm weak for her, weak for the enemy. All I can think of is how tight her pussy squeezed my fingers the other night, how ready she was for me. I know she's weak for me, just like I am for her, but it *can't* happen, *won't* happen, not ever again.

She hands each of us one, but I refuse to take it. I refuse to take anything from her. I wouldn't have even punched Clark if it wasn't for her. She makes me insane with need, with jealousy, with rage. Clark has no trouble taking his ice pack and holds it to his jaw while leaning back in the chair, a void expression on his face.

The good thing about Clark is, unlike me, he doesn't hold grudges.

"Vance, just take the damn bag of ice, your face is already swelling," Ava scolds, holding the ice to my face like she actually cares. Pff, she doesn't give a fuck. She'd love to see me fall, love to see me broken. Angrily, and like an immature bastard, I slap the bag out of her hand, watching it spill out on the patio. She gasps, taking a step back.

Jesus, I'm losing it.

I should just fuck her already, get her out of my system. Maybe if I fuck her hard enough, I can fuck her straight from my mind.

"You think just because I fingered you one time that suddenly were friends? That I want your help? What we did doesn't mean shit...you don't mean shit. Stay the fuck away from me, or I'll make you stay away, and believe me you don't want me to have to do that," I yell, just wanting her to go away, far, far away.

Her cheeks turn a dark shade of pink and I know I've embarrassed her, sliced her deep. And for the second time today, I let her walk away from me when all I want to do is pull her in, keep her close. I shake my head before letting my face fall into my hands.

I'm the definition of a hot fucking mess right now.

"Shiitttt! I can't believe I didn't see this before." Clark chuckles beside me, the noise shocking me. "You have a thing for her. Fuck, maybe even more than a thing, considering how crazy you've been acting. It makes sense now. You've never tried to punch me, and we've shared chicks plenty of times and we've never fought, not until her." He pauses for a moment, having pieced my fucked up puzzle of a life together.

"You've got it bad for her."

"I hate her," I mumble into my hands, more to myself but Clark hears me.

"Are you sure about that? Do you really hate her or are you *trying* to hate her? It sounds like you're trying to convince yourself, even more than everyone else. It's okay to want her. She's attractive, funny, and super smart."

Just hearing Clark talk about her like he knows her irritates me. It should be me who's getting to know her, going on dates, holding her hand. But I'm too strung up on the past. She keeps telling me she doesn't know what I'm talking about and I'm slowly starting to doubt what I think is the truth. No one can hold up a front that good, not even her. She might be an actress, but when she cries, her tears are real, when I hurt her with my words her hurt is real. Every single emotion she projects onto me is real.

"I don't know anymore," I sigh. Even if she is telling the truth and she didn't accuse me that night. I still spent five years hating her. I can't erase that time, neither can I erase how I've been treating her the last few weeks.

"Look, if I would have known you had a thing for her. I wouldn't have tried to get into her panties, not that I think she would have let me anyway. She seems to be immune to my charm. It's infuriating as hell, by the way. I've never met a woman I couldn't get to take their panties off for me." He laughs softly. "She doesn't have eyes for me, Van. She has eyes for you. I see it, clear as day."

I snort, turning to face him, grimacing at the purple bruise that's developing on his cheek. "Then why are you still hanging out with her?" It's not like Clark to hang out with a girl unless he's getting a piece of ass. Even then, he fucks them and goes on his merry way. Women are expendable to Clark and he only goes for the easiest ones.

He's a hit it and quit it guy, and he's so serious about it, that he's vowed never to fall in love. I mean I'm a dick, but even I know someday I'll fall in love. It's inevitable.

"Honestly, she's really fun to hang out with. She's the first girl I actually enjoy having a conversation with. And one of the few people who can see through my bullshit. She doesn't care about her makeup or her hair, and she's honest, like almost so honest it hurts. I like her...but I don't *like* her. I see her more as one of the bros, ya know?"

I let my eyes drift closed momentarily. I would know these things if I pulled my head out of my ass, if I tried. Fuck, my heart seems to tense up inside my chest. The idea of letting go of the pain she caused me. It feels like I'm letting down my mother, letting down my father, even though he doesn't deserve an ounce of my pity, not anymore. Yeah, we bounced back from it, but we had to lose it all to get here.

"I don't think I can let this go, Clark." My admission feels like a weight is being lifted off my shoulders, but it's only one weight...there are still hundreds more.

"I think you need to. Holding onto that kind of anger, it eats at you. It's been five years, it's time to let it go. Plus, you should talk to her about it. Ask her what happened that night. Her version of it all. Maybe there's more to the story that you don't know about."

My face deadpans. He makes it sound like he knows something I don't know but he doesn't. Whatever Ava told him, it's a lie. My parents told me what she did, and they wouldn't lie to me...would they?

11

AVA

Alan, a friend of Remington and Jules, hands me another shot and I down it just as fast as I did the last one. The liquor burns less this time, my body slowly numbing itself. Now I know why people drink their problems away, because the alcohol makes you forget. Which is all I want. To forget... to let go. This is what I need, to drink my troubles away with my friends like a normal college student. Forget Vance, my mother, and my seriously fucked up life.

"Are you okay?" Jules asks, placing a hand on my arm. Her touch is gentle, and I've come to see Jules as the mother hen. Always nurturing, caring, and being supportive. She's the best friend I wish I had for the last five years.

"No, but I'm getting there," I say, gesturing to Alan to get me another shot. The boy would make an excellent bartender.

"Just ignore him, he's a man, and men are idiots sometimes."

"Girl, I wish it was that easy. It's hard to ignore someone who is living under the same roof as you, in fact, right across the hall, and then going to the same university."

"I'm sorry, Ava." Jules pouts. "You can always come hang out with me if you need to get away. Remington and I live right off campus. It's literally a block or two away. We have a spare bedroom too."

"Thank you. Really, we just met and you're already such a good friend. For once, I'm grateful Vance did something stupid, because it led me to you."

"Any time, and trust me." She leans in, her voice a whisper, almost as if she doesn't want anyone to hear her. "It might not seem like it's going to get better right now, but last year I was kind of in your shoes. I had moved here after my dad and brother died in a car accident. I had no one. I was alone and needed a friend, and it didn't help I had other issues going on." Her eyes cut to her very protective boyfriend who is standing no less than five feet away at all times. "So yeah, believe it or not, I know how you feel."

"Oh Jules, I'm so sorry." I frown and pull her into a hug. Her embrace is warm, and I'm reminded why I miss hugs so much. They're like the glue that holds you through the bad days.

"Another shot, miss?" Alan hollers from behind me and I release Jules and twist around, seconds away from telling him I'd better stop, since I feel the warmth creeping up into my cheeks already. But then I catch Vance staring ice daggers at me from across the room. I've been watching him too, and he hasn't drank a single drop of beer, or liquor. In fact, he hasn't done anything but sit in the corner of the room brooding.

Asshole. As an act of defiance, I walk over to Alan, running a hand down his arm. The touch is innocent, but I still know it's wrong. I don't like Alan, he's cute, yeah, but he's not Vance. That doesn't matter in my mind right at that moment. I still touch him, just to get a rise out of Vance, to show him there are other options out there for me.

"Sure, I'll have one more," I coo, beaming up at him. Taking the shot out of his hand, I bring it to my lips. The clear liquid sloshes against the rim and onto my bottom lip. Flicking my tongue out, I lick up the bitter liquid, a sour expression contouring my features.

Alan's gaze turns molten following the movement of my tongue. I follow the shot with a huge gulp of beer from the cup in my hand. My legs sway, the alcohol sinking heavily in my stomach. I down the rest of the beer and consider getting another when Alan opens his mouth to say something.

"Want to dance?" he asks, extending his hand out to me. Usually I'd say no, but the three shots and all the beer I've drank swirling around in my stomach are giving me a fuzzy, happy feeling and I just want to have fun and be carefree. I want to forget about the asshat across the room and if I can do that by dancing with someone else, then I will.

Taking his firm hand, I try to ignore the feel of Vance's eyes on me as we walk to the makeshift dance floor in the center of the frat house living room. A pop song comes blaring through the speakers. It's not really slow dance material, but we make the most of it. Alan holds my hands while he dances with me. It feels nice, but it's nothing like when I danced with Vance.

There's no electricity between us, no spark, no fire. Alan doesn't seem to notice or maybe he doesn't care, I don't know. He moves closer, pulling me into his chest, his hands moving to my hips as we dance. I want to have fun. I want to forget about Vance and I want to like Alan, but I can't. It doesn't matter how nice or good looking he is, he is not Vance.

This feels like a mistake. Dancing with someone while thinking about someone else, it feels wrong, like I'm cheating, which is ridiculous since Vance and I are nothing but mortal enemies and as far from a couple as it gets. I'm about to politely excuse myself, shame blanketing me when Vance appears out of nowhere, his hand wrapping around my wrist gently.

"It's time to go home," he yells over the music, tugging me off the dance floor.

"Are you serious?" Alan asks the question that was lodged in my throat.

"*Very*. Now let's go, Ava," he orders, his green eyes piercing mine. He's paying Alan no attention and I'm thankful for that. I don't want another fight to break out.

"It's fine," I tell Alan, who's giving me a weary look. "Really, its fine, I want to go home anyway," I reassure him.

Alan frowns, but releases me, taking a few steps back before giving me a wave goodbye. Vance tugs on my arm and I follow along behind him, not that I could do anything anyway. I feel bad for not saying bye to Jules, but I suppose I can always apologize later. As soon as we step outside and the fresh air hits me, my head starts to spin. I press a hand to my stomach to stop the contents inside from sloshing around.

Maybe three shots within ten minutes wasn't such a great idea. Vance's pace slows when he realizes my steps are becoming unsteady. Turning, he wraps an arm around my waist, hauling me against his side. It feels nice, nicer than I expect it to, especially after the way he acted earlier tonight. A smart girl would push him away, tell him to get bent, but I'm not smart. I'm broken, so horribly broken.

"What are you doing?" I ask him, realizing that I'm slurring my words a tad. I've been drunk maybe twice in my life. One other time back in high school with one of my friends, it also happened to be the night I lost my virginity.

"Helping you to the car." His arm tightens around me and the familiar tingle I feel every time he touches me zings through me. I want him to keep touching me, to tell me everything is going to be okay. We're not even halfway across the front yard when a familiar voice calls out my name.

"Ava!" The sound is deep, manly and it stops us dead in our tracks. Vance turns us so we're facing toward the owner of said voice. My eyes light up when I see Jules and Remington walking toward us.

They seriously are the sweetest people ever.

"Where do you think you're taking her?" Rem asks Vance, but it sounds more like an accusation than a question. Worry creases his forehead and I wonder if he thinks Vance is going to hurt me or something.

"Home," is all Vance says. It's obvious he doesn't care to explain himself, and I suppose he shouldn't have to. He might be a dick, a douchebag even, but he's not the type to take advantage of a woman.

Turning away from them, he starts to walk again, tucking me in even closer to his side. I feel protected, secure, and for one single moment, I let myself lean into his touch. My nose pressed into his shirt. He smells like soap, and spices like clove and cinnamon.

"Yeah, I don't think so, pretty boy. She's not safe with you, need I remind you of your little outburst earlier. I can't allow you to leave with her and maintain a clear conscience." At Rem's words, Vance stiffens, every muscle in his body tightening. He inhales a sharp breath, almost like he's trying to calm himself.

Shit. This is bad. I brace myself for the fight that I'm certain is to come, only this time it'll be against Remington and there won't be anyone to break them up. Wincing, I start to pull away but am surprised when Vance does the polar opposite of what I'm expecting.

He calmly turns, and says, "She'll always be safe with me. I would never let anything happen to her. I might say mean shit, cut her down, but I wouldn't ever take advantage of her or lay a hand on her. I'm a fucking man, and men don't take from women who don't want it."

Well fudgesicles, where is this guy all the time?

I'm not sure what I'm more shocked over, the words coming out of Vance's mouth or that it sounded like he might actually care about me. There's a strange kind of conviction to his tone that makes it impossible for me to deny that he is speaking the truth.

Hell, I must be drunker than I suspect if I'm thinking that Vance actually cares about me. I'm probably totally misreading the situation. What other explanation could there be for his caring behavior.

"I'll hold you to that, Van. If I hear that you fucked with her, or hurt her in any way, I'll rearrange your face with my fists. Got it?" Rem warns. He's so protective, Jules really is lucky to have him.

"I got it," Vance growls, turning our backs to them, we start walking away again.

With each step toward the car, my legs get weaker, my knees knocking together. Exhaustion seeps into my pores. Unable to stop myself, I lean into Vance more and more until my head is leaning against his shoulder.

This feels right, perfect even.

When we finally get to the car, he opens the door for me and helps me inside. I'm so tired and woozy that I can barely keep my eyes open. My eyes fall closed, and I tell myself I'm just going to doze off for a few minutes, but the next time I open my eyes, we're already parked in the driveway at the house.

Vance opens the passenger side door and holds out his hand toward me. I blink, looking up at him wide-eyed. Why is he helping me? He doesn't care about me, so why?

"What...?" I tilt my head to the side, inspecting him.

"Either take my hand and let me help you or I'll throw you over my shoulder and carry you inside. It's your choice and don't take long to decide or I'll choose for you." His voice is unusually soft, and dare I say calm. It's so unlike him to be gentle and kind that I'm almost worried this is a dream. A dream I kinda don't want to wake up from.

"Am I asleep?" I whisper, placing my hand in his. His hand is warm and I shiver at the contact.

Laughing softly, he says, "No, you're not sleeping. Why would you even ask that?"

He helps me out of the car and onto my wobbly legs before closing the door.

"Because you're being nice to me and you're never nice to me. You'd rather stab yourself in the eye with a fork then befriend me. Admit it, you would."

Quietly, he whispers, "I'm thinking maybe I was wrong about you."

Wrong about me? Of course he's wrong about me. He's been blaming me for some mysterious thing since I got here, cutting me down with his words, and giving me serious whiplash with his hot and cold attitude. He thinks he knows, knows what I went through to get here, but he doesn't have a clue, so yeah, he's wrong. Very wrong.

He walks us to the front door and unlocks it without ever letting go of me. I'm a little more awake and a little less drunk now that I've had a short nap and some fresh air.

"What's going on between us?" I blurt out before I can stop myself.

Vance is suddenly so different. Less angry and brooding but I can't figure out what's changed aside from his attitude. It's almost like he's repressing his feelings. Is he sick? Has he hit his head? It's kinda like he's the old Vance, like he's my friend and not my enemy.

Oh God, maybe I've missed him so much over the years, that suddenly now I'm imagining him being nice to me. But I can't possibly be imagining his gentle hands or soft voice. He helps me up the stairs and all the way into my room where he navigates me to the bed before pushing gently on my shoulders to make me sit.

"What do you mean what's going on with us?" he finally asks, startling me. I had almost forgotten I asked him a question.

Sighing, I blow out a big breath. "I mean, you're being nice to me, helping me..."

Rolling his eyes, he ignores my question and instead asks his own, "You need help getting undressed?"

"Who are you and what have you done with brooding, angry, Vance?"

Vance wants to smile, his lips trying their hardest to tug up at the sides.

"Clothes, Ava. Do you want them off? I'll help you if you need me to."

I don't really need help, I could probably manage on my own, but I *want* him to help me. I want to feel his hands on my skin, burning a blazing path of fire all the way down to my center.

Giggling, I say, "I bet you would..." And because patience has never been Vance's strong suit, he leans down and grabs the hem of my shirt.

"Lift your arms," he orders.

I do as he says as he pulls the shirt up and over my head. Cool air hits my heated skin, and I shiver, a light dusting of goosebumps blanket my arms.

"So bossy," I mumble under my breath.

He ignores my comment and instead reaches for my shoes, pulling them off and placing them on the floor. Green eyes meet mine, there's a hunger in those depths, but it's nothing that scares me, or even worries me.

It's a normal Vance look, intense, and possessive, and made to be felt. He gently nudges my shoulders, making me lie back on my bed. My pulse is racing, my heart slamming against my rib cage like it's trying to escape my chest and fly away.

Then he flicks the button on my jeans and pulls them down my legs slowly, so damn slowly I'm pretty sure he's trying to kill one of us. Probably me.

Once he's done, I'm left on the bed wearing nothing but my black lace panties and a bra, and somehow even that seems to be too much clothing. I want every inch of fabric gone, and I want Vance to lose his clothing too, so it's nothing but our heated bodies, skin to skin.

I twist in the bed, hoping that he won't leave just yet when the stupid underwire of my bra digs into the side of my boob. Stupid bras, who made this damn contraption anyway.

"You probably don't know this...since you're a guy and don't have a pair of tits, but bras get really uncomfortable after a while. Definitely not something you want to sleep with..." My voice trails off. I'm staring up at him, unable to remove my eyes from his smug, arrogantly, ridiculously handsome face.

"Is that right? Are you asking me to take your bra off? Because I must say, I've never had a chick ask me to take her bra off just so she can go to sleep. Most of the time, I'm not touching their tits."

I start nodding halfway through the question.

He peers down at me for a few seconds like he's weighing his options, considering if it's a good idea or not. *Do it.* I think to myself, secretly tempting him.

Do it. Touch me.

As if he's made up his mind, he sighs and leans over me, slipping a hand underneath my back. His fingers are warm, and I shiver again at his gentle caress. I arch my back to give him better access, but mainly so I can tease him by pushing my boobs into his face. I'm impressed when he quickly unhooks the bra with one hand without even seeing the hooks in the back.

"Impressive, Mr. Preston. You've got some mad skills there," I taunt teasingly.

"You haven't seen anything yet." The mischievous glint in his eyes tell me I probably haven't. Vance is way more experienced than I am. I've had sex with one guy, and it was all fumbling and awkwardness. Nothing like how I know sex with my bully, my enemy, would be.

Before he has the chance to straighten and pull away, I snake my hands around his neck and make an attempt to pull him down on top of me. He's huge, tall, and muscled. All I can seem to think about is the weight of his body on mine, our skin touching, his fingers digging into my hips while he thrusts his hardened cock into me.

Ugh, I need to get laid, and by someone that isn't Vance.

Anticipating my next move, his fingers wrap around my wrists, halting any further advancement. *Oh, shucks.* It seems the asshole as grown a conscience.

"You're drunk. Go to sleep, Ava."

"You're drunk. Go to sleep, Vance," I mock, sticking my tongue out at him.

"*Sassy.* Not much has changed about you, has it? You still make me want to throttle you," he says heatedly.

"Well, I feel the same about you too," I say before slipping out of my bra, and flinging it across the room. I can feel my nipples tighten now that they are free from the bra and I know if he would touch them, touch me, they would harden to stiff peaks.

Excitement and lust pulse through me at the thought.

"Stay with me," I whine, giving him my best pout. I don't want this precious, un-hateful moment to end between us. It's too soon. I've only got a taste of the old Vance and I'm not ready to give him up yet. "Please..." I say a second later, because the apprehension flickering in his eyes tells me he doesn't want to give in.

He exhales all the air in his lungs, and his jaw tightens. He shakes his head as if he's telling himself he shouldn't do it, shouldn't stay, but just like me, he can't let go of whatever is happening right now. So instead of leaving, he starts to take off his clothes. Gulping, I swallow down the groan forming in my throat.

His shirt is the first to go and when the simple t-shirt is pulled away, he extends it to me.

"Here, put this on." There's a seductiveness to his voice that calls out to me.

"Do you have a problem with boobs?" I tease, feeling light-hearted and free. He rakes his teeth over his bottom lip, letting his eyes run over my bare chest. *Of course he's not shy about looking.* My tits aren't huge, more like a handful each, but they aren't bad either. I mean boobs are boobs, right?

"Nah, your tits are perfect. Now put the shirt on, before I put it on you myself. I'm a man of my word, so for tonight your virtue is safe with me."

"You're so bossy, and I'm not a virgin, there is no virtue to save," I grumble, pulling on his shirt awkwardly before shoving down into the pillowy mattress.

"Virgin or not, it's not happening, so stop being a pain in the ass."

I watch him intently as he gives me my own personal strip-tease. My mouth starts watering and moisture builds between my thighs with every piece of clothing he tosses to the floor.

Once down to his boxers, he slides into the bed beside me, the bed is a queen, but with his bulking frame in it, it feels like a twin. He pulls the blanket up and over both of us. Feeling extra brave, I slide across the sheets and over to him until my body is pressing up against his side. He starts to move, and all I can think is, shit, he's about to push me away, but instead he does the opposite and slides his arm under my head the motion drawing me closer to him, if that's even possible.

"I'm sorry," I murmur, suddenly feeling like I need to apologize even though it wasn't me who made myself look like a giant ass tonight. Kidding aside, we should really talk about it. The giant elephant in the room. It's weighing heavily on both of us. I don't know Vance as well as everyone else, but I do know that he wasn't acting like himself at that party.

"Shhh..." Vance whispers as if he doesn't want to hear my apology. Pressing my cheek against his red hot skin, I inhale deeply, sniffing him. *Damnit.* Even his skin smells good like soap and cloves, and I kinda want to take a bite out of him like a chocolate chip cookie.

But even his scent can't mask the exhaustion I'm feeling. All this fighting, pretending, it's wearing me down. The wakefulness I felt a few minutes ago evaporates, and I yawn into Vance's side, none too lady-like. My eyelids droop, fluttering open and closed a couple times. I'm about to doze off with hopes I don't drool all over his chest when Vance's deep rumbling voice fills my ears.

"What happened...like *really* happened, that night five years ago?" With my eyes still closed, I answer him.

"You dared me...remember?" I ask sleepily. Maybe he did hit his head if he can't remember what happened that night.

"Yeah, and then? What happened then? What happened after that, after you went into the house?"

My brain is like a cookie jar that you can't see the contents too, my hands digging through the memories trying to place the right one. It seems to take me an eternity partially because I'm drunk, but mostly because it's not a memory I'm really all that fond of.

"I-I snuck into the house..." I take a deep breath, almost falling asleep during my pause, but for some reason, I still manage to get the rest of the words out. "I went into my parents' bedroom..."

"And?" he questions, his voice a low hum, his fingers playing with a couple strands of my hair. It's all too much, his gentle caress, body being so near, all the exhaustion, and my mind starts to shut down mid-sentence.

"I saw them..." The words come out as a whisper, so softly I'm surprised that even I hear them.

"Saw who? Who did you see, Ava?" Vance's panicked voice bleeds in my subconscious but I'm too far gone to answer him, sinking deeper and deeper into the darkness, deeper and deeper into his arms.

12

VANCE

The sun starts to peek up over the horizon, little glimpses of it filtering through the window blinds in Ava's room. I shouldn't have stayed last night, hell, I should get up and leave right now. But I can't. My body physically will not move. It's like I'm in a trance, weakened beyond measure by her presence.

After what she said to me before she fell asleep, there was no way I was going to get a wink of sleep. My mind was running a mile a minute, trying to figure out *who* and *what* she saw. I even tried to wake her up, but she was too exhausted and too drunk to open her eyes, and batted my hands away in protest. Which leads me to where I am right now.

Staring at her like a peeping tom.

Watching her sleep all night, her pink lips parted, her mousy brown hair splayed across the pillow and my chest while the tiny strands tickled me, it was worth staying for. Never had I watched another person sleep, let alone a woman. I realize then that Ava could be my first and my last. *No.* She can't.

I let my gaze fall over her bare thighs, *my* shirt riding up. Fuck, she looks good in my shirt. She'd probably look good with my cock in her too. I lick my lips envisioning it, fuck yeah, she would. My cock hardens to steel instantly, and I try and think about anything other than Ava's perfectly sized tits, creamy white thighs, or pink lips.

Old saggy tits. Clark's asshole.

Ahh, fuck what's the point. It doesn't matter what I think about, my dick knows Ava is lying next to me half naked.

Just when I think it couldn't possibly get any worse, she starts to stir beside me, her leg sliding over my thigh inches away from my dick. *Fuck.* I try to move my leg, inching it away from hers, but all she does is move closer, like I'm her personal pillow.

She snuggles deeper into my side, her knee inching closer until it actually grazes my dick. I can't help but close my eyes, biting back a groan that I know will surely wake her up. An explosion of pleasure floods my body. I can't believe that single touch felt so good.

Realizing that she's stopped moving, my lid's flutter open, my gaze dropping to her face, where I find two emerald green eyes staring back at me. A warm flush creeps up my throat. The knot of anxiety tightening in my belly.

We need to talk, but the last thing I want to do right now is talk, unless it's with my cock. Her fingers trace over my washboard abs lazily.

I damn near gulp at the sensation, my body humming. If she doesn't stop touching me, I won't be responsible for whatever happens next.

Fuck me is a bad idea. We shouldn't do this. *But I want to. I want to so bad.*

"We should..." I start, but the words are cut off, as Ava

pushes up off the mattress, and covers her mouth with my own.

For one split second, I'm shocked, so shocked I can't even move my lips.

What are we doing?

Every single rational thought that doesn't center on sex flies right out the window when she tosses a toned leg over my body and straddles me, centering her warm pussy against my abs. *Fuck. Fuck. Fuck.*

I have to stop this. I don't deserve her, and we need to talk. I go to push her away, but she sinks her nails into my chest like a kitten, the little sparks of pain taking a beeline straight to my cock. My resolve snaps and my fingers weave into her hair as the exact opposite of what I intended. Deepening the kiss instead of pushing her away. If I'm going to have her, then I'm going to have her completely, every single gasp, moan, and plea is going to be mine. Her pelvis grinds into me, her wet heat sliding over my skin.

I pull back a fraction of an inch. "If you don't want me to fuck you, then you need to stop this right now."

That's the only warning I'm giving her. If she keeps her slickness on me, or swivels her hips one more time...

"Pretty sure the entire reason I'm straddling you is because I *want* you to fuck me." The cheeky grin that forms on her lips is one I want to replace with pleasure.

"Fucking, that's all this is." My heart constricts inside my chest at the words.

She licks her lips and says, "Give me your worst, Vance Preston."

My name falls from her lips like a prayer. Now that we've got that out of the way, and my cock is straining so hard I'm pretty sure I have the worst case of blue balls ever, I reach for her and slide my hands underneath the t-shirt she's wearing until my fingers make contact with her hips.

Then I trail those same fingers downward and slide the fabric of her panties to the side revealing her pink pussy spread open for me like rose petals, each one begging to be plucked.

Perfection at its finest.

Dragging my fingers through her wet folds, a shudder ripples through me before I sink two of my thick digits into her tight entrance without warning. Her green eyes widen, squeezing together at the intrusion, and for a moment I worry I've hurt her. She said she wasn't a virgin, how long has it been since she fucked a guy?

When she doesn't say anything, the thought disappears and I pick up my pace, scissoring my fingers, angling them in a *come-hither* motion.

"Fuck, Ava, look at this pussy... so fucking wet for me. Tightening with every stroke. You want to come, don't you?"

She nods her head frantically, her chest rising and falling rapidly, her pebbled nipples straining against the thin fabric of my t-shirt. Her reaction to me is everything I had hoped it would be and more.

Pumping in and out of her tightness, I keep my eyes on hers. She fists the sheets at her sides and bites into her plump bottom lip while I stretch her to accommodate my length. She's tight, so fucking tight and it's going to be an even tighter fit.

Most of the time, I don't take the time to prepare the women I fuck. But Ava isn't just some random to me, she's everything, the beginning, the middle, and the end. And I'm going to make this good for her, even if I die trying.

With two fingers inside her, I take my thumb and press it

against her diamond hard clit. I'm ready to be inside her...so fucking ready.

Pulling my fingers out of her, I earn myself a whimper. When she comes, it's going to be around my cock, so I can feel every spasm and quiver her pussy makes.

"Don't worry, you'll get to come soon enough." Gripping onto her hips, I push her off of me, laying her down on her back. Hooking my thumbs into her panties, I drag them down her legs, my knuckles running against the supple, soft flesh.

Her shirt goes next and I throw both pieces of clothing onto the floor. Pausing for one single moment, I drink in her naked body before me. Everything about her is perfect. I want to look at her for hours, explore every inch of her body, but my cock is done waiting. I have patience but when it comes to her, I'm like a small child giddy with excitement as he reaches into the cookie jar.

Pushing my boxers down over my hips, I free my length. The head of my cock is swollen and an angry red. *Poor fucking guy.* Wrapping my hand around the angry giant, I stroke myself a few times, pleasure pulsing from my balls to the tip of my cock with each stroke.

Ava looks up at me with hungry eyes, watching me like a hawk.

Then I realize something... *Shit!*

"I don't have a condom." I groan. I have some in the car. I could go and get one, but I don't think I'm physically capable of leaving her here right now. "I've never gone bareback before, so if you're..." I let my voice trail off. I don't want to ruin this moment between us, but there isn't any way I'm going to put myself in a situation where I have to worry about knocking her up. I wouldn't ever consider fucking without a condom but in my heart, I know Ava's worthy of this moment.

"I'm on birth control," she squeaks.

Thank fucking, fuck!

I have to fucking have her. I have to be inside of her. *Now.*

"Thank fuck," I whisper.

Pressing forward, I blanket her body with mine and lean down, holding myself up with one arm so I don't crush her. With my free hand, I guide myself to her entrance and dip the head inside wetting it in her arousal before slipping it between her folds. I bump against her clit and she mewls into her hand, tilting her hips up, seeking out more friction.

"Please..." she whimpers, and I grin, loving that I hold this much power over her. That for once I'm the one driving her insane instead of it being the other way around. Guiding myself back to her entrance, I press the tip inside, slowly, so slowly. I'm killing myself as much as I'm killing her, but fuck it will be a pleasurable death.

I'm inside maybe an inch, it's just the head of my cock but it's enough to feel how tight she is, how drenched, and ready for me she is. Feeling her tightness all around me, I call on every ounce of self-control I have to not just plunge into her warmth and fuck her like a possessed beast. Sweat beads my forehead, my muscles tightening, and I can't fucking remember the last time I went this slow with someone. *Probably never.*

Exhaling all the air in my lungs, I ease into her, stretching her slowly. Her hands start to move, and I feel them everywhere. On my shoulders, roaming down my chest and abs. My lungs burn as I forget to breathe, getting lost in her touch.

Thrusting forward another inch, her hands claw at my back, trying to pull me closer, while also telling me that she needs more.

"I want to fuck you...fuck you right into this mattress, fuck you so hard that all we hear is the headboard slamming against the wall in rhythm with our breathing."

"Then do it. Fuck me. Claim me. Own me."

Gritting my teeth, I tell myself she doesn't know what she's asking of me. She's different, not some random hook up. She's made to be cradled, and kissed with slow, steady strokes, not fucked. I can't help myself though. I need her, want her...

Letting my self-control snap, I plunge the rest of the way inside of her, only stopping when my balls kiss her ass. Deeply seated inside her, I feel like I'm on top of the fucking world.

"Full... so full..." Ava hisses. I almost expect her to tell me to stop, that she's changed her mind, but she doesn't, and thank fuck.

"Tell me to stop if it gets to be too much," I grunt, pressing a soft kiss to her cheek before pulling all the way out. I give her no more time to get used to my size, and instead start fucking her like an animal, giving her long, hard, powerful thrusts, one right after the other. It's like something inside of me has taken over. I can't control myself. I'm out of control, the only thing in my sight is the finish line for both of us.

My hips swivel, hitting something deep inside of her. Her pussy gushes around my cock, her wetness dripping down my length and gathering at my base.

"Vance..." she gasps. "Oh..."

She meets every one of my thrusts, tilting her hips up, and wrapping her legs around me, pulling me in deeper. Her moans and pants mingle with mine, creating a beautiful symphony of lust and passion. I've fucked a lot of women, but nothing compares to the way that Ava feels beneath me, the way her warmth feels wrapped around my dick.

It doesn't take long before I feel her thighs quivering and her pussy strangling my cock. I pull back a few inches so I can see her face. Her cheeks are rosy red, lips parted and her eyes closed as pleasure overtakes her features.

Her tiny nails dig into the skin on my back as she fractures straight down the middle. The hollowness inside my chest fills as I watch her, my strokes slowing. I didn't think it was possible, but she looks even more beautiful while falling apart on my cock.

Continuing to thrust inside her, I extend her orgasm, and while sliding through her quivering pussy, my own release starts to build. My balls slap against her ass, and my chest heaves with each precise stroke. She feels like heaven and I know even before the moment is over that I'll need another taste of her.

"Look at me. Look at me as I come inside of you," I grind out. Those green eyes of hers flutter open and bore into mine and I swear I can feel every sliver of pain, every heartache, and every word I've ever said to her. She owns me in this moment, and as frightening as it is, I don't look away. I want to see what I've done to her, feel it.

Pushing back onto my knees, I dig my fingers into her flesh and plow into her, over, and over, and over again until there is nothing but a cosmic wave of euphoric pleasure surrounding us. Then and only then as my muscles tighten and sweat beads down my back, do I allow myself to come, filling her tight cunt with spurt upon spurt of sticky salty cum. Her small hand lifts to my chest, pressing against the organ threatening to break free there. It thumps, like a feral animal, and I collapse for a moment on top of her, feeling as if I just ran a marathon.

That wasn't sex. That was... I don't even know, but I want to do it again. Pulling out of her, I roll to the side. She's quiet, too quiet and as the lustful haze fades from my mind, I'm reminded that we have unfinished business from the night before to talk about. I meant to discuss it as soon as she woke up, but never got the chance, my cock having other ideas.

"Last night you said... you saw *them*. Who is *them*?"

Ava sits up, grabbing the sheet from the edge of the bed to

cover up. "You know what I meant." She fiddles with the edge of the sheet and I can tell she's already uncomfortable with the conversation. That's too bad.

"Actually, I have no idea what you meant by *them*. You're talking in riddles and I don't have the patience to read between the lines. So spit it out already."

Her eyes flicker to mine, and she stares at me as if I'm a puzzle piece that doesn't fit in its spot on the puzzle. My pulse races, anticipation of the unknown building. Nodding my head, I encourage her to keep going.

Thick brows draw together and her mouth pops open. "My mom. Your dad. I walked in on them fucking. You know that, right?"

The way she says it, so nonchalantly, like it's actually true… I don't know why but it's almost like her tone of voice affects me more than the words she's said. Opening my mouth, I plan to say something, anything but suddenly my tongue weighs ten tons and the words, they get lodged in my throat, clogged by an all too familiar anger.

Instead I gawk at her, waiting for her to tell me that she is kidding, *lying*, but all she does is look back, her expression wide-eyed, and on the cusp of shock. My heart sinks into my stomach, and my hands grow clammy.

"You know that, right?" she repeats, but I still can't answer. This doesn't make sense, why would my dad…*no*…this can't be true.

She's lying. My dad wouldn't have cheated on my mom. He loves, or at least loved her back then and you don't hurt people you love. Squeezing my eyes shut, I will the thoughts away. Lies, it's all lies. It has to be. I can't believe Ava, she's a vile manipulator, she told my father that I threatened her, that I was using her to steal jewelry. My eyes open a second later and it must dawn on her that I don't have a fucking clue as to what she's talking about. When I don't respond, she starts to explain the more.

"How did you not know about this? Why do you think my dad took me and my mom and left the state the next day?"

Ava asks, tears well in her eyes, but I can't react. I feel... I feel fooled, broken, like I've fucked up and there is nothing that can make it better and I guess there isn't.

"I didn't lie to you, Vance. My mother and your father were having an affair. I told my father, even though my mother begged me not to, even though your father told me what I saw was wrong. I was young but not dumb. They were having sex. They were the reason my parents' marriage fell apart. You can't fix something that's beyond repair, my father thought otherwise, and look at him now. He's in rehab, while my mother sails the Seven Seas remarried and with the man she cheated on him with."

"I..." What do I even say to that? All this time, I believed that my mother and father's marriage had ended because of the financial strain of moving and my father losing his job. I placed all that blame on Ava, calling her a liar, lashing out at her, because I thought she caused all the problems.

But she didn't... he lied. The man I looked up to my whole life lied to me. I open my mouth again to say something else, but the words never make it past my lips. The sound of the front door opening echoes through the house, followed by voices that I know all too well.

"Vance, Ava. Surprise, we are back from our honeymoon!" My father's voice meets my ears and when I look to Ava, I see the horror of what she's told me reflecting back at me.

"You... you really didn't know?" she whispers.

"No...no I didn't," I croak.

13

AVA

*V*ance pulls on his boxers, grabs his pants, and races from the bedroom.

He didn't know. Oh my God, he didn't know. I can't comprehend it. I can't believe it. All this time I thought he knew... but there's no way, the look in his eyes, the anger and sadness. I knew as soon as I saw it, he didn't know.

Which leads me to wonder what he thought had happened? Why he was so mad at me? What did Henry tell him? Obviously it had something to do with me, but what exactly, I have no idea and right now, I have no time to ask him not with our parents back.

I slip into my own clothing in record time, brushing through my hair with my fingers, and splash some water on my face in the bathroom before rushing downstairs. It feels weird to have Vance's cum inside me as I walk down the hall and toward the staircase to talk to Henry and my mother.

Vance is already standing at the bottom of the stairs, chatting with our parents when I appear at the top of the stairs. Neither one of them notices how tense he is. How hard he's trying to make polite small talk when all he probably wants to do is confront them. I don't know why he hasn't said something yet, if I was him, I would be coming unglued, bursting at the seams for answers. Not Vance, he's cool, casual, acting as if he didn't just find out the most tragic lie of all.

It might be pitiful, but even after all my mom has done, I still want her to spend time with me without fighting. All I want is my mom back, and bringing up what happened five years ago is not going to be pleasant for any of us right now, so even though I know Vance is dying for answers, I hope at the very least he waits until we leave.

"We didn't know you guys were going to be here today." I force a smile, even though I feel more like crying.

"It wouldn't have been a surprise if we would have called in advance, would it?" My mom beams at me. "And for you, young lady, I have one more surprise."

"You do?" I perk up even though I feel shameful about it.

"Yup, we are going to the spa! Just the two of us for the rest of the day. I felt bad leaving as soon as you got here, so I thought we could spend the day together."

My mom gives me a genuine smile and now I feel like crying for an entirely different reason. This entire thing is a shit show. It's hard to hate someone that gave you life, but it's even harder to know that your life would probably be as it was supposed to be had that person not made a selfish choice.

"Yes, that sounds… it sounds great," I tell her, but I can't help it when my gaze moves to Vance. His body language all but screams the pain he's feeling on the inside and the people that are the cause of that pain are right in front of him, and sadly they don't even notice.

"I'm guessing you kids got along just fine while we were gone? Seeing as we got no phone calls, and you both are alive and well?" Henry jokes, slapping a hand to Vance's back.

"Yeah, everything was great," Vance grinds out.

"Good, good. Well, the ladies are going to the spa, we should go play some golf. What do ya say, son?" Henry asks.

Vance shrugs. "I don't golf, but if you want me to go…"

"Perfect. I've got some calls to make, but we can meet up after lunch." Henry turns to my mother and presses a kiss to her cheek. "I'll be seeing you later," he whispers, and then his eyes flick to mine. "Have fun, ladies."

I stand motionlessly as my mother looks between Vance and me as if she's trying to fit the missing pieces back into place to solve the puzzle.

Finally, after she's flicked her gaze between us twice, she says, "I'm going to go and change really quick and then we can head out."

I nod my head and watch as she walks away, leaving Vance and I alone all over again. That seems to be a reoccurring thing in this house.

Staring at him, I feel the need to reach out to him, to soothe him, so I do. I place my hand on his shoulder and let his warmth seep into me. It's a simple touch, but it feels like I'm sticking my hand into the sun.

"I don't know what to say," he admits.

"You don't need to say anything. I'm just glad you know the truth now." I still want to ask him what he thought I lied about, but seeing how troubled he is already, I decide to bite my tongue. I can always ask him later.

His eyes are transfixed on mine for a minute, and a regretful shadow cloaks his face. Somehow, I get the feeling he wants to tell me that he's sorry, but the words never come. I'm hyper-aware of him now, my body buzzing when in his presence. Having sex changed something between us, but it wasn't just the sex, it was the truth coming out too.

"I'll talk to you tonight, okay?" he finally says.

"Okay." I smile. Giving in to the need to hug him, I throw my arms around him and pull him into my chest. He's a good foot taller than me, but I make it work. He dips his head down and lets it rest on my shoulder, his arms snaking around my middle and coming to rest on my lower back. He's holding me to him, hugging me back, and after that first night at the wedding, I was sure this would never happen.

We don't hug for long, or at least it doesn't feel like a long time, because I want to keep holding onto him. When we break apart, he looks a little calmer, some of the tension in his gorgeous face fading.

"Have fun with your mom," he tells me. "I'm going on a drive to clear my head before going *golfing* with my dad." Pulling out a pair of keys from his pocket, he heads for the door just as my mother calls out for me.

"You ready to go, Ava?"

With one last fleeting glance, he walks away.

"Yeah, let's go."

∼

SPAS ARE NOT MY THING, let's be real. Getting dolled up, doing my hair and makeup, also not my thing, but spending time with my mother is more important to me than my sanity for lack of girliness and since I'm desperate for even a little bit of interaction, I let her drag me along.

We do a full body massage that makes my body feel like goop, and get our hair cut and colored. By the time we're finished at the salon I've got a growling belly and look and feel like a million bucks.

"Let's go to lunch, and then we can do a little shopping. I want to get some stuff for your bedroom. Add some personal touches to it." I smile, but can't help but feel guilty. While I'm having a great time with my mother, Vance is stuck in the presence of his father, dealing with a truth that was hidden from him for five years.

Five years, he blamed me. Five long years.

We head into an Italian bistro at the mall, the hostess seating us right away.

"Are you okay? You seem...worried," my mom asks, and for the first time in three years, I see my mom look at me with genuine concern. She's not looking through me, she's looking at me, and it feels too real, too much.

"I missed you," I blurt out. "I really missed you."

"Oh, sweetheart." Her eyes fill with tears and I have to bite my bottom lip to keep myself from crying. "I know it doesn't seem like it, but I missed you too. I'd have called more often... and visited you. And the worst part is that my excuse for not doing so, is selfish. I've made many mistakes in my life, I'm not too proud to admit that, but not being there for you for the last three years was the biggest mistake of all." She pauses to wipe an escaped tear away with her finger.

"Every time I did call you, I was reminded of everything I've lost, and that hurt. It was easier not to call altogether. I told myself that it would be easier for you too, but obviously I was wrong, and for that, I am very sorry."

I didn't even know that I *needed* to hear her say those words until she said them. For so long, I was wondering why she didn't call me, why she left without coming back. I often thought to myself that it was me, that she didn't want me. So many times, I asked myself what I could have done wrong, so to hear her say that I didn't do anything wrong at all, it took a huge weight off my shoulders.

Fidgeting with the napkin in my hands, I say, "I thought maybe it had something to do with me so—"

My mother cuts me off, "God, no honey. It had nothing to

do with you. I know what I did was selfish and I'm sorry for that, truly I am." And for a moment I wonder which part she's admitting to being selfish about...having an affair or being a shit mom.

"Now tell me, how are classes going. Did you and Vance really get along while we were gone?" she asks while clasping her hands under her chin.

"Classes are good, and everything was fine. No fights, nothing." I don't dare mention the fact that we fucked in my bedroom just moments before they came home. Somehow I don't think my mom would enjoy hearing that little tidbit. And I don't tell her about Vance's house party or any of the petty things he did like share my cell phone number with the entire campus.

"Good, good. I know the situation wasn't ideal." She frowns. "And that I had to bribe you a little to get you out here, but I hope it hasn't been too bad."

Thinking about it, it could be worse. I could be homeless, living in my car, while looking for work instead of going to college. Dealing with Vance's taunts, and verbal bullshit was something I could handle, as long as I had somewhere to rest my head at night. The only person I worried about now was my father.

"It wasn't that bad, and I'm enjoying being here with you even though we haven't been able to spend much time together."

She smiles, her eyes getting misty. "Awe, honey I don't deserve a daughter like you."

No, you don't, I want to say, but don't. Then the waitress comes by the table and takes our orders. We make small talk about the design of my bedroom and how she wants us to do something together each week to make up for lost time. And because I'm desperate for her affection and love, I agree.

Once our stomachs are filled with more carbs than a human should be allowed to consume, she calls for the check. Our day together is coming to an end and the reality of what awaits me once we get home falls heavily on my shoulders. Being with my mom was an easy distraction from the chaos, but I know once we get home, shit is going to hit the fan.

I bite my tongue, stopping myself from asking her anything about it. Maybe she doesn't know that they told Vance something different than what happened. She probably wouldn't care anyway, and only tell me to move on, to get over it, that it's in the past and can't be rewritten.

But is it really the past if it's affecting your future?

"You look lost in thought, is something bothering you?" My mother's voice rings in my ears and for a moment, I forgot where I was, becoming so wrapped up in my thoughts.

I clear my throat drawing myself back to the present. "I was just wondering why Vance's parents got a divorce." I try not to sound too eager, mainly just curious.

"Why..." My mother blinks slowly. "Why would you ask something like that?" Suddenly she seems nervous.

"Oh, no reason really. Just looking for something else to bond with Vance over. He's a hard nut to crack." I smile, but it's forced, and I hope she can't tell.

"Ahh, well truthfully...I do not know. Henry and I never talk about his and Meg's marriage. We're beyond in love. Why worry about the past anyway?"

I want to scream at her...to tell her that Vance and I are currently living in the past because of her and Henry's selfishness, but I don't. What's the point? She doesn't care, and if she does know something, it's obvious she isn't going to tell me. The only way to get the answers that I want and need is to go to Vance.

"You're right. Let the past be the past, right?"

My mother smiles, and it's dazzling, happiness filling her eyes. "That's right. Continue forward, not backward."

I can't help but think about the fact that both of them got what they wanted, they ruined two families, and still ended up happily together and that's the lesson here, I suppose. If you shit on enough people, you'll always find a way to come out on top.

What kind of person shits on their family though?

14

VANCE

Somehow we make it through a whole game of golf without really speaking. I mean it's not like we just stare at each other or anything, but he doesn't ask me how I'm doing, or how it's been with him gone.

He's changed.

It wasn't really noticeable before, but since Laura came into his life, he's almost pushed me out of the picture, only dealing with me when he feels he has to. All my life, I've looked up to him, wanting to be like him, but now it feels like I've lost my compass, and I don't know which way to go. I can't look up to a man that's lied to me for years, that's responsible for my anger, my pain. Fuck, I can't even imagine how Ava must feel right now. She knows now that I had no idea, but that doesn't mean I can take anything back.

All the things I've said and done to her. Just thinking about it, and knowing that I placed the blame on the wrong person this whole time it makes me sick, physically and emotionally. There's no amount of pleading and begging, there are no words I can say to make her forgive me.

The question I want to ask has been sitting impatiently on the tip of my tongue for the last three hours, but I can't bring myself to actually ask him. I've analyzed every way this could go, and I still don't have the balls to ask him.

Mainly because I'm not ready to admit it to myself... but the truth is... I'm scared. Afraid to hear my father's answer. Sure there isn't shit he could say that would make any of this better or change the damage that's been done, but I need this, to hear him, to hear the truth spoken out loud, because right now all this feels like is a nightmare I'm never going to wake up from.

After three hours of painful silence while hitting balls around with a bunch of other rich fuckers, we walk back to the clubhouse and load up the clubs into the trunk. I know time is running out. If I want to ask him when it's just us, I'll need to do so now.

Knowing that, I mentally prepare myself for what's to come. I lock down my emotions, sliding a mask onto my face. No matter what he says, at least I'm getting the truth, right? Wrong is wrong, but I don't focus on that. My stomach knots with dread as we both get into the car. The engine roars to life and fills the empty space inside the car with a dull hum.

Sucking in a deep breath, I blow it out and ask, "Did you and Laura have an affair five years ago?"

"What?"

The shock in his voice surprises me, probably because I was expecting him to say yes.

"Did you?" No way am I repeating that question again, and especially not when I know he heard me the first time.

He gives me a befuddled expression, his brows pinching together. "Why would you ask me something like that?"

No, yes or no answer, just another question on top of all the others.

"Did you?" I repeat more urgently. I need him to say it. *Yes or no.* My knee starts to bounce up and down, nervous anxiety vibrating off of me.

"Of course not, Vance. What the hell? I loved your mother very much when we were married and never would have done such a horrendous thing."

My knee stops mid-bounce, and my gaze drops to the floor. *No?*

"No?" I croak. There's a terrible feeling inside my chest. It feels like my heart's being ripped in two, a spasm of pain shooting through me, almost like a bullet has lodged itself deep inside. My lungs burn, needing air, but I can't even perform the simplest of functions.

"No, of course not, son. Why would you even ask me a question like that?"

He said no.

He said no.

Which means...

"Vance, did something happen? Talk to me, son." My father's voice draws me back.

"A...Ava..." I stutter. A hundred things running through my head all at once. Ava's smile, her laughter, her sweet floral scent, her soft curves, her pink lips.

Everything...everything is a lie. Why can't I see her for what she is? Why did I let what she said to me affect me in such a way? I should've expected this, expected her manipulation. She lied then, and she's continuing to lie. A cheetah never changes its spots. The pain inside gives way to anger, and it floods my veins, fueling me with red-hot rage like I've never felt before.

She manipulated me.

Lied to me...*again.*

She made me think it was all real. Her tears, her pain.

"What happened? Did something happen when we were gone?" Concern overtakes his confused expression. "I tried to tell Laura it was a bad idea to let her come and live with us. I'm sorry if she upset you."

Clenching and unclenching my fists to gain some type of composure, I say, "Why? Why was it a bad idea for her to come and live with us?" I could name ten reasons off the top of my head right this second, but I want to know *why* he thinks it was a bad idea.

Maybe I can get him to ship her off somewhere, obviously not until I get done with her, but nonetheless, I'll get rid of her even if I have to send her back to her piece of shit father, crying.

"Her mother told me she's got a serious problem with lying. I guess it's something she's developed over the years, or should I say gotten better at. She's a master manipulator, Vance. She can't be trusted, not at all."

Ain't that the fucking truth. I should've seen this coming, but I was caught up in the glamour of who she was, thinking maybe beneath it all she was an actual fucking human, the friend I had cared for so much. But if there is anything this teaches me, it's that if someone does something once, and gets away with it, they'll do it again, and I guess that's what Ava was doing. Trying to gain some hold over me.

"She lied, right to my fucking face. I swear I thought she was telling the truth. She looked so genuine. She was even crying... real tears, real fucking tears," I whisper, talking more to myself than my father.

He shakes his head in disappointment. "It makes sense, she's been making up things since she was an early teen, fabricating stories so well it was hard not to believe them. Remember when she told her father you threatened her? That you wanted her to steal some jewelry so you could sell it?

Seems she's only gotten worse over time. Don't feel bad for believing her, son. She's been practicing this lying gig for so long, its second nature to her. I'll have Laura talk to her, let her know that if she does something again, she's out. I wouldn't subject you to that again. My son isn't a liar, and you've never done anything to anyone."

Every muscle in my body tightens…I'm strung so tight that once I snap, I worry there may not be any coming back from the things I'll do.

Such a beautiful fucking liar. She must think I'm stupid, an idiot without a fucking brain. I bet it's all just a game to her. Letting me fuck her, getting under my skin. Maybe she thinks she can use her pussy to control me. Teeth grinding together, my jaw aching underneath the pressure. I stop myself from punching the dashboard.

I've got to unleash the pain… find an outlet, and soon before I explode.

"You know I loved your mother. We might be estranged now, but I did love her when we were married, she gave me you, after all. I respected her too much to ever cheat on her. I'm sorry son, I really am. If I knew she was going to do this kind of thing, I wouldn't have allowed her to come."

"It's fine," I grit out, my nostrils flaring.

"It's not. I feel terrible." He scrubs a hand down his face and all over again, I feel as if I've let my father down by falling into a hidden trap.

"It's really okay, Dad. You did nothing wrong. Can we just go home? I have some plans with Clark and I don't want to be late." How I get all the words to come out without a growl, I don't know. Maybe magic.

"I'll talk to Laura. I'll fix this," my father murmurs, shifting the car into drive. The drive home is short, and he doesn't say but a handful of words, thankfully. Fire rippling through my veins, I'm ready to burn everything the fuck down.

When we pull into the driveway, I bail from the car before it's even parked. I look up at the house with murderous rage and take a step forward.

No, my subconscious says. If I walk into that house right now, as angry as I am, I'll do something I know I'll regret and when I hurt that lying bitch, the last thing I want to do is regret it. So instead I fish my keys out of my pocket and start for my car.

"Are you sure you're going to be okay?" my father asks as I stomp across the pavement, each step vibrating through my bones.

"I'm fucking fine. I'm going to Clark's, so don't wait up for me. I'll be home when I get home," I mutter and slide into the driver seat. I start the car and pull out of the driveway as slowly as I can. Once on the street, I floor it, the roar of the engine combined with my rage in my veins giving me an unnatural high.

Driving around aimlessly, I try to decide what the fuck I'm going to do. My need to make her hurt outweighs all my other thoughts.

Liar. Fucking liar. The mere thought of her makes me want to punch a fucking wall. I tighten my hold on the steering wheel, my knuckles turning white. How can I hurt her the same way she's hurt me. She used her body, her fucking tears, and my emotions to twist and turn the knife. As if her betrayal from before wasn't enough, she then drove the knife deeper by fucking lying some more. I suppose I could use her back. She wanted my dick, came on it, and sighed my name like a fucking prayer. I'll just use her body against her, her fucking want for me. She might be a fucking liar but that tight little pussy squeezing around my cock is something you can't fake.

Soft skin. Green eyes. Pink parted lips. It's all I can see when I think about her.

"Fuck her," I yell into the air beating my fist against the steering wheel.

By the grace of God, I end up at Clark's house. The place looks like a fucking mansion, but it's very similar to my house. Five bedrooms, twenty million bathrooms, and a pool that lets everyone know we have more money than we know what to do with.

Parking in the driveway, I kill the engine and escape the small space of my vehicle. I need a punching bag, a bottle of whiskey, and some pussy. I don't knock when I enter the house and why should I, it's not like he knocks when he comes to mine.

As soon as I enter the over the top foyer, I hear voices. They boom off the walls and into the empty house. They're coming in the direction of Steve, Clark's father's, office. Not wanting to impose, I hang out around the staircase, my hands shoved into my pockets, waiting for Clark to make his appearance.

"I don't understand why this girl has to stay with us? If she got a scholarship, why can't she stay in the dorms? I'm an adult, not a babysitter, surely she can care for herself."

Her? What the fuck is going on? I know I shouldn't be eavesdropping and I'm not, not really. Both of them are talking loud enough that the neighbors could hear if they wanted to.

"I told you, she has really bad anxiety and I promised her parents that I would watch out for her. Darrel is one of my friends from when I started my business, he is one of the reasons we have money now, you know the money you use to buy booze and all the other expensive shit you have? I've known him and his family for a long time and I'm doing this because it's the right thing to do. Now you'll either do as I say, or you'll suffer the consequences."

Consequences? What's Steve going to do? Take his credit cards?

"Dad..." Clark growls, and I can practically see his face, the tendons in his neck tightening.

"Emerson is a sweet girl, and you will make her feel welcome here. Don't disappoint me, son. Just do what I say."

There's a finality to Steve's voice and I know whatever his father is setting him up to do he'll do. Clark might not like the shit his father does, but he wants to be accepted by him, appreciated, seen as more than just a boy.

Seconds tick by and an irritated Clark exits his father's office, his eyes downcast, frustration riddling what I can see of his face. Obviously neither of us are having a good fucking day. Listening in on Clark's problems, I almost forgot about my own. About the con-artist at my house, about the fucking lies she spewed just this morning.

"What happened?" he asks as soon as he lifts his eyes and sees me standing against the staircase. Everything seems to fade away around me. All I see, all I feel is her, her lies wrapping around my throat, tightening, stealing my breath.

The muscles in my jaw flex. "You don't even want to know, but since you're *best friends* with the bitch, I'll tell you. Long story short, we fucked, she used her pussy and some fake tears to spin a story about how my father cheated on my mom with her mother."

Clark's gaze widens. "Whoa, whoa. That's...wow." He pauses. "And you...fucked? How was it?" Suddenly he's grinning. Of-fucking-course he worries about what it was like to fuck her instead of the task at hand.

Amazing. Sensational. Jaw-dropping. Nothing but a lie. That's what it was like.

"Tight, warm, great until she opened her mouth." I try and sound uninterested.

Clark shrugs. "That's what it's like every time. You're fucking them, it's great, you blow your load and then they open their mouth and suddenly it wasn't worth it."

"Getting off track here," I growl. I'm an impatient fucker and my chest begs for something to dull the ache taking up residence inside it.

"Dude, sorry, you said something about fucking and it's like I have a one-track mind sometimes."

My features deadpan. "Look, it was either I came here and lost my fucking shit or went back to the house and confronted her. But, right now I don't trust myself to be in the same house as her, so do you want to get piss drunk with me or do you have other plans for the day? Plans that involve the girl downstairs maybe?" I question with a thick brow raised, knowing that busting his balls will get him moving in the direction.

"Shut the fuck up." He slugs me, but I don't even feel it. Then he twists around and starts walking in the direction of his father's whiskey cabinet. "Let's go drink away your sorrows, fucker," he slings over his shoulder with a knowing grin, and just like that, I'm already feeling better. Ava and her fucking lies being a distant memory as I swim in a pool of bad choices and enough alcohol to kill myself.

15

AVA

He never came home. Never showed his face back at the house. Forty-eight hours have passed and I still haven't heard from him. I've tried to call him, but his phone went straight to voicemail. I'm starting to wonder if he's regretting what we did and maybe that's why he wasn't coming home. Part of me hopes he didn't regret it but I'm dumb. I know that whatever is going on between us isn't anything serious and I've come to terms with that fact. I'm probably going to be just another notch on his bedpost. Still, it doesn't mean he couldn't come home. This is his house after all. I'm merely an unwanted guest.

"Off to classes?" my mother asks as I enter the kitchen.

"Yup. I'll be home later. I'm meeting up with a friend for dinner," I say, grabbing an apple from the fruit basket before making myself a cup of coffee in the Keurig. My mother has been overly peachy lately, her and Henry didn't even seem to notice a change in my attitude, nor did they seem to care that Vance hasn't been home.

"Alright, sweetie. Whenever you get back, Henry said he

wanted to talk to you about something. I'm not sure what it is, but if I know my husband it's probably nothing bad." She giggles like a love sick teenager.

"Uhh, sure." I blanch, wondering what the hell he could possibly need to talk to me about. She doesn't say anything else and walks out of the kitchen without even saying goodbye. I tell myself it's because she's busy or caught up in her thoughts, but I can't keep making excuses for her. I thought after her confession at lunch the other day, her attitude toward me would change, but if she keeps acting like she doesn't care, then it's probably because she doesn't.

Slinging my backpack over my shoulder, I grab my coffee and head out of the house and off to campus. I try my best to make it through my classes without thinking about Vance, but it's nearly impossible. When I spot Clark standing on the sidewalk, two girls talking to him, I bite at the chance to ask him if he knows where the hell Vance is. I shouldn't care, but I do. I care a lot more than I let on.

"Clark," I call out to him as I close the distance between us.

His eyes lift to mine, indifference reflecting back at me. "Hey A, what's up?" His tone is cool, casual, but it's off. *Something is up.* The two girls he was talking to seconds ago, huff and stomp their heel-covered feet on the ground wanting his full attention. Who purposely wears heels to college?

"Oh, stop it. There is more than enough Clark to go around," he teases, giving them his signature panting melting smile. One of the girls sighs, and I make a gagging sound.

Clark notices and snickers. "Don't be like that, we both know you want to take a ride too."

My brow furrowed in confusion at his comment. After the few times we hung out and talked, I was sure we were past this.

"Seriously? You know we aren't like that. Why are you acting weird?"

Clark shrugs. "Nothing weird about me. Just being myself." He plucks a hair off one of the girl's shoulders and examines it just like he did the first time I met him.

"Clark," I growl.

"Go find another dick to ride. I'm sure Vance's is available. Or maybe not, last I heard I think he was balls deep inside of Sarah, but I can't be sure."

The menace in his voice tells me he knows more than he's letting on, and I flinch, retreating a step back. His dig hurts, hitting me right where he had intended to. Even if Vance and I don't want to admit it, there's something going on between us, a connection, and hearing that Vance was with another chick after just being with me, Sarah of all people, stings. The two sorority chicks beside him start to giggle. Lifting my head, I hold my chin up high.

"I don't know what you're talking about. I was just going to ask you if you had seen Vance. Our parents are worried about him," I lie.

Clark squints down at me, taking a step forward, and then another until he's invading my space. He's gorgeous even on his worst days, but right now he's downright terrifying. He lifts a hand to my face, and it's almost like he's going to touch me, but he stops a fraction of an inch away from my bottom lip.

"You've got a little bullshit left on your lip from all the lies you've been spewing. Want me to get it for you?"

Ass-fucking-hole. Instantly I know this has everything to do with Vance. Every single thing.

I can't stop my reaction. I'm angry. Hurt. Broken inside. In a fit of rage, I pull my hand back and slap him hard, right across his stupidly perfect face. A sting of pain lances across my palm at the contact. His jaw tightens and his hand falls away, balling up into a tight fist.

What happened? What did he tell Clark?

I'm missing pieces to a puzzle that seems to get larger and larger every single day. I stare in horror at the red handprint on his cheek.

Clark tilts his head to the side. "Nothing you say to me will ever make me forgive you for hurting him. We might have been friends for half a second, but you mean shit to me now."

His words cut through me like a knife and I can't stop myself from turning around and running back the way I came. This was a mistake. A huge mistake. Coming here. Thinking I could earn my mother's love. Thinking that I would fit in. I know without even talking to Vance that he doesn't believe me. His father probably told him that it was a lie. Cold tears fall from my eyes as I run down the sidewalk, nearly taking out a group of people along the way.

My chest heaves, up and down, up and down, but it doesn't feel like I'm breathing. He doesn't believe me. He doesn't... I don't know why it hurts so bad. Why it feels like my heart is breaking. He means nothing, he doesn't even care about me. It was just sex. Sex, that's all it was.

I'm going to be late for my next class, but I don't care. Maybe I won't go at all. Rounding the corner near the English building, I finally stop running and slow to a walk, my knees wobbly. As soon as I stop walking altogether, I lean against the wall. Pressing my back against the cold brick, I close my eyes and try to get my erratic breathing under control.

Happy thoughts...I need to think about a happier time, a time when things made sense, when the people around me loved and trusted me. It's been so long since I was just happy, and everything changed on that night five years ago.

"I love you." My mother's breathless voice filters through the door. Pushing the door open, I expect to find my dad home from work. Instead, I find my mom...naked...with... a man, a man that isn't my father...

Henry.

I'm frozen in place, every muscle paralyzed by shock and confusion.

"I love you, Henry..." My mother moans right before she turns her head and finds me standing there staring with my mouth gaping open.

Thinking about that night has my stomach doing somersaults. Why did I open that door? I should have just turned around and walked away. I try to push the memory away, but it has a hold on me that I can't shake no matter how hard I try.

"You don't know what you saw." Henry, Vance's father, raises his voice. My mother's crying, big tears fall from her eyes. Why is she crying? Why is Henry telling me I don't know what I saw. I know my mom shouldn't have been doing what she was with Henry. My dad loves her, and she loves him, or at least I thought she did.

"Henry, stop. She's just a kid, she doesn't understand." My mother pulls her robe tighter around her small frame, her body shaking.

"That's exactly what I'm saying. She doesn't know what she saw. Do you Ava?" His dark gaze swings from my mother and back to me. It feels like he's trying to bully me, threaten me into agreeing with him.

Which angers me.

Lifting my chin, I look him right in the eyes. "I'm telling my father, no matter what you say."

The sound of approaching footsteps pulls me from the memory, but I'm not ready to open my eyes and face reality yet. Let whoever is walking by think what they want to think. With my eyes shut, I drown out the world around me, that is until two hands wrap around my upper arms, fingers digging into my skin. I'm pulled away from the wall.

My eyes fly open and my arms flail around wildly trying to

fight off my assailant. Sucking in a sharp breath is all I can do. The scream becoming lodged in my throat beneath the shock. Not that I'd want to scream once I realize who is holding onto me.

"Vance," I gasp, catching a small glimpse of his face, having wished I didn't.

He drags me along with him down the sidewalk and around the corner. He pulls open the door and tugs me inside the building. I try and dig my feet into the floor, but there's no point. I'm half his size and don't even stand a chance.

"Where are we going?" I whimper, his hold on my wrist tightening.

Ignoring my question, he says, "You think you can lie to me, use your fake fucking tears, and pussy to change my mind about you? Did you think I wouldn't ask my father about it? I hope you liked fucking me because I'm about to use you like you used me." The tone of his voice rains down on me like an angry thunderstorm.

We pass one room where a class is in session, voices carrying through the closed door as we pass it. He tugs me farther down the hall and when we get to the last room, all chatter has ceased and I realize we're pretty far away from anyone.

I try to swallow my fear down. I don't think he would hurt me, but I didn't think Clark would say the things he did to me either. Vance drags me along a few more steps and then opens a door on the right side of the hall. He pulls me into the empty classroom, dread trickling into my belly. Then he releases me.

Turning his back to me, I can hear the sound of a lock being turned into place. My gaze swings around the room, looking for another exit. When he spins around to face me, his expression makes a shiver run down my spine. I've never seen him so angry, I've never seen anyone so angry.

"My dad told me everything," he spits. "I can't believe I let you wrap me around your finger. I can't believe I listened to your sob story, or that I fucked you. That I felt even a sliver of sorrow for you."

The darkness in his voice is startling and he takes a step toward me, which makes me instinctively take one back. I don't know exactly what Henry told him, but I know for sure that it wasn't the truth.

"Vance, I swear..." I hold up my hands to fight him off, but he cuts me off, waving a hand in front of me.

"Shut. Up. No more lies. No more words. No. More. Fucking. Talking. You used me, you used my body, my emotions, and now I'm going to use you." He takes another step forward, and I take one back, my back hitting the table behind me, leaving me nowhere else to go. Trapped. I'm trapped.

He closes the distance between us with one large stride. The air grows thick with tension, with arousal. Part of me is terrified of having him so close, ironically, another part of me takes comfort in his body being so near.

I'm equally scared and excited when he leans in, his chest pressing against mine while grinding his groin into my center, making it impossible for me to miss how turned on he is. His face is so close to mine, his minty breath fans out against my cheek as he leans in and whispers directly into my ear. "Turn around." His voice is deep and gravelly, the sound vibrating through me, leaving goosebumps in its wake.

My mouth goes dry, and I lick my lips instead of kissing him like I want to. I can feel the slickness of my folds wetting my panties. And when our gazes meet for a fraction of a second, it feels like we're seconds away from exploding into each other. The lust and carnal need in his eyes leave me breathless. He hates me, but he also wants me, and right now,

I'll take that. If that is the only way I can be close to him, then that's enough for me.

My body moves on its own, following his order as if it was always made to. I start to turn slowly, but apparently too slow for Vance because he grabs my hips and spins me around in one swift move, then dips his fingers into the waistband of my leggings, his fingers make contact with my skin and a small zing of pleasure ripples across my skin. He shoves my leggings and panties down swiftly, leaving them at my ankles.

Cool air caresses my heated skin as I listen to Vance undo his pants behind me.

"Hands on the table," he orders gruffly, and all I can do is follow his command. I place my palms flat on the tabletop.

My nipples harden uncomfortably inside my bra. A soft groan meets my ears, and I can't comprehend if that came for me or Vance. The lines between hate and want are so muddled right now it's almost like we're trying everything we can to not hate each other. Vance places a hand to my lower back to hold me in place and then I feel the smooth head of his cock at my pussy. He drags himself up and down through my folds, growling when he realizes how wet I am for him, how much I crave his touch, even if he is not gentle and loving like he was two nights ago.

"Tell me you want this...tell me you want me to fuck you."

"Yes," I whimper, just as I feel him tease over my entrance. I want him. I want him so badly. Without any warning, he slams into me, stretching me as he buries his length inside of my channel, stopping only once his heavy balls slap against my ass. There's a slight sting of pain, and I cry out with the mixture of both pain and pleasure at the intrusion.

"Vance..." I whimper, gripping onto the table for leverage, knowing that he's about to make me feel every ounce of anger, and hate he has for me. I might not deserve it, but I'll take it for him. I'll harbor the weight of his father's betrayal.

He doesn't stop to give me time to adjust, he takes me hard and fast, plowing into me like an animal. I can feel his rage with each thrust mounting, his fingers digging into my hips as he pulls me back every time he thrusts inside.

My arms give out and I let my upper body rest on the table, turning my head to the side, I press my cheek against the flat wooden surface and continue to hold onto the edge as he continues fucking me, his strokes more furious than the next.

A tingle starts to spread from my center and outward, working its way through my limbs. My legs start to shake, letting me know I'm close, my pussy quivering. I push up onto my tiptoes, trying to get him to hit that spot that I know will drive me over the edge. So close, so fucking close. I bite into my bottom lip feeling the pleasure build. I'm almost there when he slows down, nearly pulling all the way out of me.

"Don't you dare come. This is not for you. This is for me."

His hand pushes me back down on the table so I can't move my hips at the angle that I want to. Then he enters me again, his strokes are deep, so deep I can feel him inside my belly, but they're also annoyingly slow. And the pleasure I was feeling before is long gone now. There's no way I can come at the pace he's going, and I guess that's the point. He's punishing me, showing me that he has all the power.

He thrusts into me a few more times, only picking up speed the last two strokes for his own release. Grunting, I feel his cock growing, and seconds later, he comes inside of me, coating my inner walls with his cum as his fingers dig into my flesh with bruising force.

"Fuck," he grunts. "Fuck..."

A moment later, he pulls out of me and steps away. The loss of his body leaves me cold and empty all over, only the cum dripping out between my folds is left of him. I want him to touch me again. I want him to make me come. But most of all, I just want him to hold me, to tell me that he believes me and that everything will be okay.

Instead, I hear the sound of jeans rustling and a zipper zipping. I don't move. Heavy footsteps followed by the clicking noise of the door unlocking, meets my ear, but I still don't move. I'm spent, between my interaction with Clark and Vance just now I feel... hopeless, lost in a vast ocean of emotions.

It takes me a long time to get the strength to push myself up and off the table but when I do, I pull my panties and leggings up, righting my clothing. I feel dirty and used. My muscles ache, and my eyes hurt from the crying I had done earlier. All I want to do is go home and curl up in my bed, forgetting everything around me, but if I go home, I have to face Henry, my mom, and worst of all, Vance. I have nowhere else to go. I have no friends. I have nothing.

16
VANCE

I haven't seen her in twenty-four hours and I feel like a drug addict coming off a trip, unable to get more of his favorite drug. Somehow she has managed to avoid me after I fucked her bent over the table in the empty classroom. I walk down the stairs and knock on my father's office door. He looks up from some paperwork and waves me in.

"Hey son," he greets, pushing the folders of paperwork away from him.

"Hey, did you talk to Ava yet?" I really don't care if he did or not. I just want to know where she is, and I would rather not let on to him how obsessed I am with her.

"No, I'm not sure where she is. I have a feeling she's been avoiding me. My guess is she knows that she's been caught lying and doesn't want to face the consequences. I wish her father had put more effort into disciplining her."

"Okay, she must have come home sometime, it's not like she has anywhere else to go." I'm thinking out loud again. *Shit.*

"You okay?"

"Yeah, I'm fine," I lie. Fine, yeah, no. I'm not fine at all. I'm on edge, angry, and confused. Confused about the whirlwind of emotions and thoughts that I can't get in order over Ava. I can't suppress my need for her, no matter how hard I try.

"Is she bothering you again?" he asks. Half of me says to tell him she is, hell, make her disappear, hopefully forever, while the other half wants to torment her myself, keep her right where I want her.

"Nah, she's behaving," I murmur, slipping out of his office before he can ask me another question. The thing about this house is when it's quiet, you can hear everything. As I enter the hall, I hear the front door opening quietly, followed by light footsteps racing up the stairs. By the time I come around the corner, I've only caught a glimpse of her at the top of the stairs before she disappears again.

My lips curve into a predatory smile. I'm about to get my fix, my first hit in what seems like forever. The blood in my veins tingle and saliva fills my mouth. As badly as we don't want to admit we want each other, maybe we even need each other. The hate I have for her melts away, giving way to a different emotion all together when I'm inside her. But as soon as I pull out, that feeling fades away, and I'm reminded that she's a liar, a master-fucking-manipulator.

Taking my time, I walk up the stairs, one step at a time, feeling myself being pulled closer and closer to her without thought. I don't want to burst into her room as soon as she gets here. I want her to think she's safe and secure, then I'll come in and pull the rug out from underneath her, keeping her on her tiny little toes. Then she'll never know when to expect me...she'll merely have to watch her back at all times, wondering what and where I am.

I come to a stop right in front of her door. My lips form into a line, and before I pull on that tight mask that covers my real emotions, I stand there taking comfort in knowing she is only a few feet away from me. Even with the door between us, my need for her is soothed. I want her close, but far away at the same time. She leaves my brain in disarray, scrambling it like a plate of scrambled eggs.

I can hear her on the other side of the door, smell her unique floral scent, and almost feel her heat. *Almost*. After about ten minutes, my patience has worn out. As quietly as I can, I feel for the key laying on the top of the doorframe, knowing without a doubt that she's locked her door. Or at least I hope she has, if she's smart, she would.

Her trust in me is confusing. I thought she would push me away yesterday, fight me, maybe even scream, but instead, she shocked me by letting me fuck her like I wanted to. She let me use her for my own pleasure without so much as a peep. I can still remember the feeling of her quivering pussy around my cock. I wanted to let her come so badly, but that wouldn't have made it a punishment for her, and I wanted to punish her, break her so badly it was all I could feel, up until I slid inside her. Maybe letting me use her body was her way of saying sorry. As if that would be enough, it would never be enough.

She didn't have to let me touch her. If she had told me to stop, I would've even though I didn't want to, but she didn't because deep down she wanted me to use her, she wanted me to touch her, to fuck her, and I hold onto that knowledge with an iron fist, knowing I'll use it against her over and over again. Inserting the key, I turn it, listening to the small click when the door unlocks. Turning the knob, I push the door open, bracing myself for her to yell at me, maybe even push me out.

Instead, I find her room empty.

I can hear the shower running in the bathroom and my dick turns incredibly hard. So much bare smooth skin is hiding on the other side of that door. I lick my lips in anticipation and walk toward the bathroom. I test the doorknob, turning it gently, smiling when I realize it's not locked. I kind of expected her to be paranoid enough to lock the bathroom door as well. Hot steam hits my face as I push the door open.

Her perfect silhouette hiding behind the see-through frosted glass of the shower enclosure is the first thing I see when I step inside. I close the door behind me, the noise alerting her to my presence.

"Get out, Vance," she yells over the roar of the shower, much less surprised of me being here than I thought she would be, taking a little of the wind out of my sails.

Tilting my head to the side, I ask, "Why? I thought you would be happy to give me another show."

"Just go away, please. You've hurt me enough, and I don't have it in me to fight with you right now," she says in a much lower, almost defeated tone.

She sounds tired, hurt, maybe even broken. *Just as I told her she would be.* I ignore the feelings her sadness gives me. I don't have room inside me to feel sorry for her. Anger and resentment taking up too much space already.

"I bet your nipples are hard right now, your pussy dripping for me," I taunt. "I'm ready to use you again. So wash nice and good between your legs. I'm not sure where or who you've been with last night, but I don't want to catch anything."

The thought of her being with someone else has my blood boiling. She better not have been with anyone else. Not unless she wants me to go to jail for murder. Though knowing her, she'd probably tell me she did just to spite me.

"Leave, I don't want to have sex with you again."

"I didn't ask you what *you* want. I said I'm ready to use you again. Finish up your shower so you can get me off. Unless you want me to come into the shower to do it. Maybe I'll throat fuck you today. I'm getting tired of your mouth running, like you have a fucking choice in anything I do to you. It'll be a lot harder for you to talk with my cock in your mouth."

"I'm not one of your whores, Vance, and I'm not having sex with you again. I'm definitely not giving you a blow job either. If you so desperately need to get off, maybe go find Sarah. My vagina isn't taking orders from some boy that thinks he knows me."

Somehow she's grown a backbone since the last time we saw each other. I'll take pleasure in snapping that newly formed bone, along with whatever attitude she plans to give me. I own her now, her pleasure, her sadness, her pain. I hold all the keys, and I'll unlock all the doors I have to prove my points.

She turns off the water a moment before pushing the shower door open.

I've seen her naked before but still, the sight of her, it takes my breath away. There's nothing like it, her beauty is profound. Her wet hair sticks to her skin around her shoulders and collarbone, her breasts are perked up, her light pink nipples rising and falling with every breath she takes. Tiny droplets of water kiss her pale smooth skin like freckles.

My eyes wander all the way south until I'm looking at her perfect little pussy. I've got self-control and I would say I'm pretty good at holding onto it, but it takes a lot out of me to not reach out and run my fingers over her and through her folds. My hand twitches with a possessive need to touch her. And I curl it into a fist, digging my nails into my palm to stop the ache.

She steps out of the large shower stall with her head held high, that cute little chin of hers jutted out. If she's trying to prove that she's strong and unaffected by me, she's doing a shit job, and ironically, she's not a good enough actor which surprises me given all the lying she does.

Not when I can hear the light tremble in her voice and see the subtle shaking of her hands when she reaches for the towel. You'd think she would be able to give an Oscar-worthy performance every time.

I guess not...I guess a liar is only as good as the lies they're telling.

She wraps the fluffy towel around her torso, covering up the beautiful canvas I had been admiring and wipes the condensation off the mirror with her palm. Then she picks up her toothbrush and starts brushing her teeth, trying her best to ignore me. *Adorable.* As if I'm that fucking forgettable. Taking a step forward, I center myself directly behind her, lifting a hand, I skim it across her shoulders.

Try and ignore me now. I force myself to smile when I know I should be punching myself in the face, but I can't help it. She lied, she used me, and I never saw it coming I fed right into her fucking hand.

Spitting into the sink before spinning around, she slaps my hand away.

"Don't touch me," she growls, and my smirk widens.

"Oh, I plan on doing much more than touching... and it's not like you don't want it. Stop playing hard to get," I say, pinching one of her towel-covered tits.

She shoves at my chest with both hands, making me stumble back. The heat of her touch resonates through my chest. I want to pull her closer, wrap my arms around her, but I also want to see her cry, see those beautiful emerald eyes fill with tears.

"I said no! This is over. I'm done trusting you. We are done!" she yells, her chest rising and falling rapidly. I can't help but laugh at her words. She's done trusting *me*? That's rich. "Get. Out," she huffs, squeezing her eyes shut and I'm surprised at how angry she sounds. I decide to let her cool off then. I don't want to break her too fast. I'm going to draw out the pain, make it hurt as bad as I can.

"Fine, I'll wait in your room for you. But make sure your pussy is nice and wet when you get out. I'll still fuck you if it isn't, but I'd prefer for it to be, a wet pussy fucks better than a dry one," I say, even though I'm pretty sure she is more than serious about not having sex.

Too bad, I was really looking forward to using her body against her today, but I'm not about forcing her. I have other ways to get my rocks off to hurt her.

Back in her room, I look around the space, trying to find something of interest. My eyes catch sight of her laptop sitting on her desk. *Jackpot.* I walk across the room and flip the thing open, shaking my head at her stupidity when I realize she doesn't have it password protected. Cracking my knuckles, I grin like the asshole I am and start to flip through the folders on the screen and stop at the one that says *Homework.*

I open it and delete every single file in it. Then I click the *Trash* icon in the corner and empty it out, making sure she can't recover any of her homework.

Boom! Asshole deed of the day, done.

Satisfied with my work, I shut the computer and sit down on her bed, lounging on it like I own the place. I don't have to wait long before she exits the bathroom, shooting me an angry glare that's filled to the brim with flames of fire.

"I said to get out, Vance, and I meant it. Keep fucking with me and I'll go to my mom."

Her threat is laughable more than anything. I open my mouth to respond when she suddenly drops the towel in front of the dresser. *Fuck.* My cock stands at attention, growing like a weed in a second flat. I stare at her smooth ass and envision entering her from behind before I can stop myself. She starts to pull on her clothes, and by then, I finally get my mouth to work again.

Swallowing a knot of arousal down, I say, "Is that a threat?"

She turns around to face me for half a second, her eyes burn into mine and I see all the pain, all the sadness I've caused her.

"It's not a threat. It's a promise."

Then, without another word, she leaves the room. *What the...* Who the fuck does she think she is? I won't lie and say my mouth isn't left gaping open like a fish flopping out of water. She doesn't get to talk to me like that...

I lounge against her bed waiting for her to come back, but after a few minutes, curiosity gets the better of me and I get up to look for her. I check the kitchen, the living room, and even in the backyard, but I don't see her anywhere. *Maybe she left?* Though she didn't have her wallet, or keys with her when she left her bedroom.

Letting out a sigh of frustration, I tell myself she's most likely hiding from me. I'm about ready to grab my keys and head over to Clark's house when I hear voices, they're faint, but they carry through the house like a quiet gust of wind entering through a window. It sounds like it's coming from my dad's office down the hall.

Ava's voice meets my ears, it's soft, vulnerable, and for some strange reason, tugs at my heart. My jaw tenses and my heart thunders deep inside my chest. I know I shouldn't, that I should keep on track with my plans, but I can't. Something compels me to walk down the hall, like I need to hear what she's going to say, what she is saying. Stopping a few feet away from my father's office door, I lean against the far wall.

The door is not closed all the way which lets me hear right in on their conversation.

"I don't understand why we can't tell Vance the truth. It

was a long time ago, and things have changed so much since then. Please just tell him the truth." Ava's heartbroken voice meets my ears.

"I will not tell him anything." My father's voice comes through.

"He blames me. He hates me for it," she admits softly.

Of course I blame her... she's a lying...

"Well, that's because it is your fault. What kid comes into her mother's room in the middle of the night at that age? If you hadn't snuck in that night...if you would have stayed in your room that night..." My father trails off.

"I'm sorry, okay? It was a stupid game, and yes, I should have been asleep that night, but you can't really place the fault for what happened on me."

"Of course I can, you're the one who told your father. Had you kept your yap shut, I wouldn't have had to lie to my son. The way I see it, all of this is your fault."

I blink, the air stills in my lungs and for a moment I wonder if this is real. Or if this is all a nightmare. *He lied.*

"You were the ones having an affair," she snaps back, and I hear my father slam something down on the table.

"You're not to bring this up ever again. You are going to keep your mouth shut about what you saw that night from here on out or you and your mother are going to be out on the street without a penny in your pockets. Do you understand me?" My father's voice booms through the room and I feel like I just got hit by a bus.

"Perfectly," Ava says, her voice shaking like she's close to crying. I can't breathe. I can't fucking do anything. A moment later, the office door opens and Ava steps out, her head hung low, her eyes on the ground.

She takes a step toward me, but only notices me standing there when she damn near plows into me. I want her to hit me, hurt me, slice me with her words like I've done to her. I'm a bastard, an asshole, and I wouldn't doubt it if she hates me now. She was telling the truth all this time...she was the one telling the truth and my father was lying. And continuing to lie.

Her head snaps up and our eyes meet. I take in her tear-filled green orbs and forget how to breathe.

My chest hurts. I fucking failed her.

17

AVA

He heard everything. I can see it written in his features. The shock, the shame, the guilt. He finally believes me...but it's already too late. I don't think I can forgive him for what he did. It took hearing the truth from his father, not me, to make him believe it. How do I let go of something like that? It's not like what we had was anything special, not to him. He just used my body to hurt me, all while my heart bleeds for the boy I had cared for, the boy who was as close to a best friend as I would ever get.

"Ava," he whispers, his voice somber and regretful. "I'm sorry, so sorry."

I shake my head, tears slipping down my cheeks. It's too late for sorry. Too late.

"I needed you, Vance. I needed you to believe me, but you never did, and when I needed you the most, you turned your back on me. When I was already down and thought I couldn't feel any worse, you made certain I did."

A sob breaks free from my throat, and it feels like my heart is going to burst. I can't do this right now...I can't. Pushing past him, I storm through the house, grabbing my purse from the entry table before running outside and onto the front porch. Glass shatters somewhere inside the house, followed by the sound of Vance yelling at his father.

Gulping fresh oxygen into my lungs, I let it build and build.

If he would have just believed me a few days ago. If he would have trusted me, I would have forgiven him, but now? *It's too late.*

Unlocking my car with the key fob, I speed walk across the driveway and hastily get into the driver's seat. I crank the engine and back out into the road with my tires skidding across the pavement. There's no way I can stay in that house anymore, not with Henry's threat looming over me, or Vance's guilt suffocating me. I need to go somewhere, anywhere, anywhere but here.

Where can I go? I could call Jules, and go stay with her, but I don't want to involve her in my problems, plus I wouldn't ever be able to repay her. Then it hits me... *hotel.* I'll go to a hotel, the one in town at least for a short time. Until I can figure everything out.

The drive to the hotel goes by abnormally fast, even though I'm driving slow because I can hardly see through my tears that started to fall again. I park in the back of the parking lot and sit there for a few more minutes trying to piece myself back together again. Trying to put together the broken pieces enough so that I look like a normal person, at least on the outside.

When the puffiness and redness around my eyes finally vanished enough to make it look like I haven't been crying for the last twenty minutes, I get out of the car and walk inside. I'm greeted by an older man at the reception desk who thankfully checks me in quickly. I swipe my credit card and he hands me the key to my room without question.

As soon as I'm in my hotel room, I fall apart. Sobbing uncontrollably, I crawl onto the bed and curl up in the fetal position. He knows the truth, I should feel better now, but I don't. Instead I feel worse, because he only believed me after hearing his father say that he lied. He doesn't trust me, he never did, and he probably never will. I don't know why I'm so hurt by that fact. Maybe because I trusted him, I believed in him and all he did was hurt me in return. I took comfort in his touch while he took comfort in my pain. I guess I'm partly to blame because a tiny part of me had hoped that maybe, just maybe, something would come from me sharing the truth with him, from letting him have a tiny piece of me.

I think back on what Henry said, he threatened to cut my mom off and leave us out on the street penniless. I didn't tell Vance anything, but he still found out. What will Henry do now? Was he really planning to divorce my mom over this? Did he ever love her at all? So many questions. One more worrisome than the next. I don't know what the hell I'm going to do next, all I know is that my life is a complete mess.

∽

A LOUD KNOCKING drags me out of my restless sleep, and I sit up, gazing around the room disoriented. For a moment I forget where I am and how I got here. My eyes are so puffy I have to pry them open. I try and swallow, but my throat is so dry it feels like I've swallowed a handful of sand. When the incessant knocking doesn't go away, I force myself out of bed and stumble to the door. I feel like I'm hungover but without having had a drop of alcohol.

When I reach the door, my gaze drops to my lower half.

The events from last night were a complete blur but apparently I had fallen asleep on the bed without changing. Shrug. I don't care, not about anything right now.

Whoever is on the other side of that door doesn't need to know that. Straightening, I hold my head up high and grab onto the door handle, twisting, and pulling it open.

"Ava..." My mother's voice fills the room right as she pushes inside the room and throws her arms around me, pulling me into her chest. I'm taken back by her presence and just stand there motionless until her warmth seeps into me and her perfume overwhelms my senses. Then I give into her, holding onto her like a small child.

"What happened?" she gasps. "I was looking everywhere for you and only found you when I checked your credit card statement online. Why are you at a hotel?" she asks, guiding me back toward the bed. Releasing me, she turned and closed the door behind her before coming back over to where I was sitting.

She takes one of my hands into hers and the mattress dips as she sits beside me. Never has my mother acted like she cared about me, at least not in the last five years. That night changed everything. It was almost like she blamed me, kinda like how Vance did, and Henry too. It seems everyone blamed me...

"Did Henry tell you what happened?" I ask, those first couple of words gravelly sounding.

"Not really. I came home to Henry and Vance fighting. Vance destroyed his father's office, he was screaming at him, and accusing him of all these *things*. None of which make sense to me."

"Oh, Mom..." I pause, my eyes meeting hers. She truly looks confused and I understand why. Just like Vance, she had no idea that Henry didn't tell the truth. All along she's been thinking everyone knew of their affair. But no one did, no one but her, Dad, Henry, and I.

"What is it, honey?" She blinks slowly.

I examine her face, looking at her for the first time in forever. I'm drawn first to her soft blue eyes framed by long lashes. Her hair is styled professionally, glossy, and the same mousy brown as mine. She looks exhausted, worried, but at the same time has a natural glow about her.

"Sweetie, you're scaring me. Why are you in this hotel and not back at the house? Did something happen with Vance and Henry?"

Do I want to tell her everything? Would it matter if I did? She loves him and has for a long time. Plus, she's already proven where her loyalty lies. Would telling her change anything? I want her happy, but Henry is vile and mean, and does he really love her if he can toss her out onto the street without a dime?

Or did he just say those things because he wanted me to comply? Maybe he really does love my mom. She certainly seems happy. If I'm being honest, she seems happier now than she ever did with my dad.

And if I tell the truth again of what I know, the secrets, will it shatter everyone's lives again?

My mouth goes dry, and I lick my lips. "I... I just wanted... wanted some time to myself, that's all. I've been struggling with some school work," I lie, deciding that if she's going to find out, it will be from someone else.

"Are you lying to me?" The sternness in her voice grabs onto me.

"No," I lie again.

The lies keep piling up and I wonder if soon I'll be able to believe them too.

"When Vance was screaming, I heard him mention your

name, and how if Henry ever threatened you again, he would..." Her voice trails off, and I don't need to hear the rest of whatever she was going to say to know that it wasn't anything good.

It doesn't matter though. I don't want his pity, his protection, his guilt. I want nothing from someone who thought I was a liar up until they heard it directly from the source. I just wish I could convince my heart to feel the same. I'm pretty sure I was falling for him... even with all his antics.

"Did Henry threaten you?" she asks next.

"Would it matter if he did?" My eyes fall to the floor.

"Of course it would matter, you're my daughter and I love you very much. It might not always seem that way, but I do. If Henry did something, I want to know."

"Then, yes, he did threaten me."

Her mouth pops open, shock overtaking her features.

"What happened? Why would he threaten you?"

"I told Vance something, something that Henry lied about."

"In what way did he threaten you?"

"Look, it doesn't matter." I pull my hand out of hers. "It's done and over with." Shoving off the bed, I walk toward the window.

"It most certainly does matter. I will not have my daughter staying in a hotel room. You'll come back to the house with me and I'll get all of this sorted out."

"It's not that easy, Mom."

"Please, Ava. Please, come back to the house with me. I'll talk to Henry, get all this sorted out. You're doing so well, and you seem so happy."

I want to laugh. *Happy?* If she was paying attention at all, she would've seen how miserable I was. The only time I wasn't truly miserable was when I was with Vance. When I was with him, I felt like I was whole, like the storm inside me calmed. I was the hurricane, but he was the eye of the storm and together we barrel toward the shore.

"I... I don't know, Mom."

I can't stay in this hotel forever, I know that, but I also don't know what the hell to do. Being around Vance is going to be hard, especially when I know that he is going to do everything he can to make up his wrongdoings to me.

But being around Henry is going to be even harder. He showed me his real self yesterday and I doubt I'll ever be able to see him in a different light. How can I live with someone like that? Someone so selfish and careless that he would lie and deceive the people closest to him.

"Just...just do it for me, sweetie. I promise I'll do everything I can to make things better for you. I don't want to lose you again. You just got here."

The sadness in her voice breaks through the perfectly built walls surrounding my heart. I want to say no, but it's not like I have any other options. At least not until I figure out another solution. I can't go back to my father, but I could find a job and get an apartment.

"Okay, I'll come home with you, for now," I sigh. My mom's shoulders sag in relief. "But I'll be looking for a job and getting an apartment as soon as I can. I love you, but I won't be living in that mansion with him forever."

She nods her head but doesn't protest even though it looks like she wants to. If I'm going to stay, I'm going to have to find a way to get out from underneath Henry's thumb, and away from Vance. He's already broken my heart... but I'll be damned if I let him break me.

18

VANCE

Blood trickles down my hand and onto the white marble floor. I should clean the wound, patch it up, but I don't give a fuck. The only thing I give a fuck about right now isn't in this house, and that terrifies me. The thought of her never coming back. It's a real fear, something I never expected to feel when it came to her.

How could I be so stupid? How could I be so wrong...so blind? I've never wished to turn back time as much as I do now. The mistakes I made. The way I treated her. All those things are unforgivable. I'm so ashamed and the guilt is eating me alive, but the worry I feel for her right now is strongest of all. I'll take whatever pain I have to, bathe in it, so long as she's okay, so long as I get to see her smile again.

Sitting down on the cold stairs, I stare at the huge wooden doors in front of me, willing her to walk through them. I don't know where she went or where she is now. What if she's so hurt that she decides that she never wants to see me again? Fuck, I couldn't even hold it against her if she did. I fucked up. I fucked up so bad.

Thinking back at the words I spoke, the threats, the way I took her body. I curl my hurt hand into a fist, my physical pain reminding me of the emotional pain I caused her. I wish I could take all her pain and make it my own. I would gladly do so if I could.

But I can't. The only thing I can do now is make sure she is safe and happy going forward. I'll protect her from my father and anyone else who ever tries to hurt her. I'll protect her from me if I have to.

There's a hole in my chest at the absence of her presence. I'm struggling to fill my lungs with air, unable to get a full breath in. Will I ever be able to breathe again? Why am I feeling this way? It feels like I've lost a piece of my soul. I knew after we had sex the first time that I was ruined for any and all women, Ava had claimed a piece of me that no other woman had before.

Please, let her be okay.

I don't even care if she never talks to me again, if she tells me she hates my guts, all I want is for her to be back here in this house. For so long, I wanted her gone, and now, now I can't picture a life without her, now I have to have her here with me. My heart starts to beat profoundly against my ribs.

Then it hits me, all the feelings I felt for her, the hate mixed with need, with something I thought was lust. It never was... it was never lust that I was feeling. It was something else, something entirely different. It was...

The sound of a car pulling up drags me from my thoughts. Standing, I run to the huge window overlooking the driveway, my already accelerated heart rate skyrocketing when I see Laura's car. Please be inside. Please. I've never hoped for anything more in my life. If she's not in that car, then any chance of making things right is gone. Laura exits the driver's side, and I hold my breath when Ava's form appears, exiting the passenger side. My knees buckle under the relief that rips through me. I feel like a fifty-pound weight has been lifted off my chest.

She is here. She is safe.

I'll fix this. I can't take back all the words I said, all the things I did, but I can make it up to her. I just have to find a way to get her to talk to me.

"Are they here?" My father's voice meets my ear and anger bubbles up inside me.

I want to smash his face with a brick, curse him from the heavens but I need to focus on Ava right now. I can always deal with my father.

"Yes," I grit out. I'd rather him not talk to Ava at all, but he needs to apologize. I don't want her to worry about anything. "Remember what I told you, play along or I'll tell Mom everything and if Mom finds out you cheated and lied in court—"

"I know," my father cuts me off. "I know."

The front door opens, and Ava and Laura appear before me. Laura's eyes dart between my father and I before catching on the drops of blood glittering the floor.

"Oh my God, Vance, are you okay?" she asks, taking a step toward me and I wave her off before she can start her mother hen shit. I don't need anything from her or my father. In my book, they're both lying cheaters.

"I'm fine." I lift my hand, bringing it to my chest, before allowing myself to look her in the eyes. My insides knot painfully and when I do get the courage to look at her it feels like someone's hit me in the gut.

Her green eyes are filled with so much sadness it pours out of her and onto the floor. It suffocates me, wrapping around me, grabbing onto my heart with a vise-like grip. It squeezes and squeezes and I feel myself getting light headed.

You did this. Her face pales, and she blinks rapidly almost as if she's fighting off tears.

"I... I have homework to do. I'm going to go," she announces and starts toward the stairs, hurrying up them two at a time. I clutch at my chest, feeling like the organ inside of it got ripped out. I deserve for it to. I did this. Broke her. Made her run away.

"We need to talk," Laura says to my father who turns and heads toward his office.

Dismissing her just like he does me. The only difference is she follows behind him like a lost puppy where I'd go drown myself in a bottle of whiskey.

"Nothing to talk about, honey. It's all in the past. Everything is fine now." His tone is tight, and as they drift farther away, I make my move, heading up the stairs and to her bedroom.

I'm sure she doesn't want to see me. Hell, I don't even want to see me, but I have to apologize. I have to tell her how sorry I am. When I reach her door, I stare at it, trying to calm my erratic heartbeat. I'm antsy, and my hands shake as I grab the doorknob. It easily twists and with a light push, pops open.

She didn't even lock it. Either she's given up, or she doesn't care anymore. Just thinking that I could have diminished the light inside of her has my stomach in knots and my chest aching. My eyes move to the bed where I find her sitting, legs pulled tight to her chest, arms wrapped even tighter around them. It's like she's giving herself the world's biggest hug.

She doesn't even look up as I enter the room and close the door behind me. Nor when I walk over to the bed and sit on the edge of it.

"I'm sorry, Ava. I'm so fucking sorry. I've disappointed you and myself. I... I hurt you and that wasn't..." I don't even finish the thought because it was my intention, it had been all along.

I wanted to hurt her, but only because I thought she was the cause of my pain, my misery.

"Don't lie. You wanted to hurt me." She lifts her head, tear-streaked cheeks and watery eyes coming into view. "You wanted to see me broken and you promised to do it. Well, you've succeeded. Vance Preston has broken another girl's heart. Congratu-fucking-lations."

The bitterness in her voice feels like small knives digging into my skin.

"I won't lie. I did want this. I wanted you broken and hurt, but that was..." It feels like I'm going to barf. "That was before I realized it wasn't you that did this, that caused my misery."

"I told you it wasn't me," she croaks, more tears slipping down her face. I want to take her into my arms and kiss the pain away. My body reacts to that thought before I can stop it and like a crazed animal, Ava slaps at my hands.

"Don't touch me," she grits out. "Don't ever touch me again."

Then she shoves me hard, her tiny hands burning into my chest. And for the first time in my life, I know what it feels like to be heartbroken. Her balled up fists rain down on my chest like hail falling from the sky, but I can't bring myself to stop her. I want her to hurt me. I want to feel every ounce of pain that she feels. Somewhere in the back of my head, words form, and I know I need to say them even though I don't understand why or how I feel them.

I don't deserve her, but I have to tell her.

"I love you, Ava. I love you," I whisper into her ear, unable to stop myself from wrapping my arms around her.

She laughs humorlessly, struggles in my grasp and bucks against my hold. I just want to hold her, to glue all the broken pieces back together again.

"Well, I hate you," she growls, and then lifts her knee, hitting me hard in the nuts.

I release her immediately, pain radiating through my cock and up into my stomach. I grab onto my balls, gritting my teeth through the pain as she stares down at my hunched over form.

"Love isn't supposed to hurt, Vance. If you loved me, then you would've believed me. You wouldn't have had to wait to hear the truth from your father. I've been telling the truth all along. I gave you no reason to believe that I was a liar. So you can think that you love me all you want, it's too little too late."

Fuck, I knew it would hurt to hear her say something like this, but I never expected for it to feel this bad. The blood in my veins turned to tar, struggling to make my heart beat. I'd never regretted anything in my life as much as I regret hurting her.

"I'm..." My voice cracked, and her pretty lips, the ones I so badly wanted to kiss even right now curled, anger spiraling out of her, filling the space between us with heavy heartache.

"I don't want to hear your apologies, in fact, if you're truly sorry then prove it by leaving me alone. My life was perfectly imperfect before you came along, and it will be long after you. You might have broken my heart, but you will never break me."

She doesn't need me.

She doesn't want me.

I knew that before I walked into her bedroom but hearing it and thinking it are two different things. Then again, I wasn't selfish enough to worry about that right now. It's a mere blip on my radar. I just wanted her to know how sorry I am. So fucking sorry...

"I'll make it up to you."

I straighten, my nostrils flaring as I breathe through the

pain in my balls. She wipes at her eyes with the back of her hand and swallows, her throat bobbing as she does.

"Don't." Disdain as dark as the night sky drips from that one single word. "I don't need or want your half-hearted apology." She shoves me backward and I nearly trip over my feet. It feels like I'm teetering on the edge of a cliff, my life in her hands. "You can stop pretending to care. Leave me alone." She shoves me again, and this time, I take the hint and walk away, retreating backward toward the door.

With my heart in my stomach, I look at her one last time, vowing to do whatever I can to make this right. I won't stop, not until I've righted every one of my wrongs.

"I can't take the words back, Ava. I love you. I loved you for a while, I know you won't believe me, but I knew it the moment I kissed you. I felt it deep in my soul. I've hurt you, fucked up beyond measure but I'll fix this. I swear to you I'll make this right, or I'll die trying."

"Go find Sarah or someone else that gives a fuck." She sobs, and my heart shatters into a million pieces.

"I don't want anyone but you. Only you," I whisper, closing the door after I exit it.

19

AVA

"Ava!" Clark's voice carries through the trees as he calls out to me. Ignoring him, hoping he'll go away, I increase my pace to get away as fast as I can. All I want to do is go to classes, come home, and go to sleep. It's been one week since my mental breakdown with Vance and it seems to be getting easier and easier every single day.

Heavy footfalls sound against the sidewalk behind me, and I sigh into the air knowing it's a lost cause. Clark is faster and taller, so what's the point in running. I slow to a walk, and he comes up from behind me, cutting me off with his body. Clark's a big boy, tall, and breathtaking even, but he's still an asshole, and he's best friends with Vance, so that alone makes him the enemy. Crossing my arms over my chest, I stare at his firm chest with annoyance.

"If Vance put you up to this, you can tell him to fuck off."

Clark is mid-stretch, the shirt he's wearing riding up and showing off his well-defined physique. For one singular moment I'm distracted. Then my eyes catch on his face, a knowing grin forms on his lips.

"Checking me out?"

"In your dreams."

"Yes Ava, in my dreams I dream of you... on your knees, between my..."

"Stop!" I slap his arm and he laughs.

"Vance didn't put me up to this. I'm truly sorry and wanted to treat you to an excessive amount of carbs."

I tilt my head as if it will tell me how genuine he's being. "Why do I feel like you're lying to me?"

He shakes his head, a few of the longer strands of dark brown hair fall into his face. He needs a haircut, and to leave me the hell alone.

"I don't know, but I'm not." His tongue darts out over his bottom lip, and he turns on that smoldering look that makes all the women's panties go poof. He reminds me of Vance so much that it's almost sickening and I'm done with being everyone's punching bag. Done with being treated like shit.

"I'll pass. I don't have room for self-absorbed assholes in my life." I shoulder past him and continue walking, but being the persistent asshole he is, he continues to follow me.

"Look, I'm sorry. I was only being a friend to him. He told me you lied to him. How was I supposed to know what the hell was going on?"

"Maybe ask me?" I yell, louder than necessary, drawing the attention of a few lingering bystanders. Clark cuts in front of me again and I almost run into him, stopping a foot short of actually doing so.

Clenching my hand into a fist, I feel this sudden urge to punch him in the face. I'm tired of being shoved around, of being mocked, and called a liar. I don't want their apologies... I want their silence. I want peace.

"Just, let me apologize. Let me take you to have pizza. Remember how much fun we had last time?" Clark smirks that panty-melting smile of his and I hate myself for recalling the laughter, and fun we had, because truly we did have a great time that night, and as friends only.

Which is something I know he doesn't do with anyone that's a female. Stupidly, I care about Clark, but not in the way one would think. He's more of a little brother to me, an annoying, rude, cocky little brother.

"Don't make me beg. I will drop down to my knees in front of everyone. I don't care if it makes a scene, I'll do it."

I can feel my cheeks heating with embarrassment at the thought. Clark's all about making a scene and I know he'll do it.

"No!" I say in a panic, wrapping a hand around his wrist when he makes an attempt to drop down to his knees. "Jesus, no. Don't draw any more attention to us. You standing here talking to me draws enough attention as it is."

"That sounds like a compliment, A." He wiggles his thick eyebrows.

As angry as I am over everything that happened, I can't place the blame on Clark. He befriended me, took me out, spent time with me, and even stuck up to Vance in my honor.

Plus, it's not him I really want to hurt, it's Vance.

Rolling my eyes, I try and hide the smile pulling at my lips. "Carbs are my weakness."

"I know, that's why I'm using them. Thank God you have a kryptonite." He sighs like he's been spending all afternoon trying to get me to go with him.

Dramatic much.

"No Vance?" I ask, placing my hands on my hips.

He nods. "No Vance."

My gaze narrows. "If you're lying to me and he shows up, I get to throat punch you."

He beams. "Fine. One throat punch if he shows up. But what do I get if he doesn't?"

This flirtatious shit has got to stop.

"To live?"

His face deadpans. "You wound me, Ava, you legit shoot me down every single time. It's like you're immune to my charm or something."

"That's because I am."

Looking hurt, he asks, "So, it's a date?"

"Not a date, Clark, but yes I suppose I can go with you for pizza. As friends, only friends, nothing else," I sigh, and Clark does this weird little shimmy of excitement.

"I'll message you the deets," he says before giving me a quick hug. I shove at his shoulders and he releases me. Clark is too much, and knowing he's Vance's best friend, I should stay away, far, far, away, but for some reason, I can't.

I don't hate Clark. Clark isn't the reason for my pain, my heartache.

Vance is, and I should probably remind myself of that often, so I don't fall down the rabbit hole and into another trap.

∼

I FINISH classes and head home to change before heading out to meet up with Clark. When I enter the foyer, I hear voices, they're muffled, but like always, carry through the house. Ignoring them, or trying too, I grab a bottle of water and granola bar from the kitchen. I try and make my mind go blank, try and forget that he exists, but my foot hits the bottom step of the stairs at the same time Vance's voice shatters through my resistance.

"I'll bury you. I will fucking bury you so deep you won't be able to breathe. You did this to me, and you'll pay. All these years I blamed her. I said things... I..." Vance sounds hurt, heartbroken even, and though I want him to feel that way, there's a pang of sadness that ripples through me at the thought.

"You're kids, it doesn't matter. I'm sure she'll forget the things that you said." His father's intolerable voice meets my ears next.

"We're not just kids," Vance yells, the venom in his words shatters me. He's more than angry, he's on the verge of exploding. "And what happened all those years ago was because you and Laura couldn't keep your hands off each other. So while you might be able to blame Ava and me in your heads, we both know that you were the ones fucking."

A gasp escapes my lips and I bring my hand to my mouth. I've never heard him talk to his father like that before.

There's a loud slapping noise, and I hold my breath, anxiously waiting to hear what is going to be heard next. I told myself I didn't care, that I wouldn't fall for Vance ever again, but the truth is I'm not over him, not even close. My body craves his touch, craves his cruel words, his venomous rage. I've come accustomed to him, and like a drug, I can't get enough.

"Fuck with her, touch a single hair on her body and I'll ruin you. Do you hear me?" Vance's voice finally cuts through the silence.

"Yes, I've got it," Henry says.

The squeaking of a door opening has me barreling up the stairs, two at a time until I reach my room. I slip inside, closing the door softly behind me.

What was that? Was Vance protecting me from his father? I don't understand. I growl in frustration, sinking down onto the edge of the mattress. Ripping open the granola bar, I shove pieces into my mouth, because there's nothing else to do.

I try not to think about what I just heard. I try and remind myself that Vance doesn't really care about me, not like I care about him. He would've believed me if he did.

But the fact that he stuck up to his dad for me, the fact that he went against his own father... it resonates in me. It's in no way worthy of forgiveness, but it shows he's trying...that he... "*I love you, Ava...*" I can't tell you how many times I've repeated that inside my head. I can't tell you how true I wish it was.

No! No, be strong, don't fall for it. Don't fall into his trap. He doesn't care about you.

Actions speak louder than words, my brain says. Ugh, my heart and my mind want two different things. He called me a liar after I confessed to him the truth. Maybe he didn't fully believe me, but he could've asked, he could've come to me if he had questions.

But he didn't, he believed his father...

Tears fill my eyes. Feeling the need to do something, anything, I open my laptop and prepare to finish my English paper. But as soon as I click on the Word document, a new page opens. *What the hell?* Anger replaces the slightest bit of remorse I was just feeling. I check the trash icon and all the folders inside my homework file.

There's nothing... not a single thing.

He didn't. I stare at the screen. My eyes piercing the screen, willing the document that's no longer there, that I spent hours typing up to reappear. All the work is gone, disappeared, missing... the proof is right in front of me and I still don't want to believe it.

He did this, he deleted it all. Tears slip from my eyes, and I wipe them away as fast as they fall. I can't cry for him anymore. He's done so many things to hurt me, break me, and crying even one more tear for him isn't right. It's wrong, so wrong. He doesn't deserve my tears, my pain, my sadness. He deserves nothing... I'll never forgive him for hurting me like this.

Never.

20

VANCE

Clark better be right about her showing up here tonight, or else I'm going to be using my fists to rearrange his face. Not really, but I'm feeling a little on edge with all the shit going on, so a fight wouldn't be a bad idea. Bloodying someone's face seems like fun right about now. My life is starting to feel like an atomic bomb that's waiting to go off.

Tick tock. Tick tock.

An explosion is coming, and I need to be ready for it, but I also need to make shit right with Ava. Never in my life have I tried more for a girl, but then again, Ava isn't just any girl, she is *the girl*.

Ava has been avoiding me at all cost. She told me through her mother that if I come in or near her room, she will move out immediately. I tried to 'run into her' at school, but she somehow managed to outsmart me. I haven't seen her in days and it's fucking killing me.

Shoving my hands into the pockets of my jeans, I walk down the sidewalk, a nervous energy encompassing me. Will she talk to me? Push me away? Slap me? The way she acted toward me earlier, it killed me. She ripped my heart out and fed it to me like I was a fucking dog. I thought maybe, just maybe telling her I loved her would change things, but it didn't. It only ignited the hate inside of her.

Not that she shouldn't hate me. I'm man enough to know I fucked up. I can admit that to myself, to her, but all I want is to make things right. There's a sign up ahead in the shape of a pizza slice, flashing brightly into the night.

Slice It is written across the piece. I slow, exhaling all the bad energy out of me. If she's here, then I'll owe Clark big time. If she's not, then I'll lose my fucking mind and bury myself in another bottle of Jack Daniels. As I pass the huge glass window while walking to the door, I gaze through it looking for her.

There are three or four ladies in the place with dark brown hair, but they aren't her. My hands balled into fists in my pocket. I'm seconds away from breaking something when I catch sight of her and Clark in a corner booth off to the right. Mousy brown hair, pretty green emerald eyes that sparkle with happiness that I can see, feel from here.

She's laughing at something Clark says and this strange thing happens as I stand there like an outsider watching them. *He deserves her. He's what she needs.* I have no idea where the thought comes from, but it terrifies me, because deep down, I know it's true. I don't deserve her. She deserves better, someone that's not a loose cannon with a shitload of baggage.

For a split second, I actually consider walking away when I notice Clark leaning into her face. Lust fills his eyes, and something snaps inside me.

He'll never love her, not like I do. Maybe I don't deserve her, but neither does he. He's incapable of love. Unlovable as he says. The courage builds and I open the door, walking inside, the smell of tomato sauce and freshly grated cheese fills my nostrils.

The place is a seat yourself one and so I do, I walk over to where Ava and Clark are sitting, soft laughter emitting from the booth. It feels like I'm intruding and probably because I guess I am? Clark's face falls as soon as he sees me coming. Did he not expect me to show up? He's the one that put this together. Maybe he didn't think I was serious about winning her back? I know he's got his own shit going on, so maybe it's that?

"Clark... what's going on? Are you okay?" Ava's concerned voice filters into my ears right as I make my appearance known to her. Sauntering up to the booth like a broken-hearted puppy, I gaze down at her. The air thickens. I can't breathe. I'm suffocating. In my own misery, in the pain of my actions.

Murder flickers in Ava's green eyes and without warning, she reaches across the table with a closed fist and socks Clark right in the throat. Caught off guard, Clark lifts a hand to his throat and starts to cough like he smokes five packs of cigarettes a day. His coughs grow louder, and I can feel eyes on us, attention gathering.

"You're a liar! I asked you if he was going to come and you said no," she growls, her pink lips curling in anger.

I knew he wasn't going to tell her I was coming, because if he did, she wouldn't have shown up, but I didn't expect her to punch like that.

"You punched me..." he croaks, chugging his entire glass of soda, though he doesn't sound shocked by her actions. I can't help the smile that christens my lips. Ava's gaze turns to me, anger, sadness, and hate, they all mingle in those beautiful eyes that are piercing mine like daggers.

"What don't you understand? I don't want anything to do with you. You got your wish, Vance. You hurt me, you made me hate you. Or maybe that wasn't enough for you? Have you come to deliver more hate, more cruel words? As if deleting three weeks' worth of homework wasn't enough for you?"

Fuck. I've forgotten about doing that, and I'll need to reach out to her professors so that I can get her some more time to complete the assignments, but right now I need to talk to her, even if the only reaction she's going to give me is one of anger.

"I wasn't lying to you when I apologized, and I'm sorry about the homework. I'm an idiot, a fucking piece of shit, whatever you want to call me, I'm probably it."

"And how would I know that, that you're sorry? I'm not touching the name calling. I'm trying to be the adult in this situation."

She blinks up at me in disbelief.

"You... You wouldn't know that. I know I don't deserve your forgiveness, but I have to try. I want to know everything, what happened that night. I want to explain myself to you, make you understand why I did what I did."

Bitter laughter emits from her throat and Clark's gaze widens because just like me, he knows we're drawing attention.

Shoving up into a standing position, Ava wiggles out of the booth looking like she's going to bolt. But she doesn't, instead, she exits the booth and stands toe to toe with me, she blows out a frustrated breath, but all I can smell is her, all I crave is her.

"I don't care why you did it, Vance. And you're right, you don't deserve my forgiveness. Someone as cruel, as horrible as you, doesn't deserve the love that I could give. All you deserve is to wallow in your own sorrows."

With a hard shove to the chest, she pushes past me and walks away. My throat tightens, what the fuck do I say to that?

"Go to her, fix this shit," Clark orders, rubbing at his

throat with his hand. I have a million things I want to say to him, but it's not him I need to talk to right now. It's her. Turning, my feet move all on their own, slapping against the floor, and then the pavement when I get outside. What the fuck am I going to say to her that I haven't already? I spot her up ahead, crossing the street and run right at her. My heart racing inside my chest. I have to fix this. I fucking have to.

Reaching out for her, my fingers land on her shoulder, forcing her to turn around, and she does, she whirls around like a raging bull.

"Leave me alone." The molten lava in her words burns. It burns like I've actually been burnt by fucking fire.

I stare and stare another second, beautiful, so fucking perfect. She's an angry vixen and I have to have her, as selfish as it is, I need her. So I do the only thing I know I can do, the first thing that comes to mind. I kiss her.

She tastes like pizza sauce, and my lips mold to her full ones in a way that makes me want to kiss her all day long, that makes my cock stiffen in my jeans. Her hands press against my chest, her tiny fingers gripping onto the fabric, pulling me closer.

Yes! She still wants me.

I feel like a firework igniting, getting ready to blast the sky with an array of colors. I have to have her… I have to consume her like she's consumed me. Guiding us backward until she's pressed against the nearest wall, giving her nowhere to escape I deepen the kiss, my tongue slipping into her mouth, my hands moving up her body and to her rosy red cheeks. With her lips on mine, there's no talking, no chance of either of us saying something we can't take back.

"What the hell!?" she gasps, pushing me back, breaking the kiss.

Her chest heaves, so does mine. My eyes drop down to her lips. I want to kiss her again, kiss those swollen lips of hers.

"I told you to leave me alone, not kiss me. Leave. Me. Alone."

"You want this. You want me. Admit it." I lick my lips, my insides burning for her, only her. No one can compare to the way she makes me feel. She brings out the worst in me, while I bring out the best in her, and together we can fix all the fucked up pieces of our life.

Her eyes fill with sadness. "I wanted you. Past tense. Before you showed me that I'm nothing to you. That I'm just someone you can use for a good time, and disregard once the last aftershocks of pleasure have rippled through you. Before you called me a liar after I told you the truth."

My mouth snaps open, my response on the tip of my tongue, but she shakes her head, tears glistening in her eyes.

"You only want me because you know you fucked up."

My brow furrows in confusion. "I love you, Ava. I've never loved anyone, not in the sense of actually *loving* them. You're the first girl, outside of my mother, I've ever cared for."

She shakes her head in disbelief and places a hand to my chest, gently pushing me backward. The organ beneath her palm pulses, pumping blood, reminding me that it beats for her and only her.

"Stop trying, stop caring, and stop apologizing. Just stop." Cruel anguish coats her words. Her eyes squeeze shut, and when they open a moment later, I see tears streaking down her pale cheeks. "You don't know what love is, because if you did, you wouldn't have hurt me the way you did. I don't want you, Vance. I. Don't. Want. You."

The words sting, they hurt so badly my knees wobble as they pass her lips. She's lying, she has to be. What we have doesn't just disappear. I can't be the only one feeling the magnetic pull between us.

"Go find Sarah, tell her you love her, go be with any other girl at this school, but please, leave me alone. Seeing you, listening to you, it kills me, Vance. It kills me and I can't do this with you anymore. I don't want to play your sick little games anymore. I quit."

My nostrils flare, and my muscles tighten. "I don't want Sarah, and I never have. She was always going to be a fill-in until I found the one person that mattered. I haven't touched her since before we had sex." And that's the truth. I wanted to fuck someone that night at Clark's when I was piss drunk, but I couldn't bring myself to do it.

Ava rolls her eyes, swiping at the tears on her face. "That's not what Clark told me, not that it matters anyway. It doesn't change anything. I don't want you. I won't date or be with someone who treats me like garbage one second and tells me they love me the next. I'm worthy of more than that."

Clark. Fuck him. Of course he would say something stupid. The bastard doesn't know when to keep his mouth shut. Frustrated, I sink my fingers into my hair. I can't let her walk away from me. I can't.

"I can't leave you alone. You mean too much to me. You're fucking everything. You're my universe, just please let me tell you what happened, what my father told me. Let me tell you the truth. Let me save us." I'm begging now, close to dropping down to my knees and pleading with her. She looks skeptical and I await her response with bated breath.

Her pink lips part and it looks like she's going to say something, anything, when the sound of a cell phone ringing fills the space between us.

No! Please, don't answer it, please don't answer it, I silently plead.

Ava pats her jeans until she finds her phone pulling the device from her pocket. Panic flashes across her face and dread fills my gut.

"What's wrong?" I question, covering the space between us with one huge step. Her bottom lip wobbles and her eyes widen.

"My father, he's calling me…"

"Okay?" The inky dread I was feeling moments ago dissipates a little.

"He's supposed to be in rehab, not using his cell phone." Still, I don't understand, but she doesn't give me the opportunity to ask another question. Instead, she presses the green answer key and holds the phone to her ear, and I swear I can see her slipping right through my fingers.

21

AVA

"Dad?" My voice trembles through the speaker of the phone. Vance stares down at me, a frown on his lips.

"Baby girl. It's so good to hear your voice. God, it seems like it's been forever since I've seen or heard from you." I grip the phone tighter to my ear.

"Where...where are you? You're supposed to be—"

"I know where I'm supposed to be," he cuts me off, his voice raised in a tone that tells me he's been drinking. When he drinks, he gets mad, and when he gets mad, shit goes to hell.

"Dad," I try and keep my voice calm, neutral, even though inside I feel like I'm a plane spiraling out of control, headed straight for the ground. "Dad, tell me where you are? I'll come get you, help you."

"Ha, no can do, sweetie. I'm going to right my wrongs. I just wanted to let you know that I love you before everything ends. I know you blame yourself, think that it's your fault, but it isn't.

You were always the best thing that ever came from your mother."

I blink, confused by his statement. *Right his wrongs?* What is he talking about?

"Dad, what's going on? Tell me. Please, just tell me," I plead, the muscles in my stomach tightening painfully, so painfully that I lean against the nearest wall.

"I love you, Ava," he whispers, and then the line goes dead.

I blink, pulling the phone away from my ear to look down at the screen. I stare at it, mouth gaping open for several seconds before I realize he just hung up on me.

"Oh God..." I whisper into the air and redial his number, but it goes to voicemail. "Shit, shit, shit!!"

I pull the phone away from my ear and look at the screen, waiting for something to happen that could make all of this go away. How did my life become such a mess? My father, Mom, Vance. It feels like I'm on a downward spiral. Damnit! I thought my dad was getting better at that facility, not worse, but he definitely sounded worse.

He sounded like he was saying goodbye, almost as if he was going to... *No!* I shake my head as if it will make the thought disappear. He wouldn't hurt himself, would he? Or worse, someone else?

"What's wrong?" Vance's voice makes me look up from the screen, my eyes clash with his concerned ones. I almost forgot he was here.

"I...I don't know. I need to find my dad. Figure out where he is, if he's okay," I say, my feet already moving in the direction of the car.

"Wait, where are you going? Where is your dad? What happened?" Vance asks, his voice tight as he follows me closely while I speed walk down the street.

I can feel my lips trembling, I'm breathing but there isn't any air filling my lungs.

"Ava, where are you going?" He repeats his question, sounding even more nervous.

His panic is making me panic, and... *Where am I going?*

"I don't know!" I yell, throwing my hands up in the air.

"Okay, calm down. You look like you're about to hyperventilate. Slow down for a sec and tell me what's going on. Talk to me."

We reach the car then, but instead of getting into the driver's seat like I had planned, I stop. As badly as I don't want to listen to Vance, he's right. I'm about to hyperventilate, the tightening in my chest getting worse. Leaning against the side of the car, I suck air into my lungs. In through my nose, and out my mouth, the air swishes until the tightening in my chest becomes bearable again.

"I don't know where my dad is, but he sounded like he was going to do something...like hurt himself, or someone else. He was drunk and he was telling me that he loved me and that he was going to right his wrongs...whatever that means. I don't know. He sounded bad. I have a bad feeling. This is terrible, horrible, and I don't know how this happened. How did this happen?" The panic is rising inside me, cresting against my sanity.

Vance places his strong hands on my shoulders, and I don't have the strength or willpower to shrug him off. Right now, his touch is a welcoming one, a healing balm on the pain.

"Shhh, beautiful. It's going to be okay. We'll figure this out," Vance assures, his green eyes soft, his lips smooth, full. I focus on those lips, imagining how they felt against mine, how I want to kiss him again now.

Vance clears his throat, a gentle smile on his lips. "Why don't we go home and see if we can get some more information. Maybe we can call the rehab facility he was at? Ask your mom if there's anything we can do?"

My chest stops heaving, and I feel less like I'm going to pass out now.

"Good idea," I quip.

Truthfully, I know I need to keep a leveled head about this, driving around like a crazed person looking for him isn't going to fix this, even though it feels like losing my shit would be the easiest solution right now.

"Why don't you get in the passenger seat and I'll drive us home?" Vance suggests while already guiding me to the other side of the car.

I should push him away, tell him I can take care of myself, but when I reach up to swipe some loose strands of hair away from my face, I notice how much my hand is shaking. Even as stubborn as I am, I know it's best to just let Vance do the driving.

"What about your car? Didn't you drive here?"

"I can get it later, don't worry about that," he says, his voice oddly reassuring and calm, too calm. He opens the door for me and helps me inside before reaching over to buckle me in. Part of me wants to push him away and tell him to stop but the other part, the part that is winning right now, is taking comfort in him taking care of me.

The drive home goes by in a blur, and I continue to dial my dad's number in hopes that he turned his phone back on, but all I get is his voicemail. By the time Vance parks the car in the driveway, I must have called him at least thirty times.

He kills the engine and I get out of the car, thankfully without his help. I'm weak enough as it is right now, anymore of his touch and I'll be a melted piece of butter on the pavement.

"I'm going to call the rehab facility my dad was staying at

and see when he checked out and why," I mutter out loud, more to myself than Vance who is walking up to the house beside me. I don't want his help, not really. He's done enough horrible shit to me, the last thing I need to do is make myself look even more fragile.

As soon as I open the front door, I can hear my mother's chatter coming from the kitchen. I follow her voice like it's a beacon of light, my feet dragging across the floor.

"Mom, something happened," I blurt out when she looks up at me. My heart hammers inside my chest.

"Susan, I'm going to have to call you back," she tells her friend and hangs up, worry creasing her forehead. "What's wrong?"

I'm vaguely aware of Vance's presence beside me. It makes me feel stronger, and less like the delicate piece of glass seconds away from shattering that I am.

"Dad... he... he called me, he checked out of rehab, and he didn't sound good. He was drunk and saying weird stuff. I'm really worried about him. He hasn't reached out to me since I left and..." My mother's expression changes from concern to annoyance and my voice trails off at the sudden change.

"Ava, I know you worry about your father, and that's fine and all, but he's an adult. A grown man. It's not your job to worry and take care of him. We helped him get into that facility for you, and only you. I know it's hard, but he had his chance. There is nothing else we can do for him. There's no helping someone that doesn't want to help themselves."

Panic grips onto my heart, she doesn't care. She doesn't care. Why am I not surprised?

"There must be something...he needs me," I whine.

"He needs therapy, but therapy only works if he wants it to work and by leaving the facility we sent him to, he's proven he doesn't want care, nor does he want to get better. He needs to help himself, Ava."

She's right, I know that, but she doesn't have to be so cruel. Had her and Henry made a different choice, had they not been so selfish, maybe this never would've happened.

"I don't care. I'm still going to call the rehab facility and ask them what happened," I tell her.

She shakes her head but doesn't say anything else. Not that I would expect her to. She's said all that she has to say. Turning, I exit the kitchen and head for the staircase with Vance hot on my heels.

"I can help you—" he interjects.

"No," I interrupt him. "I don't need your help."

"Ava—"

"I said, I don't need your help," I repeat as I run up the stairs.

He sighs but doesn't make a move to follow me. Thankfully. Which is good because I need to concentrate on finding my father and I can't concentrate on anything with Vance sitting next to me. It's like a haze forms over my mind and my emotions go haywire with him near and I don't need that right now. I need peace, silence, and a clear mind. I need to help my father, because even though my mother let him down, I won't.

∽

TIME TICKS BY SLOWLY. Twenty-four-hours has passed since my father and I's last conversation. I've been on edge ever since then. The lack of sleep I got because of worry hasn't really helped matters either. I'm grouchy, irritable, and still have no idea what's going on with him. I can't focus on anything, which only angers me further.

Between classes, I've managed to call the rehab place twice

but all they could tell me was that he checked himself out yesterday morning without any reason. They advised him not to, but he told them he was capable of making his own choices.

When I wasn't happy with the answer they gave me, I asked to talk to one of the therapists there and he told me that my father was doing great up until a couple days ago, and that he was surprised that he had left so suddenly.

It didn't make sense to me. The puzzle pieces weren't fitting in their spots.

"Class dismissed." Professor Hall's authoritative voice pulls me from my obsessive thoughts. "Please leave your papers on my desk on the way out, and remember, you lose ten percent of your grade for every day that it's late."

Well isn't this craptastic.

He wants the paper that I *don't* have because some asshole decided to delete it, aka Vance. I could almost cry. The amount of pressure on my chest making it hard to breathe. There's probably an ulcer the size of Alaska in my stomach from all the anxiety I've been having, and now I have to add this onto the heaping pile of cow shit.

Gathering up my books, I stuff everything into my backpack. Dragging my feet, I make my way up to his desk, dreading that I'll have to explain myself to him. Never in my entire life have I been late handing in work. My grades have always been the most important thing to me, the only thing that mattered.

"Mr. Hall, about my paper..." I start, eyes cast down, shame written all over my face.

"No worries, Ava, I already know. Mr. Preston came in early this morning and explained to me about your laptop. I'll give you a ten-day extension, and not a day more, get it to me as soon as you can."

"What?" I blurt out, lifting my gaze to Mr. Hall's.

He lifts a questioning brow. "Are you okay, Ava? I told you that I was giving you a ten-day extension and you say what?"

Oh shit. "No, no, that's not what I mean. I'm sorry." I shake my head flustered, embarrassed, and ashamed.

If it weren't for Vance, I wouldn't be in this stupid situation. Gripping onto the edge of my backpack, I take a step back and mutter a *thank you*, before escaping the confines of the room. Chewing on my bottom lip, I walk straight to my car and drive home. I try and call my father a couple more times, hoping, praying that his phone will be back on, but I get the same monotone computerized voicemail.

Beating a hand against the steering wheel, I roar in frustration. He's all I have left. The last person on this planet that cares about me and there's nothing I can do to save him. I wonder what he's doing right now, where he is? If he has somewhere to stay? I know he's an adult, but I can't help but worry for him.

Moisture fills my eyes and when I pull into the driveway of the mansion, I park my car and wipe at my eyes, willing the pesky tears away. With my backpack in hand, I walk into the house, joyful laughter fills the space, and I tighten my hold on the strap against my shoulder. Their laughter grates on my last nerve and I snap like a rubber band pulled too tight.

"What's so funny?" I ask, voice clipped.

They're both standing in the kitchen, my mother near the stove, cooking. While Henry stands off to the side, a glass filled with brown liquid in his hand.

"Oh nothing, sweetie." She looks up at me, smiling.

She's smiling, and I'm dying inside. Why does it always feel like she and Henry are getting exactly what they want while everyone around them suffers?

"How can you be happy?" Bitter anger boils inside me, filling my veins with an angry venom.

"What's not to be happy about?" Henry pipes up, and I swing my frigid gaze to his, acid burning up my throat.

What's not to be happy about?

"While I could name off a long list of things I'm not happy with, starting with my father missing, which neither of you seems to care about," I spit, bearing my teeth.

Henry squints his eyes at me, and instead of responding, takes a drink from his glass, a glass that he looks like he wants to toss at my head.

My mother of course gasps, her eyes widening with horror as if I've slapped her.

"I'm getting very tired of your attitude. I've tried to be understanding but…" she starts to lash out, but I don't give her the chance to finish whatever ridiculous shit she was going to make up. I wonder if she even believes the shit she says.

"Both of you did this." I point my finger at my mother, and then Henry. "It was your selfish choices that drove a wedge between your marriages. If you hadn't fucked each other, maybe our families would be whole. Maybe my father wouldn't be missing, and maybe I wouldn't be in this deranged jail cell."

I'm past angry, and more in the murderous rage bracket.

"Ava Marie!" my mother scolds as if I'm a child, her face paling at my spoken truth. So far, I've never called her out on her bullshit, but I'm done, so far past done I don't care what happens to me anymore. Put me on the street, take it all away. At least when it's over, I'll still have myself. I turn on my heels, my sandals squeaking across the floor as I stomp out into the foyer.

"You will not talk to your mother like that, not in my house," Henry bellows behind me, and I can't help myself, I turn around, lift my hand, and flip him off. If he thinks he's going to try and father me, he has another thing coming. I'll jump off the side of a cliff before I let that happen.

"Go fuck yourself, Henry," I sneer, wanting to wipe the floor with his face, but instead stomp up the stairs and into my room slamming the door so hard that it rattles. Shucking off my backpack, I toss it into the corner on a chair and kick off my sandals. Then I sink into the mattress and wish for it to swallow me whole.

Tears start to fall without permission and a sob pushes past my lips, the noise breaking the silence around me. *Alone.* Always alone. I have no one, nothing, my mother doesn't care about me, my father is missing, and Vance... Squeezing my eyes shut, I try and forget about him. About his scent, the way his body feels against mine, and his words.

I love you.

I would never tell him, never, but I love him too.

22

VANCE

My fingers throb, and my eyes burn, but I finally finished the English paper for her. Most think I'm dumb and that I don't know my ass from my head, but I do. I just don't apply myself. Thumbing through the freshly printed pieces of paper, I count them ensuring they're all there before stapling them together. I would never put so much work into one of my own papers, for her, on the other hand, I stayed up until almost midnight so I could finish this. Professor Hall might have given her ten days, but I want this off her mind.

Opening my door, I sneak across the hall to hers. All I plan on doing is going into her room quietly to lay this on her desk so she has it in the morning, but when I grab the brass doorknob and turn it slowly, pushing it open gently, a soft sob meets my ears. The noise is earth-shattering, raw, and a cry for help. I open the door enough to slip into the room. It's dark, but I can see enough to make out the bed.

I put the paper down on the desk and step closer. Ava's sobbing quiets down, but I know she's still crying by the low sniffing noises she's emitting. I should ask her if she is okay? If there is anything I can do. But I'm not stupid. I know she'll just send me away.

She doesn't want to admit that she needs anyone, and especially not me. Staring down at her unmoving form, I wonder if she would push me away if I slid into the bed next to her? Maybe she would just let me comfort her while pretending I'm not here. I've never comforted anyone in my life, mainly because I never had the need or urge to do so. Not until her.

Weighing my options after standing in her room for two minutes like a creep, I finally decide to try it. Without lifting the blanket, I crawl onto the bed, kicking my boots off, each one hitting the floor with a loud thud. If she notices, she doesn't say anything. Biting my bottom lip, I scoot closer, waiting for her to tell me to leave, to fuck off.

I don't stop until my body is touching hers and even then, that's not enough for me. Wrapping a heavy arm around her slim waist, I nestle her into the spot against me, the spot that I'm sure was made just for her. She stiffens for a few seconds before relaxing into my touch. Breathing her in, I let her floral scent calm me. A moment later, she starts to sob again, heavy bursts of what I can only describe as pain rip from deep within her chest.

I want to say something, anything, but I don't know what. Instead, I hold her tighter, burrowing my face into her hair, letting her know that I'm here, that I'll always be here if she'll have me. I hate myself for hurting her, for breaking her more than she already was.

"When will the pain stop?" she whispers, her voice hoarse.

"I don't know. I've asked myself that a thousand times in the last five years." There's a long moment of silence and then she clears her throat to speak again.

"Sometimes..." Her voice is thick with emotion and I feel her sadness, her pain, it pricks at my skin, it suffocates me. "I wish I never chose dare that night. I only chose it because I wanted to prove to you that I wasn't a baby, that I could do one little dare. Now that I think about it, I see how stupid that was."

I smile into her hair, thinking of how even back then she had me wrapped around her finger. We were joined at the hip, where she went, I went. We were strictly friends, but I hungered for more. I wanted it, and if she had stayed, if everything hadn't fallen apart, she would've been mine a long time ago. I knew it. Hell, I would've made sure of it.

"I've blamed myself every day for telling my father. I've blamed myself, knowing that telling him ruined everything, and even now, I blame myself more after finding out that your father hid the truth from you, that he lied and placed the blame on me."

There's a vise-like grip on my heart and it's squeezing so tightly that I know at any second it will burst, leaving me a bleeding massacred mess.

"I don't fault you for being angry with me, for wanting to hurt me, for thinking I did this to you, to your family," she whispers, and it's so soft I almost don't hear her speak the words.

God, she's wrong. So fucking wrong. I'm at fault. What I did was wrong.

"None of what I did was okay, and no amount of words or apologies will take that back. I hate myself so much for hurting you, Ava, and I'll never, never, forget it."

"If I could... I would..."

A shrill scream pierces the night air, causing both Ava and I to shove up into a sitting position on the bed. *What the hell?*

Another scream follows the first and before I realize it, I'm jumping off the bed and rushing for the bedroom door.

"What was that?" Ava whispers, following closely behind me.

Glancing over my shoulder, I press a finger to my lips. She nods her head, eyes wide, fear slicing through them. Turning, I pull the door open, then I step out into the hall. I can hear the sound of feet scuffling across the floor downstairs. What the fuck is going on?

"Here, give me the gun, Greg." Laura's voice wobbles. "You don't want to hurt yourself or anyone else with that, do you?"

Gun? Greg? Ava pushes past me and starts down the hall, but I reach for her, my hand circling her wrist and pulling her back against my chest. She shifts in my arm, a protest on her lips when her father's voice pierces the air.

"First you take my wife, then you take my daughter..." Greg slurs.

He's drunk and he's got a gun. That's a deathly situation and one I'm not going to let Ava put herself in the middle of.

"I have to go to him. I can get him to calm down," Ava whispers, a frantic look in her eyes.

I know she wants to help her father, but I refuse to let her put herself in that kind of danger.

"I didn't take anything, and you're supposed to be at the rehab facility. We can't help you if you don't let us," my father says.

"Help?" Greg snorts. "You never wanted to help, it was me who helped you. Me, who gave you and your family a place to live, and you..." The pain, the hate it's suffocating. "You stole my wife, you made me this way."

Ava whimpers into my chest. I move us down the hall and closer to the landing that opens up into the foyer. Releasing Ava, I go to maneuver her behind me, but she catches me off guard and bolts for the landing, reaching it before I can stop her. My heart leaps into my throat when my eyes catch on the scene taking place in the foyer below us.

"Dad," Ava croaks and starts down the steps.

Watching her walk away from me and toward her father somehow feels like the end. Once she reaches the second to last step, I spring into action.

"Sweettthearrrttt…" Greg slurs, his eyes are bloodshot, and I can smell the whiskey on his breath across the room.

The barrel of the gun catches in the light as he whirls it around, and somehow, all I can see is his finger on the trigger. Time stands still but also moves a million miles a minute. At the same time I reach for Ava, my hands grabbing onto her shirt pulling her into my chest and turning to shift her so she's behind me, the blasting of a gunshot rings out through the air. I don't even feel the bullet enter my back, lodging itself deep inside the skin.

All I feel is heat, searing, burning outward from the wound. My lungs deflate, like a balloon. I sag against Ava, barely keeping myself upright, my knees knock together as Laura and my father both lunge forward at the same time but in different directions.

My father tackles Greg while Laura throws her arms around me and Ava like she could somehow shield us with her tiny body.

"Oh my God, Vance is shot," Ava yells. "Call 9-1-1!"

Staggering backward, I manage to sit down on the bottom step of the stairs, refusing to let go of Ava. Greg groans on the ground only a few feet away from us with my dad holding him down on the ground. Wetness coats my skin, my t-shirt soaking it up.

"Laura, you need to call an ambulance," my dad orders, and for once, I hear fear in his voice. Letting go of Ava and me, she runs into the kitchen, only to reappear moments later with the phone already pressed to her ear. A wave of dizziness washes over me and light-headedness starts to come.

"Hello...yes, someone is shot. My ex-husband broke into our house and he had a gun and my stepson was shot..." She's talking so fast, I'm sure the person on the other line is having trouble understanding her.

Shot. I've been shot.

"My husband tackled... Yes... he took the gun from him..." Laura says, looking down at Greg and my father. Swinging her gaze to me, she continues, "Yes, he is conscious...but he looks really pale...and there is a lot of blood..." Laura's eyes widen to the size of saucers. "He's bleeding, there's... Yes, hurry. Please...hurry."

Ava sits next to me, her body pressed against mine, her hands pressing over the spot that hurts the most. Forcing myself to breathe, I let her sweet floral scent fill my nostrils. My eyes drift closed, and silence settles over me.

"Don't die, Vance, please don't die," she whispers in my ear over and over again. I try and lift my hand, open my mouth to soothe her, but I can't. It's like my mouth is full of cotton, my limbs no longer working.

"Vance..." Ava calls out to me, but the inky darkness calls to me. It pulls me under with each labored breath that passes my lips. "Vance, please don't go to sleep. Stay awake, stay with me." The sadness in her voice makes me want to reach out to her, to tell her it's all going to be okay, but is it? Is it all going to be okay? I don't know.

The wetness against my back bathes my skin. Sirens sound in the distance inching closer to where we are but somehow farther away at the same time. Like the undertow of the ocean, I'm pulled under, sinking deeper, and deeper.

"Please, Vance," Ava pleas. "I love you, you can't die, you can't."

She loves me. I force my lips to turn up into a smile. *She loves me.* Her words are the last thing I hear before the heaviness of the dark becomes too much to fight.

If this is the end, than it was worth it.

At least it was her voice I heard last, her touch I felt last.

~

Darkness surrounds me for a long time, or at least it feels like it's a long time. I'm floating somewhere between sleep and wakefulness. There's a tightening in my chest, but it's not pain. I don't feel any pain and for some reason, I find that odd. I think I should feel pain, but I can't remember why. My brain feels like it's been thrown in a blender, a thick fog clouds my thoughts, making it hard to string together what happened.

The first thing I notice, other than the darkness, is a low, steady beeping sound somewhere close to me. I can hear my heartbeat, and not just in my ears, but outside my body.

It takes an enormous amount of effort to peel my eyes open, but when I do, I just want to close them again. There's a light so bright it might as well be the sun shining down on me. My eyes strain to see, and I blink a couple hundred times.

"Ahhh," I groan softly, so softly it's more like a wheeze than an actual groan.

When I'm finally able to take in my surroundings, I quickly realize that I'm lying in a hospital bed. A familiar whimper meets my ears and my gaze swings in the direction of the noise. Across the room, a small body is curled up in the recliner. *Ava.*

Like looking into a kaleidoscope, a flurry of images flood my mind. Greg. The gun. Ava in danger. The gunshot. The heat, and pain. *She loves me.* She. Loves. Me. I should be worried about the fact that I was shot, but all my thoughts are consumed by her, by her words.

"Ava…" I call out to her, my throat raw, feeling like gritty sandpaper. She stirs, her green eyes blinking open ever so slowly. When she notices me awake, her eyes widen, and she jumps out of her chair almost tripping over her own feet.

"Vance, oh my God. You're awake," she says, her tiny hand clutching onto mine like I might disappear into thin air.

"No way you're going to get rid of my ass that easily."

Her pretty pink lips form into a frown. "You scared me. I thought you…" Her eyes fill with tears and I've never seen her so pale, so well… worried. "I thought you were going to die. The whole way to the hospital, you were out, and then when they took you into surgery."

"Shhh…" I soothe, cupping her cheek. "I'm here, alive and breathing so no more crying babe." There's no way in hell I can bear to see her cry right now. Not when I already want to hold her in my arms, but can't. I try and sit up, but there's a piercing pain that lances across my back.

"Fuck," I growl, gritting my teeth. I feel like my back is nailed to the bed and with every move, my flesh is being ripped out.

"Just, don't move. They had to sew you up, and you don't want to pull your stitches."

"Where's…" I start but pause, guilt flashes in Ava's eyes.

"The police took my father away. My mom and your dad went to the police station after you got out of surgery and the doctor told us you will make a full recovery. The bullet missed all major organs, but you did lose a lot of blood, and that's why you passed out."

"I'm fine, I'm just glad it's me in this bed and not you." Seriously, I don't think I could handle seeing her in pain like this.

"And I wish it was me instead of you," she murmurs, her eyes cast down at the ugly hospital gown I'm in.

"Don't say that, I more than deserved to get shot after the way I've treated you. Now we're even." I wink playfully.

Ava sighs deeply. "How did our lives become so complicated and messy?"

"I'm not sure, but I can promise you that I'll try my best to make it as uncomplicated as I can from here on out. Gunshot, or no gunshot I still want you and now I know you want me too."

Ava opens her mouth looking as if she's about to disagree, but she's interrupted with a light knocking on the door a second before it squeaks open a foot.

A middle-aged nurse with long blonde hair peeks inside, her lips turning up into a smile when she spots me in bed. "Hi, Mr. Preston. I'm glad to see you're finally awake and talking."

She pushes the door all the way open and steps inside. Grabbing the clipboard hanging on the wall on the way, she comes to step directly beside me.

"I'm glad as well," I tell her. "Thanks for fixing me up."

"That's what we're here for. How is your pain level right now?"

"Manageable." The last thing I want to do is mention my pain. All I want to do is get out of here and go home.

"Good, lean forward and let me take a look at your back."

Gritting my teeth, I do as she asks. She leans over me, pulling up the back of my gown to check the wound. Her hands are gentle, and for the most part, I'm not in much more pain.

"Looks good. I'll let the doctor know that you're awake, and that you're handling the pain well. You'll need to eat something and keep it down, but if the doctor says so, you'll probably be able to go home today."

"Thank you," I murmur, as she writes something down on the clipboard and heads back toward the door.

"Of course if you need anything before I return, then hit the call light button attached to your bed. I'll be back in a little bit with something to eat." She gives both of us a heartfelt smile before slipping out of the room, closing the door behind her.

As soon as she's gone, I turn to Ava. She's worrying her bottom lip between her teeth and I groan, my cock hardening at the image. Reaching for her, I tug her into my chest, and practically onto the bed.

"I might have been out of it, but I heard you say *it*."

"Say what?" she asks coyly.

"Don't play dumb. I know you love me. I heard you say it. You can't deny it."

"You didn't hear anything, it must have been your imagination."

Liar.

"I love you, Ava. I'm sorry for hurting you, for everything that happened, for our lives being as fucked up as they are. I'm sorry. You deserve better than me, one hundred percent, but if you'll have me. I'll spend every day making it up to you."

"We don't have to talk about this right now," Ava mumbles, and I grab her by the chin forcing her to look at me.

Bright green eyes pierce mine.

"Yes, we do. I could've died." *You could have died.* I can't even say those words out loud. "We've already wasted so much time. I don't want to waste another minute. I want to spend every minute of every day going forward with you. I want to hold you in my arms when I fall asleep and wake you up with my tongue and fingers every morning."

"What kind of drugs did they give you?" she asks, her eyes lighting up with amusement.

"They didn't have to give me anything. I'm already on the best kind… the kind that makes your heart beat real fast and butterflies flutter in your stomach."

"I don't think that's a drug."

"You're right." I lean into her face, so close I can press my lips to hers. "It's not a drug, it's called love, and it's far more powerful than any drug I've ever heard of."

"Is that right?" she whispers breathlessly.

"Yes, fuck yes…" I growl before pressing my lips to hers.

23

AVA

Henry and my mother make an appearance just as the doctors are discharging Vance. We decide to discuss what happened when we get home so as not to make a scene in the hospital. Vance, for the most part, remains quiet, his hand in mine gathering a few stares, those including our parents. They help me get him into the car, and I slide in next to him.

I try not to think about the conversation we are about to have, I don't want to hear them tell me what's going to happen to my dad. I know what he did was wrong, so wrong, and I realize how serious this is. Breaking and entering, threatening with a deadly weapon, shooting Vance...the crimes are stacking up. He's going to end up going to prison for a long time and I know he isn't innocent, but he's still my dad and deep down, I know he wouldn't have ever intentionally hurt Vance.

Chewing on my fingernails absentmindedly I let my gaze fall on the houses and trees that whoosh by in a blur. My mind is so wound up, that I flinch when Vance gently takes my wrist and pulls my hand away from my mouth, interlacing our fingers. I stare down to where our hands are joined. Never did I think we would be together, and now, now it's surreal. The thought of losing him, for a short while there, I was consumed with fear. I didn't know if he was going to be okay, there was too much blood, and it was...

"Calm down," Vance leans in and whispers, his breath fanning against the shell of my ear. Goosebumps blanket my skin and I feel myself leaning into his touch.

"I thought I lost you." The words expel from my lips easily.

"Shhh, you didn't. I'll never leave you," Vance says as we pull into the driveway. Henry parks as close to the front door as he can. Together we half carry him up the front steps and into the house. By the time we make it up the stairs and into his bedroom, he's cursed twenty thousand times and I'm breathing like I jogged up the Empire State Building.

Once we get him settled in bed, propping him up with five pillows, our parents start the dreaded talk.

"We didn't want to talk about this back at the hospital because we weren't sure how it would turn out, but we decided to press charges against Greg," my mother says nervously. Vance remains quiet, blinking up at her. It's hard to read him, and not even I know how this is going to pan out. "We asked the judge that they not put him in jail, but instead make him go to a mandatory rehab facility where he can get the help he needs."

"Good, because no matter what happens, I still blame the two of you," Vance says, emotionless.

"Son, what happened isn't—"

"No, shut up. I don't want to hear another lie come out of your mouth. In fact, I don't want anything to do with you. Greg never would've found himself in a situation like this had you not made the choice to sleep with his wife. You and Laura are the cause of everyone's pain, and I hope you both can live with that."

Tears well in my mother's eyes, but I can't bother to feel sorry for her. Vance isn't wrong. While everyone else has suffered, they've lived this great life, always having each other, always putting their needs first.

"We didn't... I mean, we love—" Henry starts again, but Vance cuts him off once more.

"I told you what I wanted. Leave me alone, leave Ava alone, and you can go back to your precious little life. Fuck with either one of us, and I'll tell Mom you lied. I'll ruin you, bury you."

Henry gives my mother a panicked look before walking toward the door. My mother, of course, follows behind him and I wonder if she ever really cared about me? If she wanted me here because she wanted her daughter here or because she felt obligated to give me a place to live? Not once did she stick up to Henry in my defense and even now, she's like a weak dog.

"Whatever you want, son. It's yours."

"Good," Vance snarls, and both my mother and Henry walk out, closing the door gently behind them. Once we're alone, I feel his eyes on me. I turn to look at his face. His nostrils flare, and his emerald green eyes seem brighter.

"Come here..." he orders, pushing himself up toward the headboard.

"You can't do that, you're going to pull your stitches," I scold, pushing up from the desk chair. I take a seat on the side of the bed, but obviously that's not close enough because he grabs onto me and hauls me against his chest.

"Vance!" I squeal.

"Be mine. Be with me, Ava. I've fucked up. I know I did, but I promise you there is good in me. I will make this right, I'll treat you right, and I will make you my number one priority. I want you to move out of my dad's house and in with me. I want everyone to know that you're my girlfriend and that I love you."

It all sounds like a dream. I never thought Vance would care about me, let alone love me. But, I guess hate can't grow when you cut off its only source of sunlight.

"I...I want that too, but we don't want to move too fast."

"We can go at whatever pace you want, but I won't let you stay here under my father's thumb. I'm done letting them rule our lives. They've been happy while the rest of us have suffered and I'm not letting it happen anymore."

For years I've longed to be loved, I just never expected that love to be found in him.

"But what about money? I can't pay for college on my own, let alone a place to live. I'll have to get a job, which isn't a problem but..." My voice trails off. I know I'm thinking too much into this, but it's a lot of responsibility, and with a new relationship, we don't stand a chance.

Vance grins, having obviously thought everything through. "Slow down, baby. I told my dad to give me my trust fund now. It was supposed to be mine after college, but he agreed that I could have it now. There's enough money in there that we won't have to worry about paying tuition or rent. We can forget about your mom, my father, and we can live a normal life, without lies and memories of the past."

"Vance, I can't let you..."

Lifting his hand, he presses a finger to my lips, silencing me. His eyes piercing mine, softening me with one single look.

I don't want to argue with him, not after all we've been through. It should be me saying sorry, me offering to take care of him, I mean he got shot by my father.

"You can, and you will let me pay for it. I want to take care of you. Please, let me do this. Let me take that worry away from you. I owe it to you, to us."

"Okay, but only if you let me pay you back." I'll probably never be able to repay him, but I'll try.

"Oh, you can pay me back, alright." He snickers, and I feel his hardened member pressing against my ass. "You could start now if you're feeling generous."

"Stop it, you're healing. You could barely get up the stairs, you need to rest before doing any kind of activities."

Vance's face deadpans. "I got shot, baby. My dick didn't fall off."

"Well no sex, not until you're fully healed. I don't want to be responsible for any other injuries you might incur. I feel bad enough as it is."

"Don't. I'd much rather have been shot than had you shot. It was my choice, and one I would make again and again."

I lean into his face, lifting my hand, I cup him by the cheek. "Truth or Dare?"

"Truth," he says, his full lips begging to be kissed. "Always the truth from now on out."

"Maybe just one last dare?" I tease.

"Okay..." He pauses, thinking and I wonder what I've got myself into. "Since sex is off the table...I... dare you... to... kiss me."

I press my lips to his before he can say anything else, swallowing up whatever words were going to come out of his mouth next. Our relationship was never going to be perfect, but I don't want perfect.

I just want Vance Preston, today, tomorrow, forever.

My best friend, my bully, my love.

EPILOGUE

Vance

"Do we have to go?" Ava pouts, and I squeeze her hand in mine. Now I understand why Remington is so territorial over Jules. Love makes you do crazy things.

"Yes, we have to go. No way in hell am I not showing you off. I want everybody to know we are together, so no one dares to hit on you when I'm not with you."

"But, you *are* always with me." She grins. It's true, we have been inseparable for the last few weeks. While I was recovering, she played my nurse and even now that I'm all healed up, we do everything together.

My father successfully covered up the whole shooting incident. At least he got that right. Ava didn't want people to know what her dad did, and I was more than happy to help make it go away. No one besides our family and Clark knows that I was shot.

I've kept my promise to right all my wrongs, and tonight I'm going to right another wrong. I'm going to make it known to the entire campus that she's mine, and shut down any rumors that might be floating around.

"We don't have to stay late. Just long enough for everybody to see us together."

"You make it sound like I'm a trophy or something."

"Trophy wife, maybe?"

"Slow down, we just moved in together. Marriage is like a thousand light years away."

"I can wait, but one day you will be my wife…just so we're clear on that. You'll carry my last name, and then my babies." I can't help but grin, even though I know me speaking of the future terrifies Ava, I know she's it for me, and I need her to know that too.

"Okay, someday." Ava giggles as we walk up to the porch. Inside, the party is in full swing. Loud music, laughter, and chatter can be heard from the street and when we walk through the front door those noises only get louder.

I let go of Ava's hand and instead wrap an arm around her, tucking her small body into my side as we walk through the crowd. Heads turn and people stare at us while I lead us across the living room. Our relationship is still somewhat new, and the gossip about us being together will spread like a wildfire, the sorority girls wanting to get in every last word.

Spotting Remington and Jules in the far corner of the open space, I decide to go and hang out with them. At least Ava knows Jules, and they seem to like each other. I would hang with Clark, but lately he's been MIA.

"Vance," Remington greets me with a broad grin and a chin nod. Ava pulls away and greets Jules with a hug. The girls break out into conversation about classes and some new books that just released.

"I'm guessing you fell hard for the pain in the ass stepsister?"

"You have no idea. I'll never be able to forgive myself for the things I did." For some strange reason, the words just come out. Remington doesn't have the first clue what I put Ava through, so he couldn't possibly understand.

"Yeah, I put Jules through some bad shit too. I've had to learn to let go of the pain, the hate I feel for myself for doing so. I do everything I can for her now, and eventually I'll marry her, whenever she lets me." He chuckles. "There was a time when I was the bully and she was my punching bag though, and I'll never truly forget that."

Okay, so maybe I was wrong. Maybe Remington Miller did know what it felt like. My lips part and I'm about to respond when Sarah and her gang of hyenas strut up to us. Jules and Ava stop talking when Sarah stops right in front of Ava.

"Look, girls, trailer trash is here, make sure you hold on to your purses. You never know with this one,"

Sarah snickers. She had better be counting her lucky stars today that she is a girl, 'cause if she wasn't, my fist would be flying through the air right now.

"Get lost, Sarah, you're just jealous of Ava," I snap.

"Oh hey, Vance. I haven't seen you in a while," she greets me, ignoring my statement. A pout forms on her red painted lips.

Tugging Ava into my side, I make it clear to Sarah that I'm with her.

"I've been busy spending time with people who matter, you know...with my girlfriend."

Sarah's hyenas laugh like I said something funny. Sarah cuts them off with the wave of her hand, her nose wrinkling in disgust. "She's trailer trash and your stepsister. Isn't that like incest or something," she sneers.

"Stepsister. We aren't related, but I wouldn't expect you to understand that since the only thing you're good at is spreading your legs," I grit out.

"You didn't seem to mind much…" Sarah snickers and I snap.

"Don't be full of yourself. I never fucked you and I never would. Why would I want you when I have someone like Ava?"

Sarah tosses her hair over her shoulder. "Whatever, Clark still lets me ride his dick."

Is that supposed to hurt my feelings or something? Because it doesn't. I'd much rather have Ava than ever allow Sarah to touch me again.

Out of the corner of my eye, I see Ava's cheeks growing red with embarrassment. Then I lift my head and notice we've caught most of the attention in the room.

"What the fuck are you all staring at?" I growl into the crowd and most everyone goes back to what they were doing a moment before this little spat took place.

"Have fun with that," Sarah says, her top lip curling in disgust before skipping off into the crowd.

Ava slaps a hand to my chest. "You brought me here to have a sparring match with her?"

"No, baby, I brought you here so everyone knows you're mine."

"They're more like us than we thought," Jules says to Remington who grins down at her like a fool.

"Another goal for team hate to love," Remington snickers.

"What the hell?" I nudge Rem in the side, getting his attention.

"What?" he asks.

"What the hell do you mean another goal for team hate to love?"

"Oh, Jules and I had a little bet going. She wasn't so sure you would fall for the meddling stepsister, but I knew better."

"Bets get you in trouble I've heard." I wink, which causes Remington to expel another huff of laughter.

"That they do, that they do."

My cell phone starts to ring in my pocket, and I fish the thing out gazing down at the screen.

Clark.

I answer immediately. "Hey, what's up? I haven't heard from you in a while."

"Uhh yeah, sorry. I've been busy. Do you have time to help me? I'm moving and I need help with this sectional. It's a bitch to move."

Moving? "What the fuck, Clark, what's going on?" I ask.

Sighing, he says, "Look, I'll explain when you get here."

Ava having heard the entire conversation nods her head, telling me she's okay with leaving this shit show.

"Yeah, we'll be there. Message me your new address."

"Got it, see you soon," Clark says, hanging up the phone. I shove my phone back into my pocket and turn to Rem and Jules.

"Sorry, but we're blowing this Popsicle stand."

Ava gives Jules a quick hug and I give Rem a chin nod before taking my girl by the hand and guiding her out of the party. Once we make it outside and away from the loud noise of the party, Ava asks, "What's going on? Why did Clark move?"

"I don't know, but we're about to find out."

Just then, my phone chimes with an incoming text. I wait to check it until we reach the car. Then I fish the thing out and read the text Clark sent me. I know the address, the place he's living is in a condo near the country club, but why the fuck is he moving into his own place?

Shoving the thoughts away, I start the car and take Ava's hand into mine as I drive us toward Clark's place. It doesn't take long before we've arrived.

"Clark's going to live in one of these places by himself?" Ava asks astonished.

"Yeah, I don't really believe it either."

We walk up the stone walkway and to the condo that Clark told me. When we reach the door, I sigh, lifting my hand to knock. I don't get a chance though because a moment later the door comes flying open. Clark's shameful face before me.

"Hey guys," Clark says, gesturing for us to come in. The place is huge and my mouth pops open when I notice the girl standing in the middle of the kitchen, her face filled with anxious anxiety.

"What the fuck's going on?" I ask, confused. Ava blinks, and then a slow smile forms on her lips.

Running a hand through his russet brown hair, Clark says, "Ava, Vance. Meet Emerson, my girlfriend."

Girlfriend? What. The. Fuck?

"Girlfriend?" I stutter.

"Yup. Girlfriend," Clark grits out through his teeth, his eyes begging me to understand but I don't. I just don't understand. Clark doesn't do girlfriends, I mean he does other people's girlfriends, but he doesn't stake claim. He nails 'em to the bed and leaves 'em before the condom hits the garbage can.

"Emerson, this is Vance, my best friend, and Ava, my second best friend."

"Hi," she squeaks out timidly. Holy shit, she's Clark's opposite, shy, nervous, obviously innocent. Her blue eyes shimmer with secrets and I know whatever is going on here has something to do with her.

"Explain," I order, but Clark shakes his head.

"I will...later."

The End

NEXT IN THE SERIES

Secrets… they can make or break you.

I would know. I'm hiding the biggest secret of all. My scars are so much more than skin deep. They consume me, control me and every part of my life.

Then I meet him, Clark Jefferson. Six foot two inches of Greek god hotness with a smile that'll make your panties disappear. He is everything I should avoid, everything I should fear, and yet all I want is to be near him. For some reason I don't understand, he makes me feel safe.
He makes me want to break free of the suffocating fear that

claims my heart and that's one of the reasons why I agree to be his fake girlfriend.

But secrets can't remain secrets forever and as I grow closer to Clark my feelings for him grow too. Soon the line between fake and real blurs and when the past I've been running from finally catches up with me I'll have to confess to Clark the truth or let go of a love that was only ever supposed to be fake.

Find The Secret on Amazon

ALSO BY THE AUTHORS

CONTEMPORAY ROMANCE

North Woods University
The Bet
The Dare
The Secret
The Vow
The Promise
The Jock

Bayshore Rivals
When Rivals Fall
When Rivals Lose
When Rivals Love

Breaking the Rules
Kissing & Telling
Babies & Promises
Roommates & Thieves

Also by the Authors

***

DARK ROMANCE

The Blackthorn Elite
Hating You
Breaking You
Hurting You
Regretting You

The Obsession Duet
Cruel Obsession
Deadly Obsession

The Rossi Crime Family

Protect Me
Keep Me
Guard Me
Tame Me
Remember Me

***

The Moretti Crime Family

Savage Beginnings
Violent Beginnings

The King Crime Family

Indebted

Also by the Authors

EROTIC STANDALONES

Their Captive

Runaway Bride

His Gift

Convict Me

Two Strangers

WHEN RIVALS FALL PREVIEW

Chapter One

Bayshore University is not the prestigious college that I thought I would be attending. My whole life I thought I would end up going to one of the best Ivy League schools in the country, like Yale or Harvard, just like every other rich kid from my high school. Instead, I chose to attend this place. A nice but low-key University located on the west coast, hundreds of miles away from my hometown of North Woods. Most kids wouldn't choose to be miles away from their parents, but I wasn't most. I chose this college because it's as far away from my family as I can get.

As soon as I turned eighteen and I got my hands on my trust fund, I was out of my parents' house. There was no way I was going to stay another minute longer. I wanted to disappear, forget about my last name, and what it meant.

After finding out about the things my father had been up to, I didn't want a single thing to do with the family business.

"This is college, and you're acting as though someone has sentenced you to ten years hard labor." Shelby laughs. My nose wrinkles as I look up at the fortress before me. Of course, the place would look more like a medieval castle set in the Scottish Highlands than a university. Ropes of thick green ivy climb the walls like they're trying to escape.

"Maybe not ten years, but at least four, right?" I grin.

"College isn't a dick, Harlow. Stop making it so hard."

"Nice analogy. Where did you pull that one out of?"

"My ass." She grins and slams her hips into mine. I roll my eyes like I'm annoyed with her when in reality I'm grateful she is here. She really had to talk her parents into letting her attend college here. I think the only reason her dad agreed is because he's had a bad year at his law firm and the tuition is cheaper than Stanford, where Shelby was supposed to go originally. She doesn't seem to care though.

Students rush past us in a flurry to get into their dorm rooms, while Shelby and I take our sweet time. We had most of our things shipped to the college, all except our personal belongings so there's no rush for us. We spend most of our time taking in the surroundings. The University itself is beautiful, with huge oak trees, and sprawling areas of lush green grass, that I can picture myself sitting on with a blanket and a good book.

We make it to the crowded dorm and up the stairs to our room without incident. Once inside I exhale all the air from my lungs and sag down onto my small twin size bed. The dorms are small and leave very little room for privacy but that's okay. The place is close to the ocean and has a view that most would dream of.

"Okay, so I was invited to a party by a couple of guys I met over at Starbucks," Shelby says, tossing her blonde hair over her shoulder.

"We've been here less than twenty-four hours and you want to go to a party already?" I knew parties were going to happen, but I'd hoped to avoid them.

"It's a past time set forth by our ancestors, when you arrive at college you must party."

"Sounds like its set forth by Shelby." I roll my eyes.

Shelby juts out her bottom lip into a firm pout, "Oh, come on, Harlow, you only went to a handful of parties when we were in high school and now you don't want to enjoy college. Your parents are out of the picture, you can basically do anything you want."

She has no idea how wrong she is. Yes, I've managed to escape my father's clutches for now, but I'm not going to be able to hide from him and my mother forever.

"If I go will you at least wait a whole month before inviting me to another one?"

Amusement twinkles in Shelby's hazel eyes, "Mmm, two weeks tops."

"Seriously." I cringe.

"It's college, Harlow, and I'm your certified fun helper."

Shaking my head, I say, "You're not a fun helper, you're a get into trouble helper."

She taps at her chin with her finger, "Trouble. Fun. All sounds the same to me. Now, what are you wearing? Better be something sexy. We've got to grab the boys' attention right off the bat. You know college boys, all ADHD squirrel like."

"I'm not catching anything, and especially not any boys' attention."

I'd garnered enough attention from the Bishop Brothers back home. After what I did to Sullivan, I was surprised he could walk past me without wanting to murder me. Let's just say it made social gatherings a little tense.

"Your parents aren't here. You don't have anything to worry about. You're free." Shelby gets up from her bed and puts her arms out like a bird, flapping them until she reaches my bed, slamming herself down onto it, causing me to bounce and a bubble of laughter to escape my throat.

"I'm not worried about them," I lie. I'm worried about them just as much as I'm worried about the Bishops.

Actually, I'm not worried. I'm terrified. For years I've helped my father spread rumors about the Bishops. I've helped ruin their lives and for what? Nothing, it was all for nothing. I didn't know how horrible my father really was. He didn't just want their business, he wanted them gone.

At one point my hate for the Bishops started to diminish, and in its place resentment towards my father bloomed. I didn't want anything to do with my old life, the drama, the hate, the revenge. I wanted to forget that part of my life ever existed.

"Good, because it wouldn't matter if you were. Now, up. Let me see what I have to work with and then what clothing you've brought with you."

"Do we really have to go?" I bat my long eyelashes knowing damn well it won't work. I can't make myself look as innocent and sweet as Shelby does. Plus, I kind of owe it to her to at least go out once. She did, after all, move hundreds of miles away from her family to be a supportive friend.

"Yes." She smiles and I should've known that smile was going to be the death of me.

I pull on the bottom of the miniskirt that Shelby shoved me into. I'm not exactly skinny, curvy is more like it, and even though I don't have any real self-confidence issues, this thing is so short every single guy here is going to get a flash of my crotch by the end of the night.

If and that's a pretty big *if* I go out with Shelby again, she will not be dressing me.

Brushing a few strands of my silky blonde hair behind my ear I survey the crowded room. The frat house is filled to max occupancy with women and men of all ages. There's dancing, singing, and drinking games. People chilling on the couch in the living room, smoking what I'm pretty sure isn't cigarettes based on the sweet aroma that permeates the air.

"We made it." Shelby huffs, a wide grin on her blood red painted lips. She acts like she just aced a test that she's been studying for all semester. We stand together, side by side, in the middle of the room, watching as people move around it, chatting, and having the time of their lives. The longer we stand there the more attention we bring to ourselves.

I can feel eyes on me, gliding over my bare legs, and my shirt that hangs off of one shoulder. Yeah, I don't like this. Being the center of attention. Feeling out of place and a little timid, I hide behind the curtain of my hair as I turn to Shelby.

"We came, we saw, we had some fun, can we go now?" I whine, tugging on her arm. I haven't been to a party since that night. *That disastrous night.* A shiver runs down my spine at the memory, at the anger, and simmering rage that reflected back at me from all three of the Bishop Brothers.

"We'll make you pay for this, Harlow. One day you won't have your parents' protection, and then what will you do?"

Shrugging I say, "I'm not scared of you. You're weak. Pathetic. Just like your parents."

Oliver entered my bubble of space, forcing me to take a step back or be chest to chest with him, "One day, we'll get even with you. We'll break you. You'll wish you were never born."

"You'll be waiting a long time..." I sneer, feeling the fear slither up my spine and around my throat like a snake.

Wiggling my shoulders, I shake off the unpleasant emotions coming with the memory.

"Nope." Shelby pops the p, and grabs onto my hand, tugging us deeper into the house. The place is huge, similar to the mansion I lived in back home. There are priceless paintings on the walls, crown molding, and chandeliers that cost more than most cars. It reminds me so much of my old life that I have to shake away the creepy feeling slithering up my back. I did my research when selecting a college and I made certain this one wouldn't have any billionaire co-eds.

As far as I know, Shelby and I are the only two people attending this university with parents that make more than a million a year. Which leaves me to wonder whose house it is? Does another student own it? His or her parents? *Why do you even care, Harlow?*

Paranoid. I'm being paranoid. Ever since leaving North Woods I've wondered when my past would come back to haunt me. All the things I said and did. The guilt eats away at me every single day. I let my father lead me blindly into the dark. I let him feed me lie after lie. I thought I was doing the right thing, but I wasn't.

When we enter the kitchen I notice the black marble counters and stainless steel appliances. Off the kitchen is a pair of patio doors that open up to a backyard that butts up to the beach. It's beautiful really, minus all the college coeds that are liquored up.

There's a makeshift bar set up on the huge island and Shelby gets to work mixing us something to drink. *Everything's okay.* I tell myself, blowing out air through my mouth, before inhaling through my nose.

"Here," Shelby says, her pink painted nails coming into view as she shoves a red cup into my hand, the contents sloshing against the sides of the cup. I peer inside of it before bringing it to my nose to sniff.

"What is this? It smells like straight alcohol."

Shelby shrugs, her hazel eyes narrowing, "Just drink it. Live a little, will you? If you promise to have a good time, I'll promise not to push you to go out with me so much. Deal?"

Ugh, as much as I hate to admit it, she's right. I'm eighteen, a college student. I need to live a little, and enjoy the years ahead of me before they're gone and I'm forced to be an actual adult, with a job, and responsibilities.

"Fine. I'll try." I give her a weak smile and take a drink of the pink looking liquid. The burn I was expecting doesn't come and I'm pleasantly surprised by the cherry tang that's left against my lips.

"Good, huh?" Shelby asks, watching me like a hawk.

"Decent. It doesn't taste like I'm drinking lighter fluid."

"Shut up." She giggles, taking a drink from her cup. The hairs on the back of my neck stand on end and I don't understand why. Swinging my gaze around the room I look for anything out of place. *What's wrong with me? I think I'm losing my mind.*

A loud rap song comes blaring through the speakers, vibrating through the masses of bodies and into my skull, causing a dull ache to form there. A book wouldn't give me this kind of headache. Feeling as if I'll need it, I drink the rest of the liquid in my cup and hand it back to Shelby with a mischievous grin.

"Make me another. I'm going to go find a bathroom. If I'm not back in ten minutes send out a search party."

"Don't be so dramatic." She takes the cup and ushers me away. "Go to the bathroom. I'll be here when you get back."

Leaving the kitchen I notice a group of women in skirts shorter than my own enter the house. My heart sinks into my stomach at the sight. *Barbies*. Three girls dolled up like plastic dolls. Fake. Popular. Gorgeous. Every college and high school has them.

They stick out like a weed in a bed of flowers. They giggle, and toss their hair over their shoulders, batting their eyelashes at every man that looks their way, and there are a lot of men looking their way. Turning, I head for the huge staircase before they come any closer, I know their type—they'll either want to befriend me and initiate me into their clan, or they'll make me public enemy number one—I don't want to get on their radar, I want to have an uneventful, low-key college experience. Rushing up the stairs I almost run head first into a couple that is making out against the railing.

I mumble a half-hearted apology and continue in search of a bathroom. I open one door to find an empty bedroom with a large inviting looking bed in the center. How bad is it that I would rather curl up in that bed and read a book than go back downstairs and party with the other students?

When I pull the door shut behind me, a familiar scent coming from inside the room tickles my nose. I can't quite place the unique smell, something like a forest after a rainy day.

I keep walking down the hall and the next door I open is actually a bathroom. I disappear inside, locking the door behind me. It is almost as big as my dorm room. I shake my head at the size and fanciness of it all.

I use to think this is all that mattered, money, pretty things and people who look up to you. That's what my family taught me to think and there was a time when I didn't question anything my parents told me. That time is over. Now I know better.

I'm still thinking about the familiar scent in that bedroom as I wash my hands. Something about it is nagging me but I just can't put my finger on it. Looking in the mirror, I give myself a once over before exiting the bathroom. I really should act more like the other people around here. Have fun and enjoy college life. This is what I wanted. I got away from my family to be normal. All I have to do now is get out of my own head and enjoy this.

I walk back down the hall, forcing myself not to think about the bedroom with its tempting scent. I fight the urge to take another peek inside. Just as I pass it I hear the soft click of a door opening, but before I have the time to truly comprehend that someone is behind me, I'm grabbed by my arm and yanked into the room.

Screaming like someone is about to kill me I stumble into the room, losing my footing as I go. Arms flailing, I prepare myself to land hard on the ground but I'm shocked when a pair of strong arms circle my waist from behind pulling me flush to a firm, warm chest.

Momentarily I'm stunned, like a doe caught in the headlights of a car. My screams cut off, the air stills in my lungs. I can't do anything. I'm frozen in place. *What's happening?*

All I can hear is the swooshing of blood in my ears, my chest heaving up and down with panic. I open my mouth to scream again, but nothing comes out. Suddenly I'm dizzy, the smell of rain fills my nostrils once more and I realize immediately who that scent belongs to.

"Did you miss me? Is that why you're here, in my bedroom? Eager to see what we have in store for you?" Sullivan's dark voice fills the room, and a cold shiver runs through me. I notice then that he's standing a few feet away from me, but his voice affects me as if he is right beside me whispering in my ear. It doesn't matter that I can't fully see him. I don't need to. I know he's looking at me with disgust.

His room? Blinking slowly, I try to digest what he's just said? Confused I'm about to ask him what the hell he is talking about when I realize someone is still holding on to my waist. Their warm hands burning into my skin.

Spinning around I shove at the firm chest in front of me, realizing quickly its Banks, the middle Bishop brother. A sinister grin spreads across his face as he licks his lips. "I think she just missed us, why else would she come here, to our house?"

"Your house?" I finally find my voice again. It's shaky but at least I got the words out.

"Yes, *our* house." A third voice drawls, and my gaze travels across the room and collides with Oliver's chocolate brown eyes. "We bought it recently, figured it would be nicer than living in the dorms."

Dorms? Why would they be living in the dorms?

Nothing makes sense right now. This has to be a dream, no scratch that, this is a freaking nightmare. I shake my head as if I can wake myself up from it. Then I try and take a step towards the door, but Sullivan slaps a hand over the handle halting my movement.

"Not so fast," he growls, his muscled form towering over me. He's bigger than he was the last time I saw him. Taller, scarier, even more disgustingly handsome than I remember. "Let's talk. We want to tell you how this year is going to go."

What does he mean? How this year is going to go? He can't really be saying what I think he is? The Bishop brothers aren't... they can't be... My chest starts to heave, even though no air is filling my lungs. Lord, please tell me they aren't attending college here.

"I don't think she gets it," Banks taunts, devilishly.

"It's not hard to figure out. I mean, we're laying it out pretty clearly. It's a shame really. All that money and her daddy couldn't even get her a proper education." Oliver sneers.

"I'm not stupid." I try and make the words sound strong, but they come out like a soft breeze whispering through the trees.

"Right, you're only a liar," Oliver responds, his words like a slap to the face.

Gritting my teeth, I let the insult sink in. *He's not wrong, I am a liar.* Because of my father I've done a lot of things I'm not proud of. I followed him like a lamb to the slaughter, believing him with blind faith. I knew someday karma would catch up with me. That eventually, I would pay for my wrongdoings, I just never expected it to be so soon.

"Let me put it into words even someone like you can understand," Sullivan leans in so closely, I can feel the heat of his body. I can feel all three of them, their bodies drawn to mine like a magnet.

"Remember when I told you I would make you pay for what you did that night?"

Saliva sticks to the inside of my throat—like honey—making it hard to swallow. Every nightmare I've had over the last year would never have amounted to this. All three of their faces have haunted me in my sleep since that night. I regretted doing it as soon as I did it, but there was no taking it back, there was no changing the course we were headed on. It was like a bad accident, that you couldn't look away from.

As if he can see the worry filling my features his smile widens, perfectly straight white teeth gleam in the moonlight filtering in through the window blinds.

"That little stunt ruined his senior year. Got him suspended from the team. You tarnished our family name, but that was the point, right?" Oliver hisses, his eyes narrowing, his angular jaw—sharp enough to cut glass—clenching.

The Bishops' had money, but nothing could stop the local papers from printing an article about their son doing drugs and getting booted from the team. My father had hit his mark and made them bleed, and worse he'd used me to do it.

"Well, now that our family business is ruined, there is nothing for us to take over, so I guess we all have to go to college after all," Banks explains, and I finally get it. All three of them will be attending Bayshore. *This can't be happening.*

"Please... look...." An apology is sitting on the edge of my tongue, but a hand comes out of nowhere from behind me and presses against my mouth—another at my hip—effectively cutting off the words before I get a chance to say them.

I know who it is that has ahold of me, and I try to wiggle out of Banks' hold, but he just pulls me closer, until my back is pressed firmly into his muscular chest. Panic, and something else, something warm, and euphoric swirl in my belly.

No. I won't be attracted to them, and their stupid muscles, hard abs, and devilish smiles. They're the enemy, my rivals.

"Shh, Princess. We didn't say you could speak. Keep your mouth shut, otherwise, we'll find a better use for it." Banks' smooth voice tickles my ear as he pulls his hand away from my mouth. His body remains close to mine, too close, but for some reason, I don't move right away. One of his hands remains on my hip and I just stand there for a moment, letting his body heat seep into me, trying to warm the icy cold blood running through my veins.

"I told you... I promised you, that you would pay, and now it's time. It's time to pay your dues." Tears sting my eyes. *Don't cry. Don't cry.* I will not cry in front of them. I won't.

Finding a sliver of strength, I jab my elbow into Banks' ribs. He releases me, even though I know I didn't hit him hard enough to hurt.

"Is that all you've got?" he snickers.

I step toward the door that Sullivan is now blocking with his body.

"Let me go," I grit out through my teeth.

No one moves, or says a single word, it's almost like they're waiting for Sullivan to make a choice and that terrifies me. After a long second, he finally moves out of the way, a smug grin painted on his face. Waving his hand over the door and motioning me to leave, he says, "You may leave tonight, but you can never get away from us. We'll find you wherever you go, and we *will* make you pay for what you did."

Find When Rivals Fall FREE on all retailers!

ABOUT THE AUTHORS

J.L. Beck and C. Hallman are an international bestselling author duo who write contemporary and dark romance.

Also check out our website for a list of all of our books.
www.bleedingheartromance.com

Beck and Hallman

BLEEDING HEART ROMANCE

f CASSANDRAHALLMAN
AUTHORJLBECK

◉ CASSANDRA HALLMAN
AUTHORJLBECK

BB CASSANDRAHALLMAN
JLBECK

Printed in Great Britain
by Amazon